Jamie Levin
Oct 2014

Titles by Arthur James
Jason and the Kodikats (2013)
Children

HANTS

A Novel

By

Arthur James

Blackstone Books
New York, NY

ISBN-13: 9780990448808
ISBN-10: 0990448800

HANTS

Copyright © 2014 by Arthur James

All rights reserved. Except for the use in any review, the reproduction or utilization of this work in whole or in part in any form by any electronic, mechanical or other means, now known or hereafter invented, including xerography, photocopying and recording, or in any information storage or retrieval system, is forbidden without the written permission of the publisher.

This book is a work of fiction. Names, characters, places and incidents either are products of the author's imagination or are used fictitiously. Any resemblance to actual events or locales or persons, living or dead, is entirely coincidental.

Publisher Blackstone Books LLC
New York, NY

info@blackstone-books.com

To love
To men and women who love
To love that binds each day to the next
To love that survives the passing of a soul mate

The Water Boy

1

Another day was hatching in 1917 rural New England. Like a line of fire, dawn began breaking along the Atlantic horizon. Quickly the first rays of the sun passed over Portsmouth, New Hampshire on their flight inland. Gradually the Merrimack Valley, which runs north from the Massachusetts line up, through the state, began to brighten up. It wasn't long, before life started to wake along the Souhegan, a small tributary of the Merrimack River. They merged half way between the industrial city of Manchester and the town of Nashua, the state's most southern community.

Somewhere an old rooster bugled at the rising sun, calling his many wives from their dreams. Inside the house, Albert Austin had been avidly awaiting the cock's signal. After genially rolling away from his wife's side, he planted his two strong, square feet firmly on the pine plank bedroom floor. Feverishness accompanied the motion of dressing. As always, the arrival of planting inspired in him an air of youthfulness. Padding softly through the house in thick woolen socks, he stopped momentarily in the kitchen to pluck a short corncob pipe from the rack. One of the long stem clay bowls would have been preferred; however, they were much too fragile to take working in the fields. Before proceeding outside, he stooped to tug on a pair of stiff leather boots.

Overhead, a full moon, was washing away in the lightening sky. To the west, the black of night still reigned.

On the way to the barn, his thick fingers worked a twist of tobacco from a pig's bladder pouch. Today the sowing would start on the back fifteen acres, where the soil had lain fallow for three years. All his worrying had been needless. True, the early spring rains had been so heavy that, for a time, the sprouting couch grass had threatened to reclaim the earth for another year. Still, the land had drained off in time to allow a solid month of harrowing. Hardly a sprig of root had escaped being exposed to the warm spring sun. Now a fine brown soil lay waiting to be impregnated.

Last night before retiring, he had noted a line of stars parallel to the river. Usually it was a sign of good weather. Though it was his rule that the two boys would miss no school, they would both stay home today to help with the planting. The younger, Brad, who had already developed a keen interest for the land and the river, had even insisted, before going to bed the previous night. He wanted to be awakened and start the day with his father. However, the boy hadn't responded to a soft call; so Albert had left him to his sleep. If the weather held, the three of them would have the fields in by Sunday evening.

The sacks of seed were piled just inside the barn door. With a simple, but sure movement, he hefted one up across his shoulder. When the cow path, along which he walked, descended into the gully where the run-off water bubbled, he tested each foothold before advancing. It would be a catastrophe to slip and lose a single precious kernel. Besides the untold gallons of sweat to grow, harvest and thresh; there were the many long hours invested at the kitchen table during the winter nights, culling each seed by hand. As he bent over to set the burden on the ground, in the corner of the field, a brilliant orange appeared over the trees.

The pipe was spent. One sharp whack against his palm dislodged the cinders. He shook out the pear shaped seed hopper made of homespun linen that had padded his shoulder against the chafing of the burlap sack of seeds, which he had been carrying. When the hopper was spread out flat upon the ground, his attention turned to unravelling the seam, closing one of the ears of the sack of grain. He watched with pride as the golden kernels poured out of the burlap sack and into the pear shaped seed hopper.

Brimming with half a bushel of grain, the hopper's paunch straddled his shoulder. He held its neck straight out in front of him with his left hand. The steady farmer withdrew a handful of seed from the paunch. Then, with the same clean movement which sowers have practiced since before recorded time, he let fly with his arm, starting anew the cycle of generation in the world.

A half an acre of the field had already been sown, when a thin trail of wood smoke began coiling up from the trees that hid the house. It was the signal that breakfast was ready. Wendy, the youngest child, bolted from the door as her father approached and threw her arms around his lowered neck.

"Good morning daddy," she clamored, smacking her lips against one of his cheeks, when he had hoisted her up into his arms. "Ugh! You're all whiskery." She squirmed to get down. "Guess what we're having for breakfast?"

"Fried feathers and pigs tails," he joked.

"That's silly. Mummy is making us pancakes and poached eggs."

A short well-proportioned woman in a bib apron, long skirt and loose muslin blouse moved about quickly in front of a large box stove. Albert and his father had bought it in Nashua, before the couple's marriage.

"How are you this morning?" he asked, entering the kitchen.

His wife turned her heat-flushed face towards him and smiled. "I'm fine," she replied, "but you, you couldn't have slept much last night. I felt you twisting and turning several times."

"Not really," he agreed, coming from behind to wrap his hands around her expanding middle. "I was anxious to get started planting. You can't feed a growing family by staying in bed all day."

"No," she giggled, turning around in the circle of his arms to face him. "It's a great place for making a family, but not providing for it."

"What's all this special breakfast business?" he asked, stepping back.

She reached out, tenderly and brushed a lock of hair back off of his forehead.

"A woman can't expect her man to labour all day on an empty stomach. Besides," she added, redirecting her attention back to the sizzling frying pan, "a special day deserves a special breakfast."

"Where are those other two scallywags?" he asked.

"Shane is gone back to the spring for drinking water. I told Brad to put the cows in the stations and wash off their tits."

At that moment the screen door flew open with a loud bang and the two brothers came thrashing in, finally collapsing in a tangle on the kitchen floor in front of their parents.

"Get done with that nonsense this very instant," their mother commanded stamping her foot. "Where is that water I sent you for?"

Shane, in whom the mother's blood shone through the most, looked sheepishly under his eyes at his father.

"It's in the yard mom."

Hants

"Well, march mister," she shrilled, tweaking his ear, "and you," she furthered, turning to the son who resembled his father, "get those hands washed after handling the animals."

When the family was all seated, Albert looked along the table at his two sons who were still jabbing their elbows into each other's ribs.

He grinned. "Lots of energy this morning boys?"

Albert knew that nature had no weak spot. If a man were to stay in her good grace, he had better stay one foot ahead. The sooner his sons learned this, the better off they would be.

"We'll see how high you kick your heels at supper," he laughed. "After breakfast, I want you to hitch the draught horses to the flat wagon. Load those sacks of seed grain that are inside the barn door. You better take the wagon road along the bluff to the back fifteen acres. We won't take any chance of an upset in the gully. Unload one bag about every five hundred feet along both sides of the field. When you've finished, unhitch the wagon. Hook the harnesses to the harrows. Both of you will walk with the reins, so the horses don't run wild, blowing the seed every which way. Do you have any questions?"

They shook their heads no. Natalie pitied them. After all, they were only little boys. Still, she didn't interfere.

Monday morning, a week later, a light drizzle gently kneaded the countryside. In spite of broken reins, a sick horse, sore muscles and many other setbacks, they had succeeded in getting the fields planted The boys' arms were so feeble from holding back the straining horses all week that they could hardly pull on their stockings. When Albert came in from the milking, he found them dawdling at the breakfast table.

"Shane, if you and Brad harness Oscar to the buggy, while I'm eating, I'll run you into school." There was still more planting, but Albert could handle it by himself. "I'll have a word with your teacher, while I'm there, so she won't think you've been playing hooky."

A few days later during a mid-morning coffee break, Albert and Natalie were chatting together about the many chores that still had to be done.

"Something's not right with Chester," her husband informed her.

"What's it look like?"

"Colic," he uttered lowly.

"Let me see," she reflected. "My grandfather's cure for that was, boil down a pint of water in a frying pan, while saying the animal's name. Turn the skillet over and leave it on the back of the stove. The colic will be gone within a week."

Her husband smiled skeptically. "I'll leave that one to you."

Natalie was vexed and was about to reply defensively when the rumbling of a wagon sounded outside. Leaving him to his coffee, she went to the screen door to investigate. A high, board-sided wagon, drawn by a shabby grey horse had come to a stop in the middle of the yard. The reins man wore a bright bandanna about his neck.

"You back on the roads again this year?" Natalie inquired coming down the back steps.

"Why certainly missus, business is better than ever. Price of ashes went up again this spring. They can't get enough. People in the cities burn too much coal these days."

He unstrapped a square wooden shovel, and then threw back the lid on the bin where she dumped the cinders from the wood stove.

"Your mister around," the ash man inquired.

"Just in the kitchen, care to come in for a fresh cup of coffee with us?"

"Thank you, but I'll have to say no. I've already stopped for two fresh cups this morning. At this rate, I'll never get my rounds done. If you think your mister would be interested in a deal for some free firewood, tell him I'd like to have a word with him."

Hants

Albert was standing just inside the screen door. He overheard their conversation. Nevertheless, he waited inside until the silky gray powder was loaded, and Natalie had been paid. As always, the money was hers to do with as she pleased.

"Free firewood you say," the farmer repeated, opening the door as his wife folded the bills and slipped them into the pocket in her dress.

"In a manner of speaking," the ash man replied, beginning to climb aboard his wagon again. "Gentleman by the name of Shaw over on the Pond Road wants to clean some land to extend a hay field. Anybody can cart away what he cuts down. I'm just spreading the word.

"Why doesn't he just give someone a contract?"

"Don't think he knows much about running a place, sort of a gentleman farmer who has moved out from Boston."

"Which house is it?"

"You can't miss it," the old nomad drawled, "big gray stone building with fanning chimneys. I must be hustling along," he insisted, turning the wagon around. "May your harvest be plentiful."

"What do you think?" she inquired when the rattling had died away.

"It couldn't hurt to have a look see. I hate to cut too many trees off the back of this place. We might lose our watershed. As it is, I've marked a good number that will be needed for the lumber to build the new equipment shed and the lean-to on the barn."

The following Sunday, while still dressed in his dark serge suit; Albert decided to go scouting. Since Brad was equally curious, he went along. Not more than half an hour after leaving the farm, their buggy turned into a lane bound with Chestnut trees. Instantly a black and white Border collie tore across the property. Seconds later a boy dressed in knickers and long argyle socks ran in pursuit. Oscar had only started to flinch skittishly in his reins when a man's voice resounded from the direction of the out buildings.

"Fritz!"

The dog stopped in mid-stride. Head downcast, he slunk off towards the trees. His master stepped from the doorway of a small wooden building. Brad had never seen anyone with the bottoms of their trousers tucked into black spats. As his father reined in, the strange man inquired in a neighborly fashion.

"May I help you?"

Albert pushed his concealed visor cap towards the back of his head.

"Mister Shaw?"

"Yes, I'm Shaw. What can I do for you?"

"The ash man was telling my missus and me that you want to get some fire wood cut."

"Excuse me," the other man explained politely, "I don't quite understand."

While Albert filled in the details, Brad heard someone giggling. Turning around quickly, he noticed that the boy in knickers had come up and was staring at his bare feet. Brad felt his cheeks begin to burn.

Walking over to his father's side, the city boy asked in a low voice, "Who are these hicks dad? One of them isn't even wearing any shoes."

"They've come about the firewood. I'm going to take them down to show them what I want done."

The boy in knickers clamored, "I'm coming too, Dad."

"No Ward," his father insisted, "the field is wet. You'll ruin your shoes."

There followed an elaborate display of yawning and wheedling until Mr. Shaw finally relented. Albert had taken it all in, but appeared to be adjusting the harnesses. He could not understand why such an otherwise competent man would tolerate himself being run by a mere child. Whether strangers were present or not, if one of his sons attempted a similar trick, their ears would merit a swift boxing.

Behind the house, an expansive uniform field canted off towards a mixed poplar and birch grove.

Hants 9

Amid much good-natured laughing and arm waving the two men struck a bargain. During the deal making, the boys eyed each other curiously. As the men were shaking hands, Ward Shaw pranced forward in front of Brad challenging him to race back to their buggy. Brad waited for Albert to give him permission before moving off.

In spite of the head start, the city boy was out matched. He soon became winded. The farm boy, however, dug in with a straight, steady trot. Later when the Austin's had left the Shaw's place, his son bristled proudly,

"Pa, did you see how I out ran him?"

The farmer only smiled. "You ran a good race Brad, but don't talk too much about it. My motto is if you win say little and if you lose, say less."

The summer vacation was soon upon them. One afternoon, Brad came back from berry picking with his sister Wendy to find his brother Shane stretched out on the long wall bench in the kitchen.

"Shush. Don't make any noise you two," Shane said with an authoritative tone. "Mom left strict orders for you. She is resting. You're supposed to split some kindling and clean the outside oven."

"What are you going to be doing?" Brad retorted.

"Me! Oh, I'm going down to the flats to hoe the corn."

With that, he waltzed past them and disappeared out the door.

The oven should really have been cleaned, before the chopping of any kindling was started. Splitting the short lengths of log in the afternoon sun covered his body with a thin film of sweat. When he did get to the outdoor oven, the clouds of soot stirred up by the scraping and sweeping settled onto his arms and face and chest and back. Rubbing at it only made matters worse. When Natalie woke up from her afternoon nap, she found her youngest son standing on a kitchen chair looking onto the mirror above the sink. He was scrubbing at his face with a horse grooming brush.

"What are you doing?" she exclaimed. "You're filthy. Your father left word for you to hoe the corn."

"Hoe the corn!" he exclaimed. "Shane told me he was to do the corn and I was to do the oven."

"Shane was supposed to do the oven, because his arms are longer than yours, and he has done it before. You know that. When are you going to stop letting your older brother pull the wool over your eyes? You have to learn to defend yourself, even against your brother. Grow up boy and stop being such a baby."

Then she started to laugh, "I swear, you're blacker than the ash man."

"It's not funny mom. It won't come off."

"Here," she said, handing him a bar of soap and a brush. "Go down to the river and give yourself a good scouring."

The Austin place was about seven miles west of the town of Milford along the Souhegan River. It was called Hants. Albert's father had named the property. He never tired of explained to those who asked, 'New Hampshire is named after Hampshire County in England'. The local English gave their county a nickname, Hants. Albert's father liked the name and called his farm the same.

The main part of their land, along with the house and buildings, was north of the North River Road. About ten acres of the property were located on the fertile flood plain between the road and the river. The family called it the flats. For the past several years, Albert had been putting corn in there, after the spring swell on the river had passed.

Shane was nowhere to be seen in the corn. A discarded hoe lay between two furrows. It wasn't until the boy had finished washing that he spied his brother, asleep in the grass, further downstream. Shane jumped up with a shriek, when a well-aimed splash of water fell across his face.

"You were supposed to do the oven."

"Was I?" came back a mocking taunt.

Hants 11

"You know it."

"You've still got a black nose," his brother teased, skipping out of range of the second volley of water.

Like it or not, there was no time for holding grudges. They were a team. The work had to get done. The incident was soon forgotten.

One morning after chores were done, the younger brother suggested, "Let's go exploring today."

"Whereabouts," Shane asked?

"We've never gone very far north of the farm."

"Then we should find out what's up that way."

The brothers crossed the bottoms of several other farms, before arriving at the tree line. They penetrated it, but in most places the woods were unbroken. After a time, a swamp cropped up which necessitated a long detour towards the west. When finally they started walking north once more, Shane caught sight of what appeared to be a road.

"Do you see that? What say we follow it for a while? At least until it comes out some place. That way we'll know where we are."

"Okay, I'm game. Let's cut over and pick it up. I'm tired of walking on this soggy ground anyway. What time is it?"

"Almost 1 p.m.," his older brother replied stowing his pocket watch away.

It was no ordinary road. Two splinters of steel rested upon wooden cross ties that were themselves set in a bed of gravel that travelled away in both directions as far as they could see.

"Trains drive along here," Shane boasted. "The teacher showed us pictures of roads like this."

His younger brother pressed him, "Why haven't we ever heard a whistle blow?"

"The house must be too far from here," Shane surmised

"Have you ever seen a real live train before?"

"Only in picture books," his brother informed him.

"Shane, I'm starting to get hungry. Why don't we eat lunch, if noon time has already passed?"

"Good idea, I was about to say that myself."

They sat down on one of the rails, before unfolding the heavy, brown waxed paper in which they had wrapped slices of homemade bread spread thickly with molasses. The food was so good. They didn't even notice the feeble wail of a whistle away in the distance. It wasn't until they could feel the vibration coming up from the rail, through the seat of their pants that they became aware of the horrendous din, which was growing quickly in intensity. A curve in the track prevented them from seeing far. However, they both stared awfully at the plume of white smoke approaching rapidly over the treetops.

"What's that?" Brad asked earnestly.

"I don't know," Shane yelled, springing to his feet, "but let's get out of here."

The older boy fled far into the trees. His younger brother stopped short in the high grass, flattening himself against the ground. His body trembled with excitement as he watched, first the huge slanted fender; then the rest of the hissing steam engine appear around the bend. He pressed his palms over his ears, yet his eyes devoured all. At the same moment the caboose passed out of sight, Shane crept up to his brother's side.

"That was close."

"Where did you go?" the younger boy demanded.

"I was right behind you."

"I thought I saw you go in among the trees," Brad insisted with a slight air of superiority in his voice.

"Not me," the older brother declared angrily, "I was right behind you all the time."

Wendy was getting tired of watching for her brothers. They had been gone over six hours. She hadn't forgotten a word of what her father had told her, before he left hurriedly in the buggy. She was about to go back into the house, when she spotted the two of them laughing and talking, as they walked towards the barn.

Hants 13

"Hey!" she yelled, waving her arms in the air. "Hey, you two," she screamed running towards them. "Shane! Brad!"

They stopped and waited until she caught up to them.

"I have instructions from Dad for both of you. He said for you not to go into the house except to keep the kitchen stove going."

"Why?"

"While you were gone a stork came with a baby. Mommy tried to tell him she didn't want it. He beat her with his wings and said she had to take it. I heard her screaming. There's blood. Papa went to town for the doctor and Mrs. Nelson."

The boys looked at each other apprehensively and then darted towards the house. Their sister called after them.

"Papa said that if you came back before he arrived, you were to keep the fire going and to bring lots more water down from the spring."

Upon their first return trip from the spring, the brothers were confronted by the spectacle of Dr. McGillivray alighting from his carriage. He was mantled in a long, canvas overcoat with deep side pleats. A full crown, silk derby, with a rolled brim, covered his head. At the same time, their father was helping a short dumpy woman down from the family buggy. It was Mrs. Nelson, the village mid-wife. Seeing his sons with pails in their hands, Albert said to them,

"You got my message?"

"Yes, Pa," they replied in low voices, then anxiously asked together, "is Mom going to be all right?"

"She's going to be fine," Mrs. Nelson answered them. "It's only a baby."

"We'll be needing lots more water," their father instructed them, "but first take care of these horses. Put Dr. McGillivray's in the visitors stall."

Once he had scrubbed up and donned his white smock, the doctor examined the mother. Between Mrs. Nelson and himself, they were able to quiet the parent's anxieties. Within an hour, the womb was open. As the head appeared, experienced hands, covered with a light sterilized cloth, took hold of it and drew lightly. After the birth, the mid-wife washed down the infant girl with warm water. She swaddled it and then tucked it into a wicker basket which had been arranged on a chair in front of the open oven. After the men had gone into the kitchen, she fussed about the mother.

"We don't want the children to see all this," she clucked, gathering up the cloths that had been soiled red by the delivery. "I'll run and put them straight into the fire."

She returned with a juniper berry tea. Before the children were allowed to enter their parent's room, a dressing of melted butter, camphor and black pepper was applied to Natalie. The boys and their sister stared at their mother's blanched face and the dark blotches under her eyes.

"Are you all right?" Wendy wanted to know.

"Oh, yes, my little dear, Mom is going to be fine now," she smiled reassuringly. "I have some good news for you. You have a new baby sister."

"Is she my real sister?"

"She is as much your sister as Shane and Brad are your real brothers."

The following Sunday the nursling was bundled up well and taken along to church to be christened. Albert didn't breathe easily until he heard the bells ringing in the steeple overhead.

The season progressed steadily. Towards the end of July, the first crop of hay came on and was ready to be cut. Natalie's sister Loraine, her husband Rod and their children came over from the town of Nashua to help with the harvest. On the first day of the haying, the brothers-in-law and Shane moved forward into the field, with long even strokes of their scythes. Brad and his cousin Bill followed with forks, pitching the swaths of hay up into wind-rows. Later in the morning they were joined by Bill's sisters, Meg and Sybil. Using long

Hants 15

handled, wooden rakes, the girls gleaned what the boys had missed. Wendy kept busy, helping her mother and aunt in the kitchen or carrying cold ginger cordial out to those in the field. During one of their breathers, Brad confided in his uncle Rod,

"Shane and I found a secret train track in the woods north of here. While we were there, one of the trains went by. It was the biggest thing I've seen in my whole life."

"Was that the day little Dora was born?" his father inquired.

"Yes Pa."

"No wonder you two didn't hear me calling you. That must be seven or eight miles from here. You know where they mean Rod."

"Is that the place they call the Moccasin Trail?" his brother-in-law inquired.

"That's it," Albert affirmed. "Did you boys know that your grandfather worked on that section of track?"

"Why is it called the Moccasin Trail?" Shane pried.

"At that time the land was very swampy," his uncle resumed. "My father-in-law said the swarms of black flies and mosquitoes were so thick, they blocked out the sun. Not many men wanted to work there. The contractor hired a crew of Indians to do the job. He said they were the most rugged men he had ever seen in all his life. I've heard tell the track is still as dependable as the day it was laid."

Having been brought up in town, the brothers' cousin was too sophisticated to be impressed by steam engines.

"If you thought that was big," Bill boasted, "you should see the trains that go through Nashua."

"I've only seen one train in all my life," his cousin said.

"You have!" their uncle exclaimed.

"It's the same with both of us," Shane added.

"Why don't you come to visit us this summer?" Bill suggested. "I'll show you everything."

"Sure," their uncle agreed, "but take turns, so your father is not left all alone."

"Can they come back with us tomorrow?" Meg and Sybil piped together.

"Who is to come first?" Rod wanted to know.

"I'm not as interested in machines as my brother," Shane interjected. "Besides, I promised a school friend I would go to see him on Wednesday."

"Then it is settled," their uncle declared.

"Make certain to be back here next Saturday morning," Albert reminded him. "This hay will be dry enough to start turning over."

"There won't be any problem," Rod assured him. "We've decided to give you a hand again next weekend. Haven't we girls."

"Oh, yes," Brad's cousins drawled while smiling at him. The day the younger Austin returned from town; he talked straight through supper.

"You should have seen it Shane. The trains are huge. They cut right across the streets. Special gates come down to stop the cars and buggies and people when they go through."

"Brad, don't talk with your mouth full," his mother chided.

"How do trains work, Pa?"

"I couldn't say for sure," the usually unhesitating parent replied. "I know that they are operated by engineers. You'll have to ask your teacher when school starts."

"That's what I want to be when I grow up."

"What?"

"An engineer," the youth beamed out loud.

"You told me that you were going to be a farmer," his mother reminded him as she started to nurse the baby.

"It all seems very mechanical to me," Shane scoffed.

"So!"

Hants

"Country people aren't mechanically minded," Shane continued. "We live too close to nature. If we decide to educate ourselves, usually we become poets."

"I can try, can't I?"

"Nobody can stop you from trying," his father said. "But be careful you don't turn out like your uncle Rod. Look what fifteen years of sitting in an office has done for him. And stay away from poetry. I've heard it doesn't pay very well," Albert added looking under his eyes at Shane.

After the haying, the Austin's hardly seemed to turn around, before the season came to a climax. The oats on the back fifteen acres were ready for reaping. To bring that in, Albert had struck a mutual harvesting agreement with the Matthews, who lived on the next farm.

Several years ago, old Mr. Matthews had signed the farm over to his son Paul, who was of the same generation as Albert; however, he still lived with his son's family and helped out as much as his health would permit.

On the morning that the harvest was to begin, the Austin's and the Matthews formed two small groups on the edge of the fifteen acres that were to be cut. Albert ran a whetstone along a sickle blade where he had spit upon it, while he waited for his neighbors to finish their pipes. When their pipe bowls had been tapped empty against boot heels and everyone seemed ready, he contemplated his field for a long moment. The father in him wondered if his sons remembered being pulled along behind the harrowing team during the spring.

"Let's take it in!" he exclaimed in a deep excited voice.

Shane and his brother cut a roadway directly across the parcel of land. The older men worked along the edges. By mid-morning, everyone except grandfather Matthews was bare to the waist. In defiance of the blazing late August sun, the old man's one-piece woolen underwear was buttoned right up to the neck.

Stooping or kneeling, they all made their way forward. Each time a flashing sickle sunk in among the stocks of grain; there resounded a dry snap, as the ears struck against each other.

When the two teams had repeated the same motions, during the same amount of time on the Matthews' same sized field, they returned once again to the Austin's' farm. The grain that lay in the field had to be bound. Paul and his son moved ahead of the others, arranging the spears of cereal in orderly bundles, with all the ears aiming in the same direction. Brad gleaned the stocks that had been missed. The grandfather, now clad in a heavy leather apron for protection against the thistles mixed with the grain, followed with Shane. Working together, they tied the bundles with switches of young hazel, which had been cut and looped during the summer. Albert brought up the rear, raking the sheaves into stooks, so rainwater would run off quickly.

A scorching Indian summer quickly seasoned the harvest piled in the fields. Albert decided to do a little spot threshing so as to have an idea of how much grain could be expected.

"While you boys take the wagon back to pick up a dozen or so stooks, I'll dig out the flails and replace their swingle thongs."

Later they gathered on the hardwood-threshing floor in the barn. When the butts of the stocks of oats had been arranged against the grain box in a row about six inches deep, the Austin's each picked up a long handle from which dangled a short striking bar. Back and forth, again and again, they whirled the bar in the air, then brought it thwacking down into the pregnant heads of grain. Once the ears of grain were exhausted on one side, the row was turned over, and the beating began anew. Albert swept the grain and the chaff up into a heap at the end of the floor, for winnowing during inclement weather.

While Shane put away the threshing tools, Brad helped his father gather up the straw and stack it up

Hants

outside along the south wall of the barn. It would be used during the winter as bedding for the animals.

"I told the Mistress at school that I wanted to be an engineer when I grow up," Brad told him.

"Still thinking about that?"

"Oh, yea," his son exclaimed.
"What did she have to say?"

"She said I'll have to be good in arithmetic and science. Also, she said I'd have to go to school in Nashua, when I finish at Milford. The Mistress said she would give me extra work and also correct it for me, if I was really interested."

"That would take up a lot of your time. You would have to choose between going exploring with Shane on the weekends or sitting more long hours on a wooden chair with a pencil and paper."

"I know. Mom says if I have all that extra time on my hands, I should help you more."

"Never mind about me," his father reassured him.

"I'm not very good in arithmetic."

"Sometimes it takes a special tool to do a special job. The important thing is to get the tool so you can do the work."

As the harvest season was nearing the end, the local women began passing the word about the district setting the date for their annual supper. The young women and spinsters argued about details. The homemakers stopped it all by stepping in and taking over the actual preparation. As every year, there were lots of yams and boiled sweet corn, apple pie and wedges of local cheese. Most people hadn't finished eating when the fiddle player started to test his bow on the thwart of his instrument.

About an hour after the dancing had started, Shane was nowhere to be seen among the swirling people. To please his mother, Brad went searching and came across his older brother lying in the back of a hay wagon with one of the local girls.

He felt embarrassed. They were kissing. She was giggling. The younger brother left quietly and returned to tell his mother that he couldn't find Shane.

Brad had never danced in his life; however, he wanted to know what it felt like to squeeze a girl up close to him, just like his brother was doing. He narrowed his choice down to one of the girls whom he had seen at the school in Milford, then just walked up and took her by the hand. She didn't resist. When the dance was over, he pulled her in close to him. She giggled, then drew away smiling.

All Hallows Eve came fast upon the heels of the harvest supper. There were no ghost riders the length of the Souhegan, like the legendary headless horseman who drove the Yankee schoolmaster Ichabod Crane out of Tarrytown N.Y. Along the Souhegan River, there were only local hellions who burnt haystacks and turned over outside toilets. Last year the Austin property had been hit, but since the dog had been replaced soon after, there had been no visitors this year.

Ten days before Christmas, the first heavy storm of the season had worked its way out of hurricane Judy and came up through the New England States. It left six inches of wet packing snow in its wake. As if by magic, mundane daily concerns gave way to thoughts of the approaching festivities.

Albert left off threshing and splitting wood. Having selected and slaughtered a prime hog, he stretched it out along a ladder and strapped each of its four feet to the rungs. Once the ladder was standing up vertically against the barn wall, the blood drained quickly from the fleshy carcass into a basin. Natalie used this to make pudding and pork pies. One side of pork was dutifully wrapped and delivered to the relatives in Nashua, who had so generously helped with the haying.

Sylvie Matthews held a party the Saturday before Christmas to which the Austin's, the Franklin's, the Harvey's and several other couples were invited. She greeted Natalie at the door, kissing her once on each cheek then started to help her take off her overcoat.

"Oh!" she exclaimed. "I just love your dress." It was made of navy blue cloth and ornamented with hundreds of tiny white rosettes of baby ribbon. "Is it one of your Christmas presents?"

"Yes, I must thank my husband for that."

"Don't thank me," Albert protested, "thank my father."

"What does your father have to do with it?" the women laughed.

"He always said, if you adore her then you must adorn her."

Both women made big eyes at each other then hustled into the parlor to meet the others. Albert could smell baked rabbit pie coming from somewhere. He went to investigate and was met by Paul Matthews, who handed him a tall glass of a slightly clouded, dark liquid.

"Here try that."

Next morning the head of the Austin family languished over a cup of coffee after breakfast.

"Shane can you manage the barn chores by yourself? I think I'll have breakfast before going out today."

"I think so, pa."

"Not feeling so well?" Natalie chirped, when their son was gone.

"Not at all," her husband moaned.

"You know how potent Paul's home brew is. I even warned you."

He avoided her eyes.

"Never mind," she sympathized, "I'll mix you up a glass of mustard and water. That should clear up your indigestion."

The Austin family was still seated at the breakfast table on Christmas morning when a loud tinkling of rein bells was heard in the yard. From beside the far window, Wendy immediately announced that a large two-seated sled, drawn by two huge black horses had entered the yard. The suspense was transient.

Natalie's sister, Judith, was the first to come rushing through the door. The short waisted, high-spirited woman flung her arms about her younger sibling. Her five children and her husband, Leo, followed her.

On Christmas Eve, they had come over from Lowell, Massachusetts to visit Leo's parents. Judith's children had begged to go to visit their Austin cousins who were not too far away. Their grandmother had said why not, as long as they were back for dinner. She even told them that their grandfather had a sled in the carriage house that had its runners fitted with ball bearings. It could even be used on the roads that had bare patches between the sections of snow.

Everybody seemed to be talking at once. Natalie bustled about clearing away the remains of breakfast. Suddenly, Leo added to the hubbub by pumping out short quick blasts on his accordion. It was enough of an invitation. The children began to push back the furniture. Dancing partners were chosen fast regardless of age. Once they were winded, Leo stopped playing.

Judith was the first to come back to normal.

"Now look you five. You just had to see your cousins, so why don't you all bundle up and go outside. We adults have lots to talk about."

"Do you like to toboggan?" Shane asked.

"There aren't any good hills in Lowell," a cousin replied.

"We've got a beautiful run here. It goes down through the orchard."

When the youngsters had gone out, the two couples settled down at the kitchen table to play cards and catch up on family gossip. Albert brought out a bottle of choke-cherry wine he had been saving for just such an occasion.

"Cheat! Cheat!" his spouse shrieked slamming her hand of cards down. "I saw that."

"You're imagining things," her husband protested.

"No, no, fast fingers," she insisted. "That's the one Paul Matthews showed you last Saturday night. I saw you two practising it over in the corner."

Albert dealt again to keep everyone happy, and they played a dozen or more hands without further outcries from Natalie.

Suddenly their game was interrupted by someone pounding on the kitchen window.

"Mommy, mommy, come quick," Wendy Austin clamored. "Cousin Nancy has hurt herself."

Judith's face became ashen. "Oh, Leo!"

The brothers-in-law jumped up and tried to squeeze through the door together. Leo went down on one knee beside his daughter who lay sobbing on a sled.

"We were sliding down through the orchard," Shane explained hurriedly. "Nancy must not have seen the apple tree coming up. She stuck her arm out."

"You weren't being careful enough," his father growled.

"It wasn't the boy's fault," Leo said.

"Regardless of fault," his mother interrupted, "she has probably suffered a mild shock. Laying there in the cold is no place to be."

Once Nancy's outer clothes had been removed, everyone saw the ugly fracture protruding from her left forearm.

"It must be broken," Judith declared. "It will have to be set as soon as possible. Where is the nearest doctor?"

"Milford," her sister replied.

"It's on our way. Gather everything up Leo. I'm sorry that we can't stay longer sis."

"There is no sorry. I would do the same."

"Come to see us in Lowell in the summer. I'll write you."

Natalie and her husband and children watched from the upstairs window until her sister's sleigh had disappeared from sight.

It was unusual to have much snow in that part of New England. However, the Souhegan River was just at the beginning of the high country, which leads up into the northern part of the Appalachian Mountains. As such, Hants was on the edge of a snow belt. It snowed regularly during the six weeks that followed Christmas. Along with all the other farmers who lived along the North River Road, Albert tried to keep a track open, the length of his property, wide enough for a horse to pass. On the days the wind blew the snow off the iced up river, the boys would strap blades onto their winter boots and skate into the school in Milford.

When the threshing was finally completed in the barn, the farmer started to winnow the mountain of grain, which was piled up at the far end of the threshing floor. It was strictly a one-man operation. He arranged himself near the loft door, holding the five-foot-wide, saucer-shaped van, with both hands. It was made of a thin lightwood and attached to a long hardwood handle. Over and over, the mixture was tossed upward into the breeze coming in from outside. When a hard metallic sound testified that the entire husk had blown away, the grain was emptied into the grain bin.

By the third week of March, the sap began to run in the maple trees. After months of threshing and winnowing, Albert welcomed the change of tasks. There was a maple grove on the property, back of the fifteen acres upon which oats had been planted. Sugar season began. He tapped each tree on the south side, and then fitted the hole with a wooden spile and a lath bucket. At first the run was meagre. They lit a fire under the evaporator pan, once every second day. However, within a week, a gallon or more of the liquid was dripping from each spout every day and the fire hardly ever went out. Wendy took to tarrying about the sugar shack in the evening, watching her brothers tend the fire.

"May I have some," she asked slyly.
"You just had some," Brad protested.
"But it's all gone."

Hants

"Go get a shovel full of snow then," her brother relented.

He poured a ladle of thick steaming syrup over the snow. It immediately thickened. His little sister twirled the taffy substance around a splinter of wood then skipped back to her bench.

Each year, when the roads started to dry up; the farmers ploughed up the stretch along their frontage. This worked out the deep ruts left behind by the early season movement of wagons. Since both of the draught animals had lost shoes collecting the maple sap, Albert decided to take them to the blacksmith before undertaking his share of the roadwork. Being a Saturday, he asked his youngest son if he wanted to tag along,

"Sure!" Brad bubbled.

"While you're there young man," his mother said, "stop around at the general store and pick me up some rosin and coarse salt."

Discarded ploughshares, rusting wheels and heaps of scrap iron littered the yard of the forge shop. Inside, odd shaped steel patterns hung down everywhere from the rafters. At the back of the shop, three enormous squared logs enclosed the base of the forge. In front of it, a Herculean man wearing a thick leather apron worked with bare arms. His rusty hued skin rippled over muscles resembling cords of steel. Straining with effort, he maneuvered two pairs of tongs, encircling a wooden wagon wheel with a metal tire hoop, three inches wide and a quarter of an inch thick. His movements cast fantastic shadow figures across the workshop.

"Morning William," the farmer shouted.

"Morning," the blacksmith hollered back, while hoisting the wheel into a water trough. "Problems, what can I do for you today?"

"Nothing serious," the farmer replied, "just the shoes of my work horses."

"How many horses did you bring?"

"Two."

"No problem, I've booted fifteen horses, all four feet in one day. They will be ready for you by noon."

"That will be fine. My son and I have a few other errands to tend to."

"Let's go and unhitch them," the burly craftsman suggested, starting towards the door.

When the beasts were let loose in the corral, Brad whispered to his father.

"Ask him yourself," his father replied.

The boy cleared his throat. "Sir!"

"Yes son."

"Why is that horseshoe nailed up over your shop door?"

"That is a tradition which dates back to the days of the first blacksmith. They say the devil presented himself and insisted on having his cloven hooves shone. Before the smith would perform the task, he extracted a pledge from the evil one to never enter a doorway over which there was a horseshoe."

"Let's go," the elder Austin said trying to hide a smile, "I'm going to take this halter over to the harness maker. Run along and take care of your mother's order. I'll meet you back here, a little before noon."

As well as being the owner of the Milford General Store, Mrs. Johnson was also the village's most avid gossip.

"Good morning," she greeted Brad, as she shuffled back behind the high counter upon which was located the brass-plated cash register. "Let me see now. You're one of those Austin's from out along the North River Road."

"Yes missus, I'm one of them."

"What do you need today, son?"

"I don't need anything. It's my mother who needs a few things."

"And what's your mother doing today?"

"She is doing her best," the boy replied, having been drilled on the answers he was to give to outsiders who pried into family affairs.

Hants

The shopkeeper persisted, "Is there going to be a new addition to your family again this year?"

The boy resisted more forcefully, "My mother told me not to be a leaky bucket."

The gossip understood. There were no more questions.

Because it was time to make the family's yearly soap supply; Brad's mother needed rosin and coarse salt. Since the onset of the cool weather the previous fall, she had stored away all the grease and bones coming from the kitchen. The soap was prepared in a cast iron cauldron that was suspended over a fire in the back yard, from a hook attached to a three-legged steel tripod. When the salt-water solution had boiled around the bones and fat long enough, Natalie Austin would ladle out the thick gluey mixture and spread it into moulds to cool and harden.

After the younger Austin boy finished the eighth grade at the Milford primary school, he decided to go on to the next level. His older brother chose to stay on the farm a while longer. It meant a big change for the younger brother. He would have to move into the town of Nashua where the collector high school for Hillsboro County was located.

Nashua was the county seat. It was named after the Nashua River that runs through the city. The Nashaway Indians of Lancaster, Massachusetts named the river. In the Penacook language, Nashua means 'beautiful stream with a pebbly bottom'.

Natalie's sister Loraine agreed to take the boy five days a week for the cost of his food. His cousin Bill was overjoyed. The first day of school arrived and Brad felt uneasy sitting in the auditorium.

"Why are you still sitting there?" A pedantic looking man snapped from the front of the high school auditorium. "Come up here instantly, young man."

Brad didn't know that he was being addressed.

"I mean you there young man, you with the sheepish look."

The youth stumbled through a row of empty chairs. His heavy leather boots echoed like horses hooves on the hardwood floor. He stopped short at the side of the stage. Cold pearls of perspiration trickled down over his ribs. He smiled in self-defence.

"Wipe that stupid grin off your face," the schoolmaster ordered. "Why haven't you gone with the others?"

The stricken youngster stuttered then whispered that he hadn't heard his name.

"What's that?"

The reply was the same.

"Can you make any sense out of him, Miss Williams?"

"He says that he didn't hear his name, Sir."

"Well what is his name?"

Brad spoke up, "Austin, Sir."

"Austin. Here it is on my list. One of the first names I called. Brad Austin. Do you think he's playing games with us?"

"I don't think so, Sir," Miss Williams replied. "From the looks of him, I'd say he's just in from one of the rural districts."

"Rural districts," the schoolmaster chuckled, "we'll see what they taught him out in the sticks. I'll bet he doesn't make it past Christmas."

"Tell the hick to go to room five on the second floor."

All the way up the stairs, Brad fought against the urge to turn and run from this place. Once seated at his desk at the back of room five, the boy began to size himself up against the rest of the students. He felt at a distinct disadvantage, even inferior.

At supper, his uncle encouraged him, "Don't underestimate yourself boy. The only difference between you and them is that they were brought up in town, and you were brought up on a farm."

His aunt Loraine joined in, "Just ask your cousin Bill about them. They are all so conceited, "she said picking at his coarse woolen work shirt. "You'll catch on in time, if you just stick with it. In the meantime, we can do something about these old fashion duds you're wearing."

Back home in the country for the Christmas holidays Natalie's sharp tongue criticized.

"I told you so. Stay here on the farm with your Pa. Be a good boy."

One morning after hauling the milk cans out to the road, so that they could be picked up by the wagon, which passed from the local dairy, Brad went back into the barn to continue with the chores. The usually silent father leaned against his pitchfork while filling his pipe.

"It's true," he nodded. "I miss your steady hand around here."

"Maybe I should stay to help you out," his son offered.

"I'm not saying that," the farmer protested, spitting out a long steaming stream of tobacco juice. "Nobody ever said that what you are doing was going to be a bed of roses."

"What do you think I should do, Pa?" the boy pleaded.

"That is not for me to say," his father hedged. "Nevertheless, the way I see it, life is a hard struggle. If a man doesn't stick at it, he gets nowhere. Quitting now could start a habit that would stay with you for the rest of your life."

He threw a few more forkfuls of soiled bedding up into the manure bucket before adding,

"Besides, you're learning something. That will always be useful to you."

He was still undecided about returning to high school in town, until the day Shane mocked him,

"So my little city slicker brother, I hear you're not going back."

"I don't know yet," the younger brother mumbled.

"Anybody who likes work like you was cut out for the farm."

"Somebody has to do it. I don't see you straining yourself."

"I do my share while you're in at Nashua polishing the seat of your pants. Besides, I don't intend to kill myself. This isn't my land. I'm not going to work myself to death."

It was Shane's 'city slicker' taunt that tipped the balance. At the start of the second term, as he was walking into the first class of the New Year, one of the boys caused the other students to burst out laughing when he heckled,

"Hey, everybody, look at that. The Hick came back."

On the second of September 1925, after a prolonged breakfast, a well-knit, no longer adolescent went back upstairs, to arrange the rest of his belongings. A short while later he descended carrying two carpet bags. Natalie's eyes were moist, when she set a small shaped cap on his head. She thought to herself. Who would ever have dreamed that one day she would be sending her little boy off to university, in a double-breasted jacket, peg-top pants and a starched collar?

"Don't forget your prayers with all that high learning you'll be doing."

"I won't."

They moved out onto the piazza.

"You write to let us know how you're getting on."

"I will," he rasped, leaning over to kiss her cheek. "Bye mom," he added, pretending not to notice her reddening eyes.

Seeing his son walking towards him, Albert left off hoeing earth up around the turnips, which were planted on the flood plain, across the road from the farm.

"Well, you're off," he snorted when they met.

"Yup," his offspring confirmed, "it's finally time."

"It's Dr. McGillivray who's picking you up?" the father verified although he already knew it was. The young man nodded

Hants

"The Doctor should be along any moment now. When he heard that I had been accepted at Dartmouth, he told his son to tell me I could ride upstate with them, if I didn't mind sitting in the rumble of his car. You know pa; I can still remember the first time I saw the Doctor the day Dora was born."

"How many from Milford are going up to Hanover?"

"There are two of us," his son replied.

"But you are the only farmer's son."

A noisy clatter became audible approaching from the distance. Looking down the river, they watched an open touring car, as it became more visible. It resembled an ancient chariot, trailing a plume of dust behind it. The driver wore a long military style duster and a leather helmet. When the machine came to idle, the driver lifted his goggles and yelled over the motor.

"Morning Albert," then tipped his hat

"Morning Doctor," the farmer nodded.

This was the first time that father and son shook hands, man to man. When the elder Austin retracted his hand, he left something round and hard, around which his son's fist closed.

"My only advice is just keep persisting. If you do that, you can't help but succeed."

"I will Pa. I promise."

It wasn't until after the car began to move away that the young man opened his fist. His father's special 1900 American eagle silver dollar lay on the palm of his hand. He looked back to wave thanks. Everything was lost in the dust. Late in November 1925, Albert Austin fell dead, lifting a sack of grain.

***

A Bouquet of Daisies

2

The silhouette of two individuals stopped in front of the pebble glass office door. Lester Marshall, or the Major, as close associates called him was at least a foot taller and a hundred pounds heavier than his companion. The Major looked dilapidated. His short-trimmed, white beard couldn't hide his sagging jowls and double chin. His baggy sports jacket should have long since been replaced. This fact was all the more obvious since he was standing beside a younger man who was dressed in a new tan, over plaid suit.

"They're not really a bad troop, son," Marshall explained. "If you happen to see knitting needles sticking out of their desk drawers from time to time, don't pay any attention to it. When there's work to be done, they get it done."

He pushed back the door and strode forward. A stout woman, with a russet jabot cascading down over her bodice, rose from her desk and came to meet them.

Hants 33

"This is Ethel Morris," he said, introducing her. "She is ...let's say, the unofficial straw boss."

After the Office Manager, it was Miss Fulton who left the filing cabinet and came to shake the young man's hand. Marshall wound up the introductions with a bombastic crescendo.

"And this," indicating a slight attractive girl who had been typing, "is our Miss Sylvester."

"Pleased to meet you, Sir," she half whispered, then offered a hand. Brad Austin accepted it. The introduction had startled the young woman. Her previously blanched complexion freshened. Intuitively, she lowered her eyes.

With one arm wrapped around the younger man's shoulders and the other gesturing towards a solid brown door on the other side of the office, Lester Marshall bantered, "That's where you can dig in later on. For now, come on into my office. There are a myriad of details to work out."

Before he closed the door behind them, he slipped a piece of paper into his secretary's hand. "Ethel, that's how his name is spelled. Would you please have them paint it on the door of that spare office?"

Angeline Sylvester settled back into her chair not saying a word. Idly she smoothed down the creases of her plain, plum-gray dress. She vaguely heard her co-workers clucking at their desks.

During its early days of empire building, the widely stretched Alabama Paper Corporation had filled its resident-manager positions through the old boys system. Fidelity was all-important. As these men retired, very often people who had come up through the industry replaced them. Since the Neutrality Act of 1935 had kept the United States out of foreign military involvement, the domestic paper market had stayed very competitive. Because of this competition, a higher premium was now put on competence, when recruiting and promoting, as opposed to personal contacts.

Nobody knew how long the present situation would last. The international scene seemed to be deteriorating. Everybody remembered Roosevelt had said, 'an epidemic of lawlessness was spreading' and had suggested that, 'as with epidemic disease, it might best be met by quarantine.' However, at the Nashua division of the Alabama Paper Corp., it was business as usual.

On September 15th, 1937, the managers of the north-eastern mills had held their annual convention in Boston. After a lobster dinner, those attending relaxed in the deep couches and comfortable chairs of the hotel lobby in which they were assembled. They watched early evening strollers on the walkways of the Common, on the other side of Tremont Street. Hal Hamilton from the Troy, N.Y. mill addressed the man who sat in an easy chair opposite him, "Glad to see you again, Major. How are tricks in your neck of the woods?"

"Ah," sighed Lester, "Some days I don't know whether I'm coming or going. All these never ending responsibilities are getting a little beyond me. It's a bit my own fault. I've never really taken much interest in the mill. It just seemed to run itself. My secretary has kept the paper moving. All of a sudden we seem to have fallen into what they are calling a technology gap. I should have spent less time on the golf course and more time in the office."

"You can't really blame yourself," his colleague replied. "We spent our formative years in the Marines. We learned how to manage men, not machines."

"Maybe you're right," Marshall agreed, feeling better already.

"What you need is a plant doctor," Hamilton continued. "I had one a few years ago. Like you, I hadn't been doing my homework. He set the place right for a generation. Let me tell you about this fella."

"We picked him up a few months before the Crash. He was fresh out of engineering school and a very handy man to have around when the machines went down. He worked out a system which cut our repair time in half."

Hants 35

"Where is he?" Lester blustered. "Sen... Send him to me."

"Would if I could old buddy," Hal smiled. "Fact of the matter is, I haven't seen him for several years."

"What happened to him?"

"Regional sent him to some little place in Maine," the manager from Troy replied. "One of the company's men got into the market over his head. When his creditors closed in to take back his house, they found him strung up in the basement."

The Boston meeting had been six weeks ago. The plant doctor now sat across the desk from Lester, talking about his past experience. At length, the resident-manager had heard enough.

"I really must get ready for an appointment shortly," he interrupted. "Is there anything further you would like to add?"

"Not that I can think of right off hand," Austin admitted.

"Good, glad we've got the introduction out of the way. Now then Brad, I won't beat around the bush with you. As we discussed during our preliminary interviews, you were hired to be groomed as second in command here. We don't want to ruffle any feathers, and I have to justify everything. Head office is not Boston, it's in Alabama and you know how those Southerners are. What I think we will do is run you through the different departments so you can get a general overview. I want you to file a report with follow up suggestions on every operation. I can send a copy of that to head office. Is that fair enough?"

"It sounds perfectly reasonable to me."

"Come along then," Lester said, rising to his feet, "we'll let the girls know what we've decided. After that, the rest of the day is yours."

Marshall's office was symptomatic of everything that was the matter with the mill. It took three women to do the work that one had done twenty years ago. Lester surveyed his staff. Obviously, he couldn't interfere too much. That might upset the apple cart.

The girl, he thought. She hasn't been here too long. She can't be indispensable yet.

"Miss Sylvester."

"Yes sir, Mr. Marshall."

"Miss Sylvester, in his new capacity, Mr. Austin is going to need a sort of a...someone to hold down the fort while he is out making his rounds. It's nothing out of the ordinary, reports and the telephone. You could handle that couldn't you?"

"Oh, I think so sir," she replied hesitantly, looking at Mrs. Morris.

"How does that sound Ethel?" he questioned, catching the glance.

She thought a moment. Angeline was very useful when it came to getting massive amounts of typing done. However, it wasn't like she was going to be changing offices. The thought of reports made her shudder. She knew that Roxanne Fulton was not too keen on all the typing that would be involved in getting the reports out.

She flattered him. "That's a wonderful idea Mr. Marshall!"

He sensed her moment of indecision.

"Of course, Miss Sylvester, you will continue to answer directly to Mrs. Morris."

"Certainly Sir," the young woman assured them both.

"Then it's all settled," he boomed. "We'll see you early Monday morning, Brad."

"Good afternoon ladies," the new engineer said briskly, then took his leave.

That weekend he spent a lot of time walking around, getting reacquainted with an old friend. The town of Nashua didn't recognize him. However, a few faces in the doorways were familiar. On Sunday afternoon, he sat alone in the shade across the street from an old two-storey red brick building. He could still remember the first day that he went there. The Principal had laughed to his assistant, saying that he'd bet the

Hants

Hick wouldn't make it through to Christmas. All through high school his classmates had made fun of him. If it wasn't the Hick then, it was the Hillbilly or the Country Boy. How he had been glad to leave that place and go to Dartmouth.

"Good morning Miss Sylvester," the young engineer said hesitantly as he closed the pebble glass door of the plant's administration office behind him, on Monday morning.

The office had been reorganized over the weekend. She sat behind a desk that had been repositioned to the right of the empty office. Now the words, Operations Engineer were painted on the door in large letters. They were followed by Brad Austin in a smaller point.

"Good morning, Mr. Austin," Angeline said. "Mr. Marshall was on the phone just before you came in. He would like you to go to see the yard Superintendent, Mr. Frost. You need to wear a hard hat in the yard. I put one in the bottom drawer of the filing cabinet in your office."

"My office?" he asked puzzled.

"Yes," she replied getting up and going around her desk to the newly painted door, "this is all yours," She smiled, swinging it open.

Brad felt awkward being here alone with this young woman. He quickly found the hard hat and started to retreat the way he had come. Ethel Morris and Roxanne Fulton were just coming in.

"Here he is," one of them squeaked. Then, "Good morning Mr. Austin," they sang out in unison.

"Good morning ladies," he replied trying to step around them.

"Where are you off to so early, in your fancy hat?" Ethel inquired.

"I'm going down to see the yard Superintendent."

"Do you know where to look?"

"No, but I'll ask someone."

"There is no need to ask someone," she laughed, taking him by the elbow to lead him towards the window. "Angeline, where are your manners?"

"He started to leave, before I could think about it, Mrs. Morris."

"If you go down between those two buildings where that truck just went, you'll come into the area that they call the yard. At this time of the morning, Mr. Frost is usually somewhere around the woodpiles. He doesn't work on the weekends, and the Saturday and Sunday crews usually leave logs strewn all over the place. He wears one of those fancy hats like you've got on."

"Thank you very much, Mrs. Morris. I am sure that I'll have no trouble finding him now."

Angeline watched through the slats of the Venetian blind as he disappeared between the two buildings. This morning she hadn't felt that same awkwardness in his presence. Of course, she felt more confident, wearing a new velveteen jumper.

In spite of her twenty-five years, Angeline Sylvester was exceedingly naive about life. Her notions about men and women had been gleaned from the plots of popular love novels she had read when in confinement. During her eighth summer, her body had been flooded with tuberculosis microbes, while taking a drink from a tin mug, which had been chained to a playground tap. She had lived a shadowy existence in the confines of the TB Sanatorium south of Manchester, during the sixteen years that followed that fateful event. Since being declared cured, she lived with a widowed aunt in the little village of Milford, North West of Nashua, along the Souhegan River.

Irrespective of her aunt's remonstrance regarding her health, Angeline, was determined not to stay a recluse. To fill in the long hours at the sanatorium, she had learned to use a typewriter and had taken secretarial courses by correspondence from a Business College in Manchester. When she saw an advertisement in the Nashua newspaper for an office assistant, there had been no hesitation.

Hants

In the plant yard, Austin came up quietly behind a stocky foreman who watched two men doing a clean-up job.

"Mr. Frost."

The overseer swiveled from the waist. "You must be the new engineer," he said, extending his right hand. "Mr. Marshall told me that you would be around sometime this morning."

"Got a problem with the weekend crews?" Brad inquired as he pointed to the tangle of logs.

"Actually it is not the men's fault, but we rile them about it."

"What do you mean?" Brad inquired.

"I don't want to mention any names," he stipulated, "but it gets darn annoying at times. There seems to be a lack of co-ordination. Last year we ran out of wood and the paper machines were down for a week. This year it's like a tidal wave, and I've been told more is on the way."

Austin could hear the men, who were pushing logs onto a chain drive, talking among themselves.

"I've seen him around some place before," one of the mill workers commented.

"Couldn't have been in town, I've lived here all my life," his team mate replied.

"I'm sure it was in town," the other man continued.

"You've got me."

Superintendent Frost kept talking to Brad, "Have you been inside yet?"

"No, not yet."

"Wait until you get a closer look. There is no direction. The place just runs itself on the men's work experience."

"That door over there will lead me in, won't it?" Brad inquired.

"It sure will."

As he strode off towards the large open doors, Austin could still hear the yard hands' voices.

"You must be mistaken."

"No. I'm sure that's him. He wasn't in the same grade as me, but we were in school together."

"Now I remember. They called him the Hick. He came in off some farm. I remember now. I wonder how he got through to being an engineer."

"Lots of people from farms have got through to high places," his buddy reminded him.

"Yea but this one was real dense. He wasn't well liked either."

During the months that followed, all the facts of the various departments were carefully studied. The Operating Engineer's reports often subtly skirted open criticism. However, there was much that was constructive in them. Marshall was singularly impressed with his new assistant's grasp of every process. In fact, though he admitted it to no one but himself, he learned more about the operation in the six months of appraisal than he had during ten years of residency. One afternoon, the Major, was skimming through the first half of an analysis of the coating operations, which Miss Sylvester had typed. He chuckled loudly to his secretary, who he could see through the open door of his office,

"Ethel, this is astonishing!"

"Are you sure?" she hedged.

"Definitely," he assured her.

Mrs. Morris glanced towards her young assistant. Recently, the girl had abandoned her ponytail for a trendy chignon style. The older woman felt a pang of sympathy. Although the two women had never had an intimate conversation, Ethel was sure that the work alcoholic engineer saw her as little more than another item of office furniture.

For her own part, Angeline's emotions often bordered upon frustration. All his politeness didn't excuse the sin of failing to notice when she was wearing a new dress. Hadn't she poured over these infernal reports, until they were perfect?

Hants 41

Angeline had been her parent's only heir. Purchasing an automobile was one of the first things she had done when starting to pick up the strings of her life after sixteen lost years. The choice had fallen on a 1937 coupe. With its fanning front fenders and louvered hood, the car had the appearance of a crouching animal ready to spring. Going home that afternoon, she found that pushing the accelerator flat to the floor proved to be an excellent way to purge one's self of pent up stress.

"Well how was Mr. aloof today?" her aunt Avis quipped when she arrived. "Did he notice that you were decked out for spring?"

"Who needs Brad Austin anyway?" Angeline huffed contemptuously, throwing her sweater onto a chair, before continuing on through to the dining room. "You've set three places?" the niece remarked inquisitively.

"Yes," affirmed her aunt, "I'm sure Ward Shaw knows how to appreciate a lady."

"He's coming here?"

"He called at your office, but you were gone," the elderly woman explained. "It seems there's something about some bonds that must be signed. I told him to come out to have supper with us, if he had nothing else planned."

Ward was the lawyer who had acted as trustee of her estate, while she was in quarantine up state.

"I better go freshen up," Angeline trilled skipping up the carpeted flight of stairs. "If we're having a dinner guest."

Shaw was an ambitious young man. At the end of his legal practical, he decided to stay on with a local firm in Nashua, instead of heading for the well paid business work in Manchester or the lucrative government contracts in the State Capital at Concord. The senior partners had left the bothersome job of chasing down clients, to get their signatures on a document, to Ward. Now many of them contacted him directly, when they had minor legal matters to be taken care of. Angeline

Sylvester was one of these. She knew that she had to invest the money wisely, which had been left to her, but she preferred to leave the paperwork to someone else.

This evening Ward had some forms regarding the reinvestment of interest that was coming due as a part of the inheritance. After the supper was finished, Mrs. Neville told them to take their papers into the parlor, while she prepared the coffee. When the tray arrived, Shaw was just snapping up his brief case. The women were delighted to have this diversion in their otherwise evening-for-two, even if it meant momentarily abiding by his talk about international relations.

"It'll be over before the year is out," the pretentious young attorney crowed as one hand unbuttoned the vest that was now beginning to pinch as a result of having over eaten.

"Why whatever do you mean?" asked Avis, leading him on as she set down a cup in front of him.

He took the bait and proceeded to pronounce authoritatively, "Hitler doesn't stand a chance. He'll have to surrender."

"I am sure the President would be very pleased," Mrs. Neville said coyly. "He was speaking on the radio the other day and said that Americans have no business getting involved, as it's only another European conflict."

Angeline wasn't interested in what they were saying; however; she didn't want to look the dumbbell. She racked her brains for a scrap of news that she could repeat. There was no pause in her aunt's and Ward's conversation, so she simply blurted out,

"What do you think will happen to Austria now that it has been annexed?"

Ward was taken aback. He sat up straight, twisting one end of his rat-tail moustache then professed, "They will never keep it." It only took one look at Avis's expression to know that his bluff was spreading thin. Still, he managed one last remark, before she could unmask him, "but Mrs. Neville, you seem to be

Hants 43

somewhat of an authority. What do you think will happen?"

"Oh, I'm not really an authority," she spluttered, being caught off guard, "I only like to listen to the President on the radio. He has such a nice voice. I've heard what they are saying about Austria. If we Americans are going to stick to our policy on isolation, I don't think that we should form rigid opinions or take stands, which are too opinionated. If we do, we might end up having to defend them. You know Mr. Shaw; somebody always ends up dying, when somebody decides that opinions have to be defended. Anyway, a busy man like you must talk to a lot of people in the run of a day. Tell us, have you heard any talk around town concerning this engineer who is Angie's new boss. I believe his name is Austin, Brad Austin."

Ward couldn't resist. He was once more easily flattered.

"He can't be a joiner," their guest conjectured. "I haven't seen him around any of the clubs."
"That's because he is always working," Angeline interjected, before thinking. Then after reflecting a moment, she added inquisitively,

"Then you have heard of him?"

"You know what small towns are like, Angeline, especially in New England. Excuse me Mrs. Neville," he added smiling at her. "'First, does he have a wife?' If not, 'Maybe he's an odd fellow?' Then, 'How does somebody his age just show up in town?' Somebody always says, 'Well maybe he has been in prison,' and then when he hasn't just got out of prison, someone always suggests, 'Maybe he carries a gun.' When they get through all that, usually a few of the local divorcees want to know if he has any money."

"And if he doesn't have any money, then nobody wants him," Angeline piped up.

"It's a sad fact about our society ladies; if a man doesn't have any money then he doesn't need a wife. But, once he gets a little cash, it is no longer a question of who, but only when, no matter who."

Angeline blushed, and her aunt coughed a bit too forcibly.

"Anyway, Ward, what have you heard?"

"Down at the boat club, I heard one of the members say that he went through Nashua High. Somebody said that they remembered that he took first prize in physics in his final year. He was a year ahead of me, so I don't really remember much about him. Also they were saying...but you don't want to know all that."

"Sure we do."

"Everybody burst out laughing when one of the fellas yelled out, 'Here comes the Hick.' He was off a farm, and the boys from town mocked him. Even I was the object of some of their jokes. My dad was sort of a gentleman farmer, who paid his bills with money that he had inherited."

The women weren't interested in the past. Mrs. Neville redirected her question, "Perhaps he has found a lady friend?"

The young lawyer looked puzzled then confessed, "I wouldn't know anything about that. However, yesterday I stopped by to see Howie Gordon. You probably don't know of him, but he is sort of an odd job man about Nashua. I was seeing him about moving a few sticks of furniture out to the cottage I've rented for the summer along the Merrimack. It Howie who told me that he moved to a lot of things from the railway storage shed to an old house, just outside of town, for your Mr. Austin."

"I didn't know he had rented a house," Angeline laughed. "He certainly is hush, hush about these things around work. Do you know what the house looks like?"

"You've probably driven by it many times, if you ever take the Boston Road. It's an old ivory brick place, south of town, set back from the highway, down near the river."

Even though Shaw hadn't gone to Manchester or Concord to practice, he was by no means slow. He sensed that the two women were pumping him. It was

Hants 45

as if they were using him as a pass through to another man. He resented it. Before either of them had the chance to come back with another question, he redirected their conversation,

"Angeline, did you know I have my boat in the water now?"

"You mean your rowing boat?"

"No, my sail boat, the rowing canoe is stored on a rack in a boat house, except when it is being used."

"I didn't even know you had a sailboat," she exclaimed.

"It's small," he expounded. "It has a drop keel. You can't use a fixed keel in the Merrimack. There are too many shallow spots. I rent a berth in the Marina at Thornton's Ferry. It's all sanded and varnished now. I should be going out Sunday."

"I simply love the river," his client informed him.

Ward couldn't have been more pleased. "Now there's something I didn't know," he confessed tactfully. "Come to think of it Angeline, there are a lot of things I don't know about you."

This time it was Avis Neville who was taken in by their guest's seemingly innocent comment. "There's only one way to find out more about her young man. You'll just have to invite her out in that sailboat of yours."

Ward Shaw wasn't listening to a word the elderly woman was saying. He was a very practical person. He had only accepted her invitation to supper earlier during the day, because it would afford him a chance to get better acquainted with his client Angeline Sylvester. While driving to Milford from Nashua, he had been consumed by the idea of her inheritance just sitting there collecting interest. There had to be a better way to manage the money. Now his thoughts were running away with themselves. How brilliant of me to have mentioned the sail boat.

"Come to think of it Angeline, that's not such a bad idea. How would you like to come out with me for an hour or two on Sunday afternoon?"

"What time Ward?" she entreated with the air of an adolescent girl.

"I'll come to pick you up around noon."

He left soon afterwards. As Avis closed the door behind him, she looked at her niece and smiled.

"Now that he is making all that money, since he has become a lawyer, it is no longer a question of who, but when."

They both burst out laughing and went to wash up the supper dishes.

Even though the clerical staff at the plant's administration office often found reasons to be disparaging towards the new engineer Austin, the manager Lester Marshall, couldn't have been more pleased with his recruit. Little by little he delegated as many of his responsibilities as possible. Ethel had to admit that there was less of a strain on her. With Lester out from under foot, haunting the fairways once more, it was so much simpler to have things taken care of by the efficient Mr. Austin. As he began to get a better feel for the operations, the men in the plant also began to rely on him more often.

Spring was getting on. The Merrimack Valley was warming up. Brad slept with the window propped up by a short piece of lath. Outside, the night air was filled with a small variety of New England bat gorging themselves on the first hatch of a long-winged, water fly. Suddenly the stillness inside the bedroom was pierced by the telephone ringing out in the hallway. The slumbering man struggled against sleep until his hand found the earpiece on its hook.

"Hello!"

"Excuse me Mr. Austin," an anxious voice apologized. "It's Ned Lyle at the mill, the night supervisor."

"Yes Ned. What is it?"

"We've had a power blackout. Everything is down."

"Have you got the auxiliary diesel generator started up?"

Hants 47

"It didn't want to turn over at first, but it's going now."

"Then you have the emergency lights?"

"No problem there."

"You can start the clean-up then. Have the men tear all the paper off the rollers. Then they can start to clean out the pits under the machines. I'll be in shortly."

"See you when you get here."

"One more thing Ned, be sure that they open all the cocks."

"Right you are, I'll see to it myself."

By the time Brad got in, the night men were getting ready to knock off. It was four hours before the electricity came back on and well into the morning, before the rollers on the dryers of the paper machines were hot enough for start-up. He stood at the control station between two of the huge machines, which had been working on an order for the Syracuse, N.Y. daily newspaper, when the power went off. As the men began to open the valves, letting the pent up steam rush into the machines, the huge rollers started to turn slowly. He watched as the lead machine tender took the soggy tail of newly formed paper. The man began to pass it over the tops of the drying rollers, then catch it on the other side and glide it underneath the next one. It was a skill acquired over time.

If the machine tender went too fast, and the damp white ribbon became too tight, the new sheet of paper would snap off. If he missed it on the downslide, a slack would develop. Either way, it would mean cleaning the rollers off and starting all over. Austin hoped everything would run smoothly. Suddenly the lead tender stepped back onto the catwalk holding his right hand with his left. He had burnt himself. The paper tail was just coming over the top of the roller. It began to loop down into the pit under the machine.

Without a moment's hesitation, the engineer jumped up onto the catwalk beside the man holding his hand. "Are you all right?"

"I've burnt myself on one of the rollers. It's not the first time. Don't worry about me; I'll go to the first aid. Look at the tail. We're losing it."

Brad stepped in between the giant rollers, tore the trailing paper off and began to glide it up onto the next roller. By the time, it was coming down the other side, one of the regular men came up to replace him, so he went back down onto the floor. As he left to go elsewhere, he heard someone jest, "I wonder if he has his union card."

When he got back to the office, Angeline was sympathetic towards him. "I heard that you didn't get much sleep last night."

"These things have a way of happening at the most inconvenient times."

"I don't suppose you had time to eat either."

"No, as a matter of fact I didn't," he replied.

"You'll have to watch that Mr. Austin. That's how a body gets run down."

He smiled at her. "I'll watch it Miss Sylvester."

She smiled back.

Spring turned to summer, and the countryside became green again. Angeline had gone out in Ward Shaw's sailboat several times, but the novelty had worn off. It was Sunday afternoon again. She hated Sunday afternoons at home with her aunt. The radio was always on. It was irritating, especially when she was trying to read. She almost wished Ward would call, but she knew he wouldn't. It wasn't the weather for sailing. She had curled up in the corner of the chesterfield with her book. Abruptly, the music from the radio stopped. A shrill whining noise filled the parlor.

"Ugh!" she exclaimed, looking up.

Her aunt was sitting on a footstool, crouched over the polished-mahogany, cabinet radio, twisting the fine tuning dial.

"Must you do that Aunty?" she squeaked with annoyance in her voice.

Hants 49

"There's a special broadcast about Germany on another station."

"Do we have to listen to all that again today?"

"This is one of my regular programs. Where's Ward today?" the elderly woman quipped.

"I haven't the faintest idea. There's too much fog for sailing today."

"There are other things besides sailing."

"I haven't seen him for about two weeks. When he brought me home the last time, I told him that if he wanted to see me from time to time, I couldn't be more pleased, but not every Sunday."

"Why did you say a thing like that?" Avis scolded.

"I'm not all that interested in sailing."

"I wish I had somebody to take me away from these four walls now and then," her aunt murmured.

"I don't mind it once in a while. I told him I had been cooped up in that TB Sanatorium so many years and had promised myself that I wouldn't become seriously involved with anyone, before I had turned thirty."

"You're a very silly girl," the older woman chided. "He's going to be a wealthy man someday."

"What do you expect?" her niece replied snappishly. "He's the first man to pay attention to me in my whole life. It's hard to get used to. I thought it would be different. Like Scarlet in this novel, I'm reading. She gets dizzy when she sees her fiancée approaching."

Mrs. Neville decided not to venture any further. "I'll keep the radio down low so it won't disturb you."

Angeline let the book close in her lap. She felt like screaming, but that would be stupid. It was just Sunday.

"What time are we going to eat?"

"Same time as usual." Avis declared.

She bit down hard to keep control. "I think I'll go for a spin in the car Aunty. I'll bring us back some dessert."

Avis was about to say, if there were too much fog for sailing, she shouldn't be out driving around; however, she swallowed her words.

"Drive carefully. Be sure that your lights are on."

"I will," her niece called back over her shoulder, then grabbed a hooded cotton jacket off the hall tree, before closing the door behind her.

It was one thing to escape the house, but where should she go. If she went north, the road passed through Amherst, before going on to Mount Vernon. There wouldn't be any shops open in either village today. She wanted to see people. By force of habit, car and driver headed towards Nashua. The ride in didn't take long. She found a small bakery open at the southern extremity of the central business district and purchased a layered strawberry shortcake. It was still early. Supper wouldn't be served in Milford until six o'clock. Why not she thought? I probably won't be able to see the place anyway with all this fog.

The house was where Ward said it would be, just south of town on a curve along the Boston Road, near the Merrimack River. She geared down into second to get a better look, while the car coasted on by. How odd she thought. What appeared to be a candle was burning in a second storey bay window. It made her think of the lighthouses she had seen along the Portsmouth coast. As the car was leaving the curve, Angeline noticed a narrow gravel road running up from the river. There were no approaching vehicles. She veered across the oncoming lane, and continued along the gravel stretch about a hundred yards before stopping and getting out.

The young woman had only walked a few feet, when she began to hear the river. It was still hidden in the mist. The gravel was soft. Several small pieces of it worked their way down into one of her flat walking shoes. She sat on a boulder at the river bank and removed the shoe. Angeline had just finished lacing up the shoe when a voice startled her from behind.

"Are you all right?"

In a panic, she whirled about and met the steady eyes of a man staring down at her.

"Miss Sylvester! What are you doing here?"

Hants 51

Relieved she explained, "Pebbles got into my shoe while walking down the road Mr. Austin."

"Do you come here often?"

She thought for a moment. She didn't want him to think that she was spying on him.

"Oh, it's not the first time I've been here. Usually the weather is better than this. I was in town picking up something for supper. It was too early to go back home. Sundays are boring, cooped up in the house. I thought I'd come for a drive out here, before going back."

She stood up. "I should be getting back. Don't let me keep you from your walk." She took a step in the direction where the car was parked.

"You're not keeping me from my walk Miss Sylvester. Actually, it was stuffy in the house. I decided to come out for a breath of fresh air. I was going to go back up that gravel road which you came down, then walk along the side of the highway to my house. I've rented the top floor of that big cream brick place, just off the curve."

"Please don't call me Miss Sylvester when we're not at work Mr. Austin," she smiled. "There I called you Mr. Austin too."

They both laughed.

"All right Angeline, I'll walk you back up to your car."

As they moved along, side by side, she noticed the droplets of mist clinging to his hair. It must be doing the same thing to mine she thought, pulling up the hood that hung down over her shoulders. When they arrived at the car, he opened the door for her.

"Care to come back to my place for a cup of coffee? That is if it won't keep you late for supper."

She thought for a moment. "I was going to stop in town at that little cafe across from the Town Hall anyway, so why not. Hop in; I'll give you a lift."

"So where is this home that is so boring on Sunday afternoons?" he asked.

"That's right; we have never talked personally at work. You don't even know where I live. It's a quiet little village called, Milford."

"Know it well."

"You do?"

"Sure, on the banks of the Souhegan between Ponemah and Wilton. My dad had a small farm along the Souhegan, a little bit south of Wilton. I went to primary school in Milford. We went to Milford for anything that wasn't available in Wilton."

"I know the area very well," she informed him. I must have passed your family's farm a hundred times. Whereabouts is it exactly?"

"Where the river bends north, there is a bit of a gully. Our place is on the flats and runs up the hill going west. Actually there are about a hundred acres."

"I know the place," she said. "It's abandoned."

Brad flushed with a feeling of guilt. "I must admit, I haven't been out to see it, since coming back to town. It has been so busy at the mill. As you know, I didn't have a car when I first came here and since I was staying at the hotel in Nashua, I really didn't need one. It was just a good walk to work.

When I decided to move out here, I bought a car. That was about six weeks ago. On the weekends, I've been going to the coast, mostly to Rye or Hampton beaches. I'll really have to go out to see the old place one of these evenings. I suppose it's a little dilapidated."

"I've never gone in, but when the leaves have fallen you can just see the outlines of the house between the bushes and trees. The lane is all grown over though."

"I have a brother who lives in Exeter, along the way to the coast. He has been keeping an eye on Hants for the rest of the family. There are four of us, two boys and two girls. I've been paying the county taxes for years now. Yea, I'll have to take a run out one of these evenings."

Angeline looked at him for a moment then smiled.

"Did I say something funny?" he probed.

"You called it Hants."

Hants

"That's what my grandfather named the place when he bought it. Hants is supposed to be a nickname for Hampshire County in England."

"And New Hampshire is named after the county." She boasted.

"That's correct," he added. "So you know your history!"

"I met a boy who lived on that farm a long time ago."

"It couldn't have been me. I would have remembered you. Must have been my brother Shane. He is quite the ladies man."

"I don't know what his name was. He never told me. It was the summer I got sick. My father was a businessman. At that time, he was contracting business from the State of New Hampshire. He had a big machine for macadamizing the roads. One summer he took a job to rebuild the river road between Milford and Greenville. It wasn't a big job, mostly just grading and ditches. He was also doing some macadamizing elsewhere. He went out along the river road about once a week to see how his foreman was doing. Sometimes I went with him. A boy who lived on that farm worked for my father's foreman. He was the water boy."

Brad's jaw dropped down. "How can you remember a water boy, after so long a time?"

"Oh, I've never forgotten him. He gave me a bouquet of daisies and a tin mug of ice cold water. He was older than I was, but he had a nice smile. He called me Little Miss Muffett.

"There's the house Angeline. Pull in this drive. I rent the apartment upstairs. A widow lives downstairs." He waited until she had stopped the car and turned off the ignition. "Was your father a big man with red hair?"

She gasped for air speaking at the same time, "How did you know that?"

"He was my foreman's boss," Brad laughed then opened the car door and got out. "I drew the water that I gave to the men from my father's spring, at the back of the farm. I'll take you there and show you it sometime, if you are interested."

She got out and followed him quickly.

"You said you got sick after that," he continued. "Would I be prying...?"

"No, not at all. It was TB. There was an old pump at the playground in Milford. They said I picked up the germ from an old mug chained to the pump. Two other children did too." They began to climb the wide wooden set of stairs running up the side of the house. "I was eight and my next sixteen years were lived at the TB Sanatorium near Manchester."

"You'll have to excuse the disorder Angeline", he said meekly, extending an arm. "I haven't unpacked all the cases yet. It's just been a week or so."

She looked at him intensely, without speaking. He felt impelled to break the silence and assured her seriously, "Certainly I'll call you Angeline. It's like meeting an old friend," he added extending his hand towards her.

"Isn't life funny," she murmured thoughtfully, withdrawing her hand after shaking his.

"I'll...I'll, put some water on to boil," he said awkwardly moving towards the kitchen. "You'll have to excuse the sauce pan. There's a kettle here some place. I haven't found it yet. I'm accustomed to having someone take care of things, haven't quite got around to getting everything organized yet. There are some records and a gramophone in the parlor, if you want to put on music."

"You have music?" she exclaimed.

"Sure, here I'll show you," he laughed, feeling his confidence return. He side stepped her, leading the way into the front room.

"Mmmm what a pleasant smell, strawberry isn't it?" she murmured.

"Strawberry it is. It's coming from that candle on the window sill. An essence is fused with the wax. It was musky in here earlier. I lit it, before going out for a walk. Here you go. Popular music on the right and serious is on the left. I'll leave you to it."

Hants

She squatted down beside the record rack. What did he mean, 'accustomed to someone taking care of things'? Is there a woman? Is he a widower or could there have been a divorce? There wasn't enough light for her to read the record jackets. She stood back up and pulled the chain hanging down from inside the shade of a large table lamp. A soft yellow glow filled that side of the room.

There were many, half emptied packing cases she hadn't noticed. A wide oak desk was piled high with books. She walked over to examine them, American History, Geography and novels. Here I thought he was a walking slide rule. She laughed to herself turning back to the records.

"Let's see," Angeline murmured, "classical on the left and popular on the right. Blues and Jazz, 'Cold in Hand Blues', I remember that one." She pulled it from the stack and read the cover. Bessie Smith accompanied by Louis Armstrong. Her hand withdrew another 78. Cole Porter, 'Let's Do It'. Another Porter, 'Anything Goes'. "Oh, I know this one. It's from the musical."

"Talking to yourself," he asked coming in from the kitchen?

She spun around on her toes remaining squatted. Brad stood above her holding a large serving plate. "Not a bad selection of recordings you have here."

"Find something you like?" she handed him Porter's, 'Anything Goes'

"Good choice, one of my favorites, I'll put it on the gramophone for you," he added setting the serving plate down.

Angeline stood up and took a piece of buttered fruit bread then walked over to the desk and picked up one of the volumes laying open face down. "Have you read all these books?"

"Most or at least parts of most," he informed her.

She examined the volume in her hand, 'The Battle at Gettysburg'.

"Reading this kind of book won't help you run a mill."

"I know, but it helps me get out of the 'Slide Rule Joe' stereotype. If I hadn't read that, I would never have known that six hundred thousand uniformed soldiers from both sides died in the Civil War. It was in that book that I learned that the Civil War wasn't about slavery at all."

"No! What was it about then?" she demanded.

"They wanted to create a new Union made up of all the countries and states which surrounded the Caribbean, sort of a golden horseshoe."

The music began to come out of the horn, and the kettle started to whistle at the same time.

"I hear you found your kettle," she said smiling.

"Yea," he replied a bit embarrassed, "it was in a cardboard box under the counter. Guess I'm a bit lazy."

"Or used to a wife taking care of you," she pried cautiously

"There is no wife. What gave you that idea?"

"You said that you were accustomed to someone taking care of things."

"Oh I was referring to my sisters," he said, before disappearing into the kitchen.

Angeline began to feel more comfortable in these strange surroundings. There were two paintings on opposite walls. The one above the desk was an idyllic pastoral scene of a boy and a girl, dressed in farm work clothes against a background of rolling hills. The other was midway between the wide double bay and the corner of the room. It was also a rural scene. The artist had enclosed a demure cottage between a meandering, broken-down picket fence and the wavering of blossoming fruit trees.

She went and picked up the plate of fruit bread and brought it over to the low table in front of the couch, before sitting down. Brad re-appeared soon after carrying a tray containing two cups, a sugar bowl and a thick, white creamer.

Hants

"Hope you didn't get bored waiting?"

"Not at all, I was looking at your paintings."

"They are both rural, but I like them. The one above the desk is called, 'Spring'. It's by a New England artist named Winslow Homer. Actually it's a copy. The original is in a private collection somewhere. They're both copies, 'Spring' reminded me of myself, my brother and my sisters when we were young on our farm. The other one is by Willard Metcalf. It's called, 'The Little White House' and is so typical of a New England spring."

"I must admit, I'm a little surprised by what I'm seeing here today. Around the office, no one would ever suspect there's this other side to you. You're always so busy, talking about machines and schedules. And this fruit bread, I recognize it. They sell it at the same little bakery on the south side of town where I bought strawberry shortcake for my aunt and me today."

"I could say the same. I've never seen you not wearing a dress. And you've always called me Mr. Austin up until today. I like how you are, when you're not at work."

Angeline's confidence was buoyed up, and she pressed on, "Before you went to get the coffee, you mentioned it was your sisters who had usually taken care of things?"

"That's right. I have one brother, Shane and two sisters, Wendy and Dora. After my father died of a heart attack, my mother decided not to continue working the farm. Shane and I had both left. I was up in Hanover at Dartmouth studying engineering. My brother was down in Boston working part time and writing poetry the rest of the time."

"A poet, does he still write poetry?"

"No, we each had a small inheritance, after my father's death. I used mine to pay for my studies. He gave up working and writing poetry to become a card player and sort of a ladies man."

"Where's he now?"

"He lives in a hotel over in Exeter where he also works as a barman."

"What about your sisters?"

"As I was saying, my mother decided not to keep working the farm. It was too hard for a woman alone. She moved into Nashua with Wendy and Dora to live with my aunt and uncle. Their children had left for the army, marriage, New York City and the West Coast. They had a big empty house. My sisters stayed there, until after our mother died from pneumonia. Then they came to stay with me. At the time, I had a very well paid position in Troy, N.Y."

"Where are your sisters now?"

"Both married," he declared. "The eldest married an accountant in Troy. Dora came to live with me when I was transferred to Maine. While back visiting Wendy, she met a fella who owns a small cheese factory in a place called Canton, N.Y. It's about forty miles north of Troy. I went to their wedding, just before moving back here."

Angeline smiled at him and sunk back into the corner of the couch.

"It's your turn," he insisted. "Now that you know everything about me, I would like to know something about you."

"Me? There is really not much to tell. I am just a girl who was sick most of her life. I told you when we were in the car. I was in the Sanatorium outside of Manchester for a long time. While I was there, my father stopped doing road contracting work. He had earned quite a bit of money and bought a small furniture factory in Hudson. He drove over to Hudson every morning to run his factory and then came back to Nashua in the evening. My mother and he would take a trip to the Caribbean most winters. My father liked marlin fishing. One winter they never came back. The government notified us that their boat got caught in a squall while out fishing. They and two other couples were never found."

Hants 59

"Excuse me. I didn't mean to pry."

"You were not prying. This is good for me. When I came out of the Sanatorium, I went to live with my aunt Avis, in Milford. Then there was a job, which came up in the mill. I could have moved into town, but that would have meant leaving my aunt who wouldn't budge. She's my only family, well near family. The problem was solved by buying that great big car you admire so much." She smiled at him. "I saw the envy in your eyes back by the river. I have my inheritance too, but I didn't spend it up at Dartmouth."

Brad continued to ask her about herself. "That doesn't tell me very much. How about your family, the Sylvester's, have they been around these parts very long?"

She took a deep breath before going on, "My aunt Avis is the expert on who's who in the Sylvester clan, but I'll take a stab at it. I can go back as far as Charleston in South Carolina. That was my great, great, great grandfather. He had worked as a junior reporter and printer's helper on a newspaper in Charleston. Once his apprenticeship was over he headed for New York City, where he became and was a journalist for forty years. One of his sons went to Normal School.

"When he received his teacher's certificate, he and his wife who was also a teacher, moved into Connecticut. They had three boys. One of them studied agriculture. That was my grandfather. He wanted to be a farmer. His grandfather, the journalist, bought him a small place outside of Hudson that was in a tax sale. He didn't want the money repaid to him. All he asked was that he could spend his summers on the farm, as long as he wanted. He was retired, and he didn't like New York City in the summertime.

"My father didn't take to farming. When he was, young he went into the Army and studied military engineering at the same time. When he was discharged, he started a road contracting company. It was quite a good business. You know how hard the weather is on the roads in New Hampshire. And that's it."

Then she sat up straight and with a rather childlike tone to her voice chided, "One lineage deserves another." She even imitated him, "Has your family been around these parts very long?"

"You don't want to hear all that," he laughed.

"Sure I do, tit-for-tat," she chirped.

Brad could see he had no choice, if he was to retain her confidence. "OK, then here goes. My great, great grandfather was an adventurer from Europe. He had a small inheritance and decided to cross the Atlantic to see if he could double his money. On the boat over he met another man who was of the same temperament and situation in life as himself. They formed a plan to buy dry goods, when they got off the boat and go trading in the West. The two of them made quite a bit of money then turned to wagon training new settlers to homesteads in the Midwest. The first Austin settled in St. Louis and raised a family.

"They sent one of their sons to Boston to a Commercial College. That was my grandfather. He was supposed to go back to St. Louis, to take over his father's business. However, he decided he liked the east and ended up buying Hants, with a little help from his dad. He and my grandmother had one son, my dad. They spoiled him."

"My father didn't like the city so he hung around Hants. His father was annoyed because he wouldn't go to study agriculture. Also, he had absolutely no idea about farming. What saved him was his physical strength and stamina. It was a hard life, but he ran a very productive farm. He passed on shortly after I went off to first year of university. You see; I told you, you didn't want to hear about my lineage."

"Thank you!" she said.

The flip side of the recording they had been listening to came to an end and the needle began to scrape on the last threads. Brad got up and set the arm

Hants 61

on its bracket. He turned off the gramophone and switched on the radio. An announcer's voice became audible. He was talking about troop movements.

"Oh no," she sighed with resignation, "not Germany again. That was one of the reasons why I didn't stay at home this afternoon."

"We'll just listen for a minute. I want to get an update."

"I thought the President said America had no business in a European war."

"Isolation is over. The President said it himself. He said that, 'an epidemic of lawlessness is spreading' and has suggested that, 'as with an epidemic disease, it might be met best by a quarantine'."

"When did he say that?"

"He said it last fall in Chicago. We're now in the summer of 1938, and it's a whole different ball game."

The radio announcer broke in on their conversation, "And with this up to the minute bulletin, we conclude our report for today."

Brad turned the knob slightly, tuning in the signal of a station playing band music. He remained standing. His previous cheerful mood had been replaced with an air of brooding.

Angeline felt confused. She had put Ward Shaw off a little lately. That was only fair game, according to the romance novels she had read. Yet there was something between herself and Ward.

Brad Austin wasn't exactly her superior. She reported directly to Mrs. Morris. However, he was above her in the office hierarchy. Those were two good reasons why she shouldn't be too personal with him. Still she couldn't help being curious. Perhaps it was naivety.

"Is something the matter?" she volunteered.

"Excuse my rudeness," he replied, forcefully grinning back at her. "It's just that I started to think about Austria. I've never told anybody this, but I was seriously thinking of going into the Marines, just before head office transferred me here. Even then I was sure that we were going to get involved."

Angeline only smiled discreetly. It was her policy not to have any opinion on the subject. He kept pacing in front of the window. She felt uncomfortable. Suddenly he wheeled about on his heels and glared at her from across the room. She could see the agitation beaming from his eyes.

"I feel so helpless about what's going on over there," he lamented. "I want to do something. Not just listen to radio reports."

He turned back to the window and stared absently into the mist filled space on the other side of the pane. When the tension had fully subsided, he came to sit on the other end of the couch. His voice was calm now.

"I was thinking about war this afternoon by the river, before you came along."

"It's probably just the weather," she encouraged.

"Maybe, but I don't think so."

"What do you think?"

"Ever since I read what the President said in Chicago, I find myself thinking more and more this is not just another European conflict."

"And if it isn't, then what?"

"I am thirty-four Angeline. There's a fifty-fifty chance they'll accept me. I go for my medical Tuesday. If I pass it, I am turning in my resignation to Mr. Marshall."

In spite of herself, Angeline had been suspended in a pleasant euphoria since hearing there wasn't any Mrs. Austin in a closet somewhere. Now she felt a strange queasiness coming over her. It simply wasn't fair. She was only really meeting him for the first time today. Now he was telling her that he wants to go away. This wasn't the way things happened in her novels. Now she remembered how the nurses warned her that novels aren't real life, when she had been in the TB Sanatorium.

"I really should be going," she said suddenly, feeling hot flashes rushing over her. "My aunt will be wondering where I am. She didn't want me out this afternoon. She was complaining about the fog. She will have visions of me overturned some place in a ditch."

"You will come again? Better still, we'll have lunch together in town one day."

"It will have to be soon," she blurted out. "I mean if you are going to resign and go into the Marines and go to war."

Austin turned pale. "Don't mention that to anybody. It just slipped out. My mind isn't one hundred percent made up. Besides, I don't even know if they will accept me."

He accompanied her to her car. When she had backed out on to the shoulder, she leaned over to crank down the passenger window, before waving and calling out,

"Bye, see you tomorrow. Thanks for the coffee."

Ethel Morris looked up from the week's schedule she was drawing up when her assistant entered the office, slightly late, Monday morning. During the next hour, she couldn't help notice the erratic pounding of the typewriter keys. A number of times the young woman yanked the paper from the roller, crumpled it violently, and then discarded it into the wire mesh waste basket. Ethel decided to put aside her rule of non-interference.

"How was your weekend Angeline?"

"Oh, fine except for the weather."

"You and Ward couldn't go out in his boat I suppose?"

"No, as a matter of fact, I didn't see him on the weekend," she pouted.

"Is everything all right between you and Ward?"

"Everything is fine. We're just taking a weekend off."

"They can be long when you're cooped up all weekend."

"Don't I know it, especially with my aunt. Yesterday I went for a ride."

"That's what I should have done. Where did you go to?"

"As a matter of fact I ran into Mr. Austin. He invited me over to his new place for coffee and fruit bread."

"New place, you mean he isn't still at the hotel."

"No, he has rented the top floor of that old house out along the Boston Road, just at Dead Man's curve."

"Oh, I know that place. The people who own it are Thomas. She worked in the records department at the Town Hall before retiring. I heard her husband died. I haven't seen her for a while. How's Mr. Austin?"

"I don't dare tell you Mrs. Morris. Besides, it's really none of my business."

"For something that is really none of your business, you certainly seem to be letting it affect your work." Then she laughed, "I am not prying Angeline. It's just that I've been watching you trying to type for the last half-hour. It doesn't seem to be going too smooth."

Angeline felt herself blushing. She didn't stop to think. "It's going to affect you too Mrs. Morris. It's going to affect all of us." She wanted to bite her tongue, but it was too late.

In the small world of office gossip, nothing is sacred. It wouldn't have mattered if Angeline were under oath. After a ritualistic promise, not to divulge a word, Ethel found out everything she needed to know. The Major came bustling in shortly after ten and Ethel followed him directly into the inner office. The door was discreetly closed behind them.

"Great day, Ethel," Marshall boomed, pulling up the Venetian blind with a loud snap.

"You know what they say," she rejoined, putting the mail down on his blotter pad.

"What do they say?" he inquired, idly sorting through the envelopes.

"That there is always calm, before a storm."

Hants 65

Two people don't work together for ten years without understanding each other's idiosyncrasies. Lester had sensed there was something, when he noticed her closing the door, after following him in. Now she was talking metaphorically. Letting the mail go, he searched her face for a clue.

"What storm is that, Ethel? What else do they say?"

His right hand lady started slowly, fussing with the paraphernalia on the desk.

"You know I can't tell you where I heard this."

"Have I ever pressed?"

"No, but this time, not a word and no joking outside of this office," she insisted.

"Not a word."

"It's Brad," she exclaimed.

"Well, what about him?"

Ethel went on briefly to inform him of what she had heard.

"Of all the nonsense," Lester protested, before her last word was finished, "he can't do that."

"We're not at war. The Marines don't need anybody. If we do go to war, there are lots of stumblebums wandering around this country who will gladly volunteer, so they can get three meals a day and a steady pay cheque. I know what it's all about. I was a Major in the Marines."

"Still think it's a nice day?" she teased.

"Sure it is," he declared, putting his hand on hers to help her open the office window.

It had been five years since a chronic case of cancer had claimed the Major's wife, Audrey. To the end, Lester had been a devoted husband. His personal secretary and office manager, Ethel Morris, had been widowed seven years when Audrey passed on. Her husband, the editor of the Nashua Examiner, had died in a hunting accident in Maine, around Bangor.

Ethel began by giving Lester moral support until his mourning grew lighter. After a year and a half, they started to become friends. She remembered the first time that he had put his hand over hers, while she was opening the office window. It was their secret. Not even Roxanne knew at there was anything between them other than a working relationship.

Suddenly the intercom on his desk sounded. It was Roxanne in the outer office. "There's a call for you on line 1, Mr. Marshall. It's Mr. Austin. He's down in production."

"Thank you Miss Fulton."

"Not a word to him."

"I promised. By the way, do you know if Tony Edwards is still in charge at the Recruiting Centre?"

"I haven't the foggiest. You'll have to call him."

It was Friday afternoon, before Lester Marshall got back to the subject of his Monday morning conversation with Ethel.

"Good afternoon, U.S. Marines Recruiting, Major Edwards speaking."

"Afternoon Tony, this is Lester Marshall speaking."

"Hello there stranger, it must be almost two years now."

"Time flies when you are busy."

"Don't I know it! What can I do for you this afternoon?"

"It's just a little private inquiry, strictly off the record."

"Try me. I can only say no."

"It's about one of my men. I heard through a friend that he was thinking of signing up. He was supposed to have had a medical this week."

"What's the fellow's name, Lester?"

"Austin. Brad Austin."

"Hold on. I'll just be a sec. ......okay, I have the file here. First time I've looked at this. We're getting quite a few men coming through these days. They say that there's a war in the air. I'll wait until it happens. Nope, the Doc, has not passed him. My, my, he's an engineer too. The Marines could have used a man like that."

"Not passed him?" Lester feigned surprise.

Hants

"No flat feet, when we're not at war! The Docs apply the regulation to the letter. Sorry Lester, there's nothing I can do to change that."

The mill manager breathed a silent sigh of relief, "Such a shame, I heard that he had his heart set on it."

"Sorry, Major. He is not the only one. We're only taking the most fit these days, if there is no military obligation."

"Thanks anyway Tony, how about meeting me for lunch next week? Wednesday open for you?"

"Fine by me, where?"

"Does the Legion sound all right?"

"It's my favourite spot. I have to go. Someone is waiting. I'll be there about 12:15 next Wednesday."

Lester decided the good news from the Recruiting Office was reason enough to call it a day. Ethel was doing some filing when she heard him cracking his knuckles behind her.

"Remember that little cloud that blew in Monday?"

"Ugh!" she exclaimed turning around and looked straight at him gritting her teeth. Then she jerked her head towards Angeline's desk.

"I know," he half whispered, then continued, "it blew back out to sea. We'll never see it again."

"Thank God," she breathed softly.

"I'm going to call it a day. I'll see you ladies Monday."

Angeline and Roxanne half raised their heads for a second and said, "Bye."

When Ethel was sure they had returned to their work, she moved her lips without speaking, "Call me."

He winked and left.

It came as a shock to everybody when Lester and Ethel announced their plans to be married early in the fall. The rumor mill took it up. How long had this been going on? Poor Mrs. Marshall, poor Mr. Morris, some even said that it was like bigamy. Lester and Ethel had only planned to take a month long honeymoon and then return to their work. That was before they got wind of the stories going around town behind their backs. They were disgusted.

"Why bother to come back here at all?" Lester said to her one day. "We could be just as happy elsewhere and we wouldn't have these sly grins gaping at us."

"I was only waiting for you to say the word," Ethel said angrily. "I detest this little town. My house is up for sale tomorrow."

"Mine too! Where will we go?"

"I have a sister in Albuquerque, New Mexico."

"Did I ever tell you how much I've always wanted to see Albuquerque?"

She threw her arms around him and kissed him. They resigned together and left Nashua, after a small private ceremony.

***

The Thimble Game

3

With a two-fold increase in his responsibilities, it was late in the autumn of 1938, before Brad Austin eventually found the time to pay a long overdue visit to Hants. Overhead, a wide v-formation of geese flew towards the south, as his car approached the property from the east, along the Souhegan River Road. The ten-acre field along the flats between the road and the river came into view first. Immediately he noticed the gaping bald spots in the dead vegetation, which pock marked the field. The car nosed off the road onto the beginning of the lane, which was overgrown with several seasons of dead burdock and milkweed shrubs.

After crossing the River Road and stepping through the remains of a page wire fence, the perplexed man walked out onto the river flats. It was unbelievable! What had once been the most fertile spot on the Austin place was now nothing but a bed of grey clay, spotted with patches of gravel out of which grew a tangle of weeds. What had happened? A spring flood could never have destroyed an uncultivated piece of land to such an extent.

He knelt down to examine a ripple in the hard clay. Each groove was uniform. They looked very much like the imprints left behind by a tracked vehicle. There were more of them. It all became too evident. Someone had scrapped off the rich, black topsoil and silt that had built up over centuries. Angrily, he kicked at the hard ground then set off in the direction of the farm buildings leaving the raped fields behind.

The house came into view first. It was a square; two storey structure made of round field stones and mortar. A sheet of roof steel had been folded back by the wind. The black paint that once covered the steel had long since flaked away. Now there was only rust. The clapboard had turned black from exposure to the sun and rain. Not a windowpane remained. Only one shutter had survived awkwardly clinging to a rusty anchor bolt. Several other shutters leaned against the house where they had fallen. Vandals had left the front door ajar. Brad didn't want to go in. He felt a dry lump of guilt swelling up into his throat. Why hadn't he come sooner?

Going around to the back of the house, he became even more mystified. Rows of stumps rose up towards the crest of the hill, where once forty apple trees had grown. There was no path. Everything had grown over. He went down to the creek and followed it back towards the buildings.

The equipment shed was empty. Perhaps his mother had sold off some things when she moved into Nashua. The big double doors of the tall gray board barn were swung back. Several of the vertical boards were missing from the walls. He went inside. Strands of hay hung down from the loft. Even though the hay had long since dried, its warm, rich odor began to penetrate his nostrils.

He started to feel better and climbed up onto the threshing floor to look out the open upper door, back

Hants

towards the house. Only the roof showed through the trees. It was like entering another world. Memories started to come back. The brothers had come up here with their father, to flail the harvested grain.

He wondered whether the spring had gone dry. It had been a hot summer. "I should go back and see," he muttered to himself.

While making his way up through the pasture, his right foot began to hurt. The Marines had called it fallen arches. Why hadn't he gone to see a doctor? If a special shoe had been worn, the problem would have long since been corrected.

The spring was just in front of a small bush that acted as a watershed, at the back of the property. Water still trickled from the concrete spout his father had built. It was cold and had a sweet taste to it. Brad cupped his hands and went back for more several times.

Straightening up, he noticed that a trail had been cut into the bush off to the right. It couldn't have been long ago. The opening hadn't grown over yet. He went to investigate.

The puzzled man only had to penetrate the trail a few yards, before it became too evident. This was the start of their sugar bush. Here and there he saw thick maple stumps jutting out of the undergrowth. Someone had harvested the mature maple trees.

Suddenly, the euphoria, which had started in the barn, evaporated. The same bitterness came back into his mouth as when he had discovered the tractor treads on the flats. A quiet anger began gripping at his stomach. He had to see Shane.

Natalie Austin had willed the property equally to her two sons. The girls had been left what little money remained to her. She had meant for the farm to draw the two boys together. She had hoped that they would come back to it. Now it was the beginning of a wedge that would grow between them. The younger son's self-reproach began to fade. He had paid the taxes.

Why had Shane let this happen? As he walked briskly back to the car, he began to feel bitter towards his older brother.

The dusty sedan had just cleared the western outskirts of Milford, when Brad made his decision. A gas station appeared on the side of the road about a quarter of a mile ahead. There was a public telephone booth out front, near the road. The car pulled to a stop beside it.

"Yes operator I would like to phone Exeter."

"Do you have the number sir?"

"I want the main number for the hotel over there."

"I have two hotels in the directory sir, The Exeter House and The Appalachian Hotel."

"I'll take them both."

The desk clerk at the Exeter said that no one named Shane Austin was on their staff, so he tried the Appalachian.

"Yes sir, we have a Shane Austin working here. He's the bar man. The bar is only open during the evening dinner on Sundays. I know Mr. Austin isn't in his room. He went out a while ago, and he has to pass by me on the way back in. Would you like to leave a message?"

"No, that will be fine thanks. I'll drop in to see him."

It was 4 p.m. Exeter was about a two-hour drive. He could go up to Manchester and take the Portsmouth Rd. Exeter was about twenty miles inland from Portsmouth. If he stopped for supper along the way, he'd be at the Appalachian, a bit after the dinner hour. Brad pulled the car away from the phone booth and stopped by the gas pumps.

"Fill it up, please," he said to the attendant.

An hour and a half later, the younger Austin slid the plate forward upon which the fresh Gloucester flounder had been served. He was at Chester, about half way between Manchester and Exeter on the Portsmouth Road. When the waitress took away the supper dishes, he asked for the bill.

Hants

The Appalachian Hotel was an older styled building on the eastern exit of the town. It was set back from the street on a curved driveway. Four white columns supported a balcony over the front entrance. A decorative cornice extended out beyond the supports. As he parked along the curved driveway, Brad heard the tinkling of cutlery coming through the open floor length French windows, along the building's right wing.

The dining room was a large carpeted room with several chandeliers suspended over the white, cloth-covered tables. At the back of the room, a double set of swinging doors gave way to the kitchen beyond. A dark wooden bar with a polished brass foot rail ran along the left side of the room. Many different sized and colored bottles were arranged in front of the mirrored wall, located behind the bar. The older Austin was mixing a drink and didn't notice his brother sit himself down on one of the tall four legged chairs pulled up at the rail.

Shane stopped and stepped backwards, when he saw who was sitting at the end of the counter. Slowly he approached the spot.

"Brad! What brings you to Exeter?"

"I was in Portsmouth for the day. I'd heard that you were working here and decided to stop in."

"Can I get you something?"
"Coffee will be fine."

"Say you heard I was working here," his brother said pouring the coffee. "I didn't think that anybody still knew of my existence."

Brad felt uneasy.

"Yea, one of the men at work mentioned it one day. I can't recall his name."

"It's nice to be remembered," Shane said smiling. "Would you like a piece of cake with your coffee? They make great cheese cake here."

"No, I'll pass. I had a flounder for supper, and it's just starting to settle."

"So what's new? I heard you were back in Nashua. I would have looked you up, but I never go over that way. I go over to Portsmouth myself once in a while. A few of my card buddies live there."

"Still playing cards, are you?"

"Oh yea, it's just a pass time, nothing big."

"I stay away from gambling. My money is too hard come by," Brad replied sipping on the coffee.

A waitress tapped a spoon against a glass at the far end of the bar.

"I'll be right back. Just have to mix a drink." He wasn't gone long. "So how are the sisters? Either of them had any kids yet?"

"None that I've heard of," the younger brother replied.

"I would have come to the wedding, but I didn't get an invitation."

"We didn't know where to send it."

"Yea, well I was...I didn't exactly have a steady address around that time?"

"No," Brad remarked, feeling more confident, "having troubles were you?"

"Just money," Shane replied looking at him sideways, "you know cards. I had a streak of bad luck. A couple of people were itchy to get paid."

"I think you've had that problem before."

"Yea, well that is my business Brad."

"Could be that it's mine too."

"How's that," Shane asked?

"I've been out to Hants."

Shane stepped back and replied angrily, "So what about it?"

"Somebody has been hacking it to pieces. That's what it's about."

"If that's what you stopped in here to talk to me about, you can finish your coffee and move along."

"You've let somebody wreck that place Shane."

"I needed the money."

"It was left to both of us."

"Yea, well I needed my part of it fast."

"You didn't have any legal right."

Hants

"Don't talk to me about legal," Shane hissed dropping his fist down hard on the counter in front of his brother. "What some people were going to do to me wasn't very legal either."

The waitress looked down at them.

"What do you mean coming around where I'm working, bringing up family?"

"What I mean is that was our father's place. He killed himself putting it in shape."

"He wasn't the only one, little brother. I put in lots of free work on that land."

"And you mean to say I didn't."

"Listen Brad, I didn't mean to say anything, but what I am saying is get to hell out of here."

"You let them take out the maple bush. The flats are washed out."

"Look Mr. Austin, do I have to call the law. Another word and you can explain it to an officer."

Brad was just coming to a rage inside, but he caught himself. He didn't need any contact with the Police, even if there was nothing to worry about. Obviously he couldn't trust Shane. He pulled a bill from his pocket and threw it on the counter, before turning to leave. Shane laughed and jeered after him,

"Don't bother coming back little brother. Next time I'll stick the law on you."

The waitress came up and stood across from the bar man. "Was that some drunk giving you a hard time?"

"That was my kid brother."

"Whatever it was, you sure clammed him up in a hurry," she flattered.

"That's one thing I've never had much trouble doing."

"Would you give me four Irish Coffees for table number six, please?"

"My pleasure, Susan," the bar man said with a smile.

Brad arranged to have the house boarded up, and the roof nailed down. A month later the New England countryside staggered under the frozen paw of a late season hurricane. Freezing sleet covered all the roads around Nashua. Once more the problems at the mill became primordial.

The intercom on the mill manager's desk began to crackle.

"Mr. Nelson is here to see you."

"Send him in, please, Angeline."

A short, well-built man with close-cut red hair and a trimmed bushy beard came through the door.

"Morning Rod," his boss greeted him. "What's new, out in that scrap heap today?"

"Bit of the usual for this time of year," the head of the maintenance department replied, "two water lines exploded last night. I've got the shop looking into it."

"Good, good," Austin repeated pensively. "While you're here, I think that a few congratulations are in order."

"Congratulations, whatever for?"

"For the good job you and your boys have done repairing all those steam leaks. Look at this," Brad said passing him a file. "The top copy is for you. Post it in your department."

"What is it?"

"It's a report from the boiler house for last month. For the same amount of production, over the preceding thirty days, our steam bill was down ten thousand dollars."

"I'll pass your thanks along to the men," the supervisor assured him. "I have to be frank with you though. The problem was brought to Mr. Marshall's attention on a number of occasions, but he would never authorize the extra maintenance program. I suppose that he didn't seem to realize how serious the problem was seeing that he seldom came into the plant."

"We can't change the past Rod and we can't just scrap all those rust buckets today. However, if we can

Hants

keep the operating costs down like your department has done with this repair program, who knows, we may just be able to replace a few things. Seeing the success that you've had with the maintenance schedule, there's another area of waste control that I would like to discuss with you."

"What's that?"

"I came across a report in a scientific journal," Austin continued, while he rummaged through the desk drawer, "if I can still find it. Yes, here it is. As you know, at the present time when we've finished boiling down the wood chips in that black liquor solution, it gets pumped out into settling basins, before we run it off into the Merrimack River."

"I've often thought it's a waste."

"This article outlines a process called carbonation."

"I'm afraid you've got me there."

"Well, to make a long story short, if we bubble carbon dioxide through the spent liquor solution here in the mill, before we pump it out into the settling basins, we could precipitate out a salt which would make the whole thing reusable. It could be reused several times, before it would have to be discharged."

"I am not exactly sure what you are getting at."

"If we could reuse the black liquor solution three or four times, just think of the saving."

"Now I get your drift," he said with a wide grin breaking across a full set of teeth, "but where does my department come in?"

"There are a few modifications I'd like to try out on some of the equipment. Here, I've made some sketches. I want you and your department to take a look at them. Nothing fancy, we're only ten thousand dollars under budget. I'd rather use the money trying out this idea than reporting it to head office. They would only expect us to cut ten thousand every month after that."

"I understand Mr. Austin."

"Get back to me when you think that you have it worked out."

At 3 p.m. on December 24th, the thirty odd members of the office staff at the Nashua mill stopped work. Lots of things had changed since Marshall's departure, but the annual staff party had weathered its way through to another year. Angeline spotted Brad leaving the payroll supervisor with the first aid nurse and head off towards a table of sandwiches. She quickly downed the contents of her glass and picked up another from a tray, before striking off in his direction.

"And how's the big boss making out?" she giggled behind him.

He turned about with half a sandwich still in his mouth. "If I didn't know better Angeline, I'd say you were making fun of me."

"Try me," she giggled back.

"Then you have been drinking."

"It's Christmas time Mr. Austin."

"I thought we had a deal. I'd call you Angeline, and you would call me Brad."

"I remember that day Brad," she replied a little more seriously, "but tell me, can I ask you a question?"

"Sure, fire away."

"Have you ever been in love? I mean have you ever had a girlfriend?"

"Sure, I've had lots of them," he joked while smiling back at her.

"Fine, that's all I wanted to know on that subject. Now I have another question for you. Are you superstitious?"

"It all depends."

"Okay, then do you have confidence in me?"

"I think so, but what's this leading to?"

"Just close your eyes and walk in the direction I lead you."

"Where are you going to take me?" he asked, closing his eyes as he felt her taking his hand.

Hants 79

"You'll see. Excuse us Mrs. Cox. Can we get through?"

"Certainly Miss Sylvester, push over Hank they're trying to get through." A balding individual stepped aside holding his glass over their heads.

"Okay, you can open your eyes now," she declared, starting to giggle again.

"What was that all about?"

"Look up."

As he saw the mistletoe, he felt her lips come up against his then quickly withdraw. There was an outburst of cheering and clapping from everyone at the party.

"Who's next?" someone asked.

Brad took her by the elbow and guided her back to the sandwich table where they had been standing.

"You were asking about my girlfriends."

"That's right."

He smiled. "I even went so far as to propose one time. I was in about the same condition you are just now."

"You don't have to tell me about it," she said reaching for a sandwich.

"Oh, there's no problem. It was a fast summer thing, up in Maine. She had come from Europe to head up the design department of a woolen-knitting mill. She had studied textiles at school and then went on to work in design after graduating. Her company transferred her here. At the end of the summer, she was called back home, when her mother died. Her father was in a bad way, and she stayed on to take care of him. One thing lead to another, and finally she couldn't see her way into coming back."

"Fine," Angeline said giggling again. "I was only wondering. I think I'll go over to say hi to Helen. See you later."

After the New Year, Angeline settled into a winter routine. The mistletoe hadn't had much effect on her boss. He wasn't completely indifferent to her, like he had been when he first came to assist Mr. Marshall, but she couldn't detect any personal interest. She was still seeing Ward, so it really didn't matter.

Ward didn't like cross-country skiing, but she had joined a club anyway and was out most weekends. There were lots of new people. She was even invited to go into Boston one weekend by a mortgage broker who came out to ski with their group several times. She hadn't said no, just maybe some other time.

"Penny for your thoughts," Mrs. Neville burst out one morning as she was bouncing her duster over a collection of antique clocks in the parlor.

Her niece stood gazing out the bay window looking at the greening lawn around the house.

"Are you deaf girl?" the elderly woman exclaimed louder.

"Are you talking to me Aunty?"

"No, I'm just talking to hear myself think."

"I'm sorry. What were you asking?"

"What has happened to that mortgage man you were talking about?"

"Oh, the ski season is over."

"Didn't he mention something about taking you shopping in Boston some Saturday?"

"There was a mention, but you know, I am still seeing Ward. It was fine when we were all together in a group skiing. I was just not sure I would want to be alone with him all day in Boston."

"Well, where is Ward?"

"I was talking to him on the phone, while you were making your bed. He's working all day sanding down the hull of his boat."

"Girls can sand down boats too!"

"Oh, I don't want to do anything like that."

"What about, you know who at work," Avis insisted.

"That's only at work Aunty."

"I still think he has some mystery woman tucked away somewhere."

Hants

"I don't think so. There's nothing but work with him for the time being. Marshall left the place in a terrible state. Head office is starting to ask a lot of questions. Do you remember the Sunday last year I went into town in spite of the fog and brought back the strawberry shortcake?"

"I seem to recall it."

"I never mentioned it at the time, but I met Mr. Austin that day, and he invited me in for a coffee."

Avis dropped her duster and came to look at her niece. "It's odd something like that would slip your mind."

"We had a disagreement. I went out in a huff. When I got back, you were in a better mood. I decided I wouldn't disturb the calm."

Avis eyed her with a queer sort of look.

"Nothing happened Aunty, I mean more happened at the Christmas party."

"What happened at the Christmas party?"

"I maneuvered him under the mistletoe and kissed him, before he could do anything."

"And," she pried cleverly?

"And, nothing, he's still the same, well almost still the same."

"Now you're a stupid girl," her aunt laughed picking back up the bundle of feathers and resumed her attack on the clocks. "You should have invited him out here for a good home cooked meal a long time ago."

Angeline considered the suggestion for a minute, before objecting, "He's too busy. It's too hard to pin him down to a schedule. There's always something coming up."

"Excuses, excuses, girl that will never do."

"I have my pride too. I'm not running after him."

"That is not called running after dear. It's called, 'what are you doing for supper this evening Mr. Austin? I was talking to my aunt on the phone, and she has a roast on, which is much too much for the two of us.' If he says yes, give me a call, and I'll put a roast on."

Her niece looked thoughtfully at her for what seemed an eternity.

"Okay Aunty, I'll try it, but just for you," she paused for a moment and looked back out the window. There was only a thin line of snow at the base of the cedar hedge, which ran along the property border. "I guess the groundhog didn't see his shadow."

"I know, isn't it beautiful outside? I'm already starting to think about what I'll put in my flower beds this year."

Several weeks later, Angeline was starting to fit the dust cover over her typewriter one afternoon at the office when Brad came bursting in with an arm full of tally sheets.

"Is it quitting time already?"

"In five minutes it is."

"Are you in a rush to get away?"

"I'm only on my way home. I'm not going anywhere."

"I hate to impose on you at the end of the day," he stated politely. "I had meant to speak to you earlier, but I didn't get a chance to get back here."

"There is no imposition. What is it? Would you like me to type up something for the department heads meeting?"

"Actually, I was wondering if you would stay for the meeting and take down the proceedings. We're going to cover a lot of ground. I don't want to miss anything. Tell you what, I'll take you to dinner when we're finished."

"You don't have to take me to dinner. I'll just call my aunt to say that I'll be late. She'll put my plate in the oven."

Angeline picked up the receiver of the phone on her desk and dialed Milford.

"He doesn't need to take you to dinner Angeline. Tell him, he's welcome to come back here to eat with us, after the meeting."

"Hold on a minute please."

Hants

Austin had gone into his office, so she changed phone lines.

"Yes, Brad here."

"It's me Angeline. I have my aunt on the other line. She would like to know if you would come to have supper with us, after the meeting." She paused for a moment to think then added, "She's really a very good cook, much better than a restaurant. It's not a very far drive. Just over to Milford."

"Then you're asking me too."

"I suppose."

"Then I suppose I owe you one, since you're staying late."

"I suppose you do," she agreed. "What time should I tell her to expect us?"

"The meeting should be completed no later than six. Any later and everyone's attention span seems to go to zero. Tell her we will be no later than six thirty."

"Thank you," she said very deliberately, before hanging up the phone.

Avis had seen the double set of headlights swing into the yard. She was waiting on the front veranda with the door open behind her.

"Aunt Avis, I'd like you to meet Brad Austin."

Mrs. Neville accepted his outstretched hand saying, "I've heard so much about you."

"Good or bad, good I hope?" he joked.

"They say you're doing a wonderful job in at the mill."

"I have a great team. Everybody does their share; your niece included."

"Well come in, please Mr. Austin. The house will be filling up with moths, if we leave the door open too long."

The three of them stood together for a moment in the front vestibule, before Avis began to talk again, "Angeline, put Mr. Austin's things on a hanger then show him into the parlor. Would you like a martini, while I finish up in the kitchen?"

"Yes that would be fine."

"I'm sorry, but I can't give it to you with ice. The ice man doesn't come until tomorrow and what's left of the block is too stale to trust."

"I'm fine without ice," he replied, moving his shoulder backwards so that his jacket came away in Angeline's hands.

"How about you Angeline, martini for you too," she asked?

"Yes please."

"Make yourselves comfortable. I'll be back in a minute," the elderly woman declared as she disappeared down the long hall.

"Nice place," her boss exclaimed softly as he settled into a heavy armchair.

"That was my uncle's chair. He died while I was in the hospital."

"That's right. You were in for TB. I remember you telling me the day we met by the river."

"That day seems so long ago now."

"I know. I don't know what happened. I remember I had promised you a dinner that day, but the treadmill kept running faster and faster. Lately, I've even been forgetting about myself."

"Well, we're getting dinner we talked about that afternoon."

"I'm glad I accepted. It's very relaxing here."

Their conversation was interrupted by Mrs. Neville, who began sliding the frosted glass door, which divided the parlor from the dining room, back into its pocket in the wall. A tray containing three glasses lay on the corner of the dining room table.

"Here we are," she said, holding the tray first in front of him and then her niece.

"To spring," he said, before tasting the liquor.

"To spring," the women repeated.

"You two will excuse me, but I'm going to take my glass into the kitchen, while I finish putting things together."

"Can I give you a hand?" her niece asked.

Hants

"I'll call you when everything is ready to go onto the table."

"This is a very nice drink," Brad said as she was leaving.

"You will have to thank my late husband. I'm afraid I picked up his bad habits," she laughed, going back into the dining room.

It was seven o'clock when they sat down to eat. A wide shallow bowl of New Hampshire Oyster chowder came, before the main course of roast pork, potatoes in their jackets and a side dish of cranberries and greens.

"The chowder is great," their guest remarked, reaching for a slice of the warm homemade bread laid thick with garlic butter.

"It's always best during the months, which have an 'R' in them," his host informed him. She let him finish his chowder, then asked her opening question, "Angeline tells me that your family farmed not far from here?"

"Yes that's right, southeast of Wilton along the Souhegan. Not a big place, only about a hundred acres. It was called Hants, but we never put a sign out front"

"I must admit. I don't ever recall hearing tell of your people before."

"We were a close knit family. My grandfather came here from Boston. He wanted to go back to the land. It seems that there were quite a few people who were of the same mind around about that time."

"I remember, they were nick-named New England Crackers. Most of them were educated people too, but they didn't know much about farming, and they didn't make very much money from it. Where was your mother from?"

He replied, as Mrs. Neville took the empty bowl from in front of him and set it on the buffet near the dining room table. "She was from Hampton over near the coast. She was younger than my dad. When they got married, he owned the farm, the house, the equipment and animals. "His father had signed everything over to his only child and then occupied a room upstairs, until he passed on."

"I know Hampton, she commented, before switching the subject. "I suppose you have been following this war?"

"Aunty, please! Mr. Austin's supper is going to get cold answering all these questions."

Brad didn't know whom he should refuse; "I'll compromise Mrs. Neville. I know it's rude, but there are only the three of us. I'll answer between eating."

"Angeline, you should have asked Mr. Austin for supper ages ago."

"I know," Angeline replied with a look of amusement. She was so used to Ward doing exactly as she said. This independence in a man was new to her.

"To answer your question Mrs. Neville, I haven't been following the war too closely. I was turned down for the active military service and simply lost interest. As your niece can vouch, I am a workaholic. We have been introducing a new recovery system at the mill, and lately that has absorbed all my thought."

Angeline flashed a see-what-I-mean smirk, at her aunt.

"There's been a lot of smoke in Washington recently," the elderly woman prompted.

"I suppose it turns around that old question of drafting American boys for foreign wars?"

"You could say that," he agreed.

Angeline was getting desperate. She didn't want her aunt to ask him what he thought of anything. She remembered how long Ward and the older woman had gone on about the draft. "Brad, have you heard from your sisters lately?"

Both of them turned towards her with the same surprised look and asked,

"My sisters," he repeated swallowing hard.

"What do his sisters have to do with the draft," her relative asked abruptly.

Hants

"Well I was only..."

Brad rebounded easily, "Strange you should ask. They're both coming here for a week at the end of August. They want to stay at Hants with their husbands. I'll have to squeeze in some time to go out and put the place in order."

Briefly, he recounted the misfortunes that had befallen the family property. Avis offered to make some inquiries around Milford to see if there were any handymen available. The offer was gratefully accepted.

Brad didn't stay long after coffee. Mrs. Neville was in the kitchen, when Angeline showed him to the door.

"I'm very glad I came. That was the best meal I've had in ages."

"It was our pleasure."

"Your aunt is a wonderful conversationalist."

"She does tend to get carried away at times." She let her hand rest on his forearm for a few brief seconds. It was something she did with Ward by habit. She removed it just as quickly, without being conscious of what she had done.

Brad heard the door close behind him as his forearm began to heat up where her hand had been. It was a strange sensation, which lasted all the way to the car. He looked back at the floodlight lit house feeling an odd sense of pleasure.

At work, the space between them began to change. Roxanne was the first to notice.

"Have you and Brad smoked a peace pipe?"

"What are you talking about?"

"I don't know. It's just different. The chafing which always seemed to be around, when you were both in the office together, is gone."

"You're imagining things Roxanne."

"No, I'm not. Are you still seeing the lawyer boy?"

"Yes."

"Then it must be him. I'd watch myself Missy, if I were you. It isn't easy when you have to choose between two men."

"Thank you. I promise. I'll take care."

Angeline remembered how jealous Ward had been of the mortgage broker she'd met, while cross-country skiing. He had tried to talk to her about marriage, but she had put him off. She was sure there was nothing between her and Brad. They only worked together. She was sure Roxanne was reading too many romance stories and was starting to get real life mixed up with them.

Angeline watched Brad in the following weeks and months. There was nothing. She even missed meeting his sisters because she didn't want to encourage talk.

In the world at large outside the Merrimack Valley, the course of events had taken a turn for the worse. War clouds were forming. The first American Strategic Advisors went to England in the fall of 1940. Then at the end of 1941 the Axis Powers and Japan declared war against the U.S. American troops went into Europe in 1942.

In the small world inside the Merrimack Valley, the course of events took a turn for the worse in 1942. The working contract between the local Union and The Alabama Paper Company expired without being renewed, as had been the case when the previous contract ran out. Austin knew nothing about unions. He knew even less about working agreements. He had never participated in contract negotiations. He had always worked in environments that had been created by other peoples' agreements.

The resident-manager tossed the Union's notice on the desk and looked out the window, which opened on the yard leading down through the buildings. It was signed by Eric Kent. Who was this Kent? He had seen him walking through the plant. It was the shift foremen and department managers who had the most contact with him.

Brad had his own private opinion about unions. All the men really wanted were their jobs. He was sure of it. His index finger pressed the speak button of the intercom and he heard himself saying,

Hants

"Angeline would you see if you can get me Eric Kent's personnel file please."

"Do you mean Kent with the Union?"

"Yes that's the one."

"Is there anything wrong?"

"Nothing serious, I've just received an official notice from him. It seems our contract has expired with the local. I'll have to meet with the man. See if you can get me his file please."

He should have been more vigilant. Of course contracts needed to be signed. He decided against notifying the regional office in Boston. Maybe they would sign the same agreement again. Sure they would. He and Kent would sign it together.

Management and men at Nashua had always had a healthy live and let live working environment. At least, he'd been told it was so during Marshall's stewardship. All he had to do was be sure not to put Kent in a position where he would lose face. He folded the notice, put it into the envelope in which it had arrived and slipped the two into his top drawer, before reaching for the next envelope on top of the morning's mail.

The notice stayed in the back of Austin's mind during the next month. There had been nothing in Kent's personnel file: a regular person, a good employee, a family man, and three kids.

Near the latter part of April, on a Thursday afternoon, the mill manager was on his way back to his office, after talking to the department head in Packaging. It was around 3 p.m. He decided to stop in at the plant cafeteria for a quick coffee, as it was more convenient than the staff lunch room in the Administration Building. He turned away from the cashier to find a table and saw a mill hand getting up from a chair at the back of the room. The man then left by the rear door. His companion stayed seated. Brad recognized him as being Kent, who had been pointed out to him several times. He approached the table.

"Mind if I join you Mr. Kent?"

"Not at all," the union man replied politely.

"I got your note," Austin said reaching for the sugar dispenser.

"I've been expecting to hear from you," Kent replied.

"We were in year end. So many things kept piling up. Tell me Mr. Kent. Why did you send me that notice?"

"Call me Eric."

"Okay Eric, why send me the notice?"

"It's only procedure."

"What procedure?"

"Contract renewal procedure says that management will approach the Local within three months of the expiry date to begin renewal talks. If management fails to initiate renewal talks, the Local Rep will notify management within six days of expiry that the life of the contract has run out."

"Do I have a copy of this procedure?" Austin asked seeming a little bewildered.

"You should, I'd check with personnel if I were you."

"So what happens, after you send me your notice?"

"If management fails to contact the Local within thirty days of the notice, the Local Rep repeats the same notice to management by telegram."

"It must be about thirty days, since I received your notice."

"I was going to telegram you tomorrow."

"Well, let's say that this is my contact with the Local. You won't have to send me a telegram in that case."

"Fair enough."

Kent looked past the manager's shoulder and shook his head. Austin saw one of the men turn and choose another table.

"Am I interrupting something, Eric?"

"Nothing that can't wait, 3 to 3:15 pm. are my office hours. This table is my office. All the department Reps know, if they have a problem, they can stop in to see me during their break. After we talk, I go to see the

Hants 91

foreman or department head to straighten things out. It's a safe system."

"As long as I am not interrupting anything, let's get back to the procedure."

"Fine, what would you like to know?"

"What happens if I don't react to the telegram, which you are not going to send?"

"If management doesn't reply to the telegram within thirty days, I have to go up to the State Capitol and register a complaint with the State Department of Industrial Relations. They in turn notify management and the Local that the contract has expired and must be renewed. If the Local doesn't hear from management within thirty days of reception of Industrial Relation's Notice, the Union has legal grounds to strike, if it so wishes."

"How do you know if the Union so wishes?"

"It takes a three quarters majority vote to strike from the members of the Local."

"Well, I'm glad we don't have to bring Concord into this. I mean since I am now contacting you. Would you like it in writing?"

"It would be preferable. Send me a letter when you get back to your office. Back date it a day or two, so it'll be within the thirty days of the day you received my notice."

"Call me Brad, Eric. So tell me Eric, are you from Nashua?"

"No. I was born and raised in Central Vermont. I went to work in a planner mill in Manchester, when I left home. I met my wife there. She said that if we were going to marry, she needed a little distance between her and the rest of her family, so I applied here. It's not a bad place to work. The fellas in my department asked me to be their Rep. I got to know the Union a bit and decided to run for the Local Rep in the plant. This is my second term of office."

"About this contract Eric, why don't you drop by my office tomorrow afternoon and we'll sign a new one?"

"If only it was so simple. Three quarters of the local have to vote in favor of simply signing the old contract."

"They did last time."

"I know Brad, but that was the last time and this time is this time. When the previous contract had three months left in it, Marshalll notified us that he wanted to renew. He may have been slack about maintenance, but he was always on top of procedures. I guess it was his Marines training. The previous contract had a term of four years. The men still had the depression fresh in their minds, so they only renewed it.

The general trend now, in the industry, is towards three-year contracts. That's what we'll be going for this time around."

"I guess I'll have to wait until you and the men can hold a vote."

"If only it was so easy."

"What now?"

"My term expires tomorrow at midnight. I have to seek re-election in the Local."

Austin's coffee was finished.

"Then I'll wait to hear from you, when you're re-elected Eric. I have to be getting back to my office now. I'll send you that notice of reception right away. You'll get it tomorrow in the inter-department mail."

"Thanks Brad. I'll be seeing you."

Austin didn't waste the delay that the Union election gave him. The following Monday, the department heads held a special meeting. This time Angeline was not asked to stay. This time no minutes were taken. The Personnel Manager read the expired contract and then exclaimed, "Any questions?"

Paul Hamilton from Accounting and Finance was the first to speak.

"How about you Jerry, you're personnel?"

"It's wages that are worrying me. We're still working under a wage scale, which was negotiated in 1936. Most people had vivid memories of the Depression.

They were glad to be coming out of it. Wages were important, but job security was a priority."

"And I want some efficiency research conducted," Austin added.

"You'll need the union's cooperation for that. Someone always seems to lose their job when efficiency studies start."

"Then we will have to wait them out," Riley said. "Kent has been a good man. I am fairly sure he will be re-elected. He seems to be well liked."

"I hope it's not too long," the mill manager continued. "Things have a way of deteriorating the longer they're drawn out."

"What do you mean by 'deteriorating'?" A production department head asked.

"Nothing really...but, for example, this morning I was walking down between the Sulphite Mill and the Soda Mill. Someone yelled out from one of the upper windows, 'Hey Cracker, when do we get our new contract? I looked up, but all I saw was a head being pulled in."

"I wouldn't put much store in an anonymous heckle Brad," the Sulphite Mill manager said. "No offence, but I've heard them refer to you as 'The Hillbilly' and 'The Hick' on many occasions. It's just joshing. Don't let them get your goat."

"They have never got it yet, Bill. Their name calling started a long time ago, when I transferred in from Milford Primary to Nashua High."

"By the way Brad," Riley said, "what's this employee bond option plan?"

"It was only an idle reflection until this evening. I was talking to Paul about selling the men company bonds on a payroll deduction plan to help finance a capital replacement program."

"What's your opinion Paul?"

"It's a good idea, but I don't think it will work. You said yourself, we are on a 1936 pay scale. I think most of the men have every cent split four ways, long before it's ever earned."

Riley turned back to the manager. "Why did you say it was only an idle reflection until this meeting?"

"Jerry, you're only through telling of us we won't be able to sell them on bonds because every cent is already planned for and you think they're going to push for a raise. Well, a raise can't be earmarked, until they know it's coming. So, if we plan to take it back from them with a payroll bond deduction plan, they will never miss what they never had. And just think, it will be like money in the bank for them. Actually we will be doing them a favor."

"That's going to take some selling," Marketing Manager Bud Grimes chuckled.

Austin continued, "Who has ever participated in contract negotiations? I'm a beginner at the game. I'll need three people with me who know how to carry the ball."

The head of the Sulphite Mill was the first to speak; "Kent will probably come with several of the department Reps. I think you should leave the heads of the production departments out of it. We have a lot of day to day contact with the men and the department Reps. Sometimes we have to get down to the nitty-gritty and it leaves them a little sore. I think you would be better to conduct contract talks starting from a clean slate."

Several of the other men who worked in the plant were of the same opinion. Austin made up his mind quickly, once they had finished giving their opinions.

"I think the concerns which have been raised by production are very valid. So if there are no objections, I would like you Paul and you Jerry and you Bud to take me through this."

There were no objections.

Kent was re-elected. The bargaining session was set for mid-May. They decided to meet on neutral territory. One of the hotels in Nashua was chosen. It had an excellent dining room and suitable conference rooms. Town groups such as Toast Masters and the Inter Faith Unity Council used them.

Hants

Kent and three of the department Reps showed up in their Sunday best. It was obvious they felt a bit awkward in the tight collars, which their spouses had starched the night before. Austin was slightly off balance. He was so accustomed to seeing the men in overalls. He was glad he hadn't gone into this alone. After a round of introductions and declarations of good faith, Paul Hamilton read the old contract. Most of the morning was taken up discussing its pros and cons. The departments Reps were singularly well informed about every section in the old agreement. Austin kept thinking he should have been reading the contract, along with his books on History.

After lunch, Mr. Robert Coldwell, the company lawyer and Chairman/Secretary of the talks, opened the session to new business. The Union came first. As had been expected, their main argument was money and all they could get. Austin had set up guidelines of two cents, three cents and four cents an hour over the life of the contract; however, that was to be the bottom line. Hamilton and Riley opened with nothing the first year, then two cents the second year and three cents an hour the third year. As it was to be expected, the Local said the offer was either a bad joke or an insult.

Back and forth it went. Austin followed them but stayed out of the actual negotiations. They were all very good. It reminded him of listening to auctioneers. By the end of the second day, the Union was bumping up against the guidelines. He kept trying to recall how they had done it. It was like the thimble game his brother Shane had showed him one time. The pea had been there, under that thimble, but now it was here under this thimble.

With about fifteen minutes left in the second day's talks, the Chairman suggested they leave off salary for the time being and hear what the Company was asking. It was agreed, in the morning, the Company would start by expressing the modifications and additions it was looking for in the new contract.

Wednesday morning during their pre-conference strategy huddle, Bud Grimes volunteered to shoulder the employee bond option plan.

"They have had two days to get used to Paul and Jerry. Brad and I have hardly said a word. I can see by the looks that they give me every little while they think I'm just some dumb bunny salesman who's along for the ride. I think Brad should handle the efficiency studies, which he wants. They wouldn't take me serious on something like that. The replacement fund is only words. I've used a lot of words in my life. If you three see me having trouble, then you could come right in. What do you think?"

"I think it's a good plan Bud," his boss said. "What's more, I think it would be better if you came last. I'll wear them down a bit more, before they get to you."

"Don't wear them down too much," Paul reminded him. "If they give too much, they won't get it through a ratification vote. Then we'll be right back here."

Once they were settled around the table, it was Austin who spoke first.

"You've all been here long enough to be aware of the critical situation that we are facing."

Kent's expression conceded nothing. "Which situation exactly are you referring to?"

A perplexed look appeared on the manager's face. He wasn't used to direct questions.

"Good question Eric. Actually there are two situations, which are significant: the condition of the machinery and our operating procedure."

"Which situation are we supposed to be discussing?"

"The operating procedure, he replied."

The Local Rep blinked back at him with stoic innocence. "I fail to see how that pertains to the men."

"For the moment it's merely of indirect concern to them."

"So, why are we talking about it?"

Hants

"Eric, there are two sides to an agreement. This is the business side."

"Fair enough," the steward replied.

"As you are well aware, the country is now involved in a war. However, wars don't last forever and by all reports, our GI's should mop up in Europe in a couple of months. This mill was just starting to feel the competition, before our entry into the war. It has receded somewhat, but you can be sure when the hostilities are over, it will come back stronger than before. If this mill is to meet the higher wage demands, which have been voiced during the previous two days, we have to increase our profitability. At present, it is only marginal."

Kent was quick. "Then it's accepted. We get ten cents over three years."

The Chairman interrupted him; "I'm sorry Mr. Kent. It was agreed yesterday that we would move along. Wages are not on the agenda today."

"By all means Mr. Coldwell," then turning to Austin, "please continue. What is it that you want from the men, which will help meet our wage demands?"

"Before we can insure the continued existence of this plant and the employment it will provide for the future, we need much more detailed information concerning where our strengths and weaknesses lie."

One of the department Reps spoke up, "The strengths lie in the men, our expertise and our experience."

"To be sure," Austin replied.

"How do you propose to measure our strengths?" another department Rep asked him.

Austin looked directly at him and replied, "Have you ever heard of efficiency studies?"

"Hold on a minute," Kent interjected. The four Union men conferred together. Then they started.

The first speaker came back again, "Are you inferring that the men are inefficient?" They were off again. For the next hour, the argument raged back and forth about efficiency. Paul and Jerry came in to clarify points twice.

Finally, Kent called a halt; "You can't expect us to cast the men adrift on a sea of studies, without certain stipulations."

"What sort of stipulations?" Bud asked.

"Is he in this?" one of the Union men asked. "I thought he was an observer."

"Please gentlemen," the Chairman demanded, "everybody here is free to participate except me."

Once again, both sides went into the semantics of stipulations. It was noon, before they got past a definition of research. When they returned after lunch, the Union had prepared their stipulations.

"First off, we will need a guarantee that no member will have his employment terminated, as a result of any conclusions reached from the studies." Management accepted, but in return the Union had to agree to the possibility some men may be transferred.

The Local also wanted to be a full partner in the studies. The company wasn't ready to accept this. A standoff occurred. The Chair broke the deadlock by asking Eric to explain what they meant by full partner.

"We would like somebody from the Union to be present at all times. The person should be someone who is not being studied. He will receive his regular rate but won't be responsible for his regular duties. Also, he must agree with the choice of the operator to be studied. The man, who is to be the subject, must be advised beforehand."

"Wait a minute," the Personnel Manager broke in.

"Please Mr. Riley," the Chairman said sternly. "They have the floor."

"Excuse me Mr. Coldwell."

One of the department Reps continued, "And we don't want any unrealistic production targets being set as a result of these tests. We want fatigue to be considered in setting standards. Everybody knows how a person being watched has a tendency to show off a bit, trying to make a good impression."

Austin wasn't happy. He didn't want the Union having that much say. At four fifteen, they still hadn't reached a compromise. It would go on like this again tomorrow. He also wanted to give Grimes the chance he would need.

"Okay men, we aren't getting anywhere like this and there's still the question of the condition of the machinery, which we would like to bring up tomorrow. For the time being, until we come to our final wrap up on Friday, let's say that the company tentatively agrees to Union participation in the research."

Paul Hamilton breathed a sigh of relief.

The next day, Bud Grimes got the department Reps to talk to him about the machinery in their areas. He was even a little patronizing. The four individuals opposite him were still tired from the previous day's arguing. They were glad to vent their complaints on someone. So far Bud hadn't antagonized them. They even relaxed slightly, when they started talking about shiny new equipment. It didn't seem to be leading anywhere. They found themselves wishing it were true, especially when he had a chalk board wheeled in and explained the difference in profitability between the new and old machines. One of the reps took the bait.

"If we had machines like that, there wouldn't be any problem with us getting our wage demands."

"Exactly," Bud agreed, "which brings me to today's topic. Gentlemen we don't have a capital replacement fund. If a machine goes down tomorrow and can't be repaired, it stays down."

"Then Mr. Hamilton should be setting up a capital replacement fund."

"We would if we could," finance replied.

"Then what's the problem?"

"There's no extra money."

Hamilton started to explain to them how tight the situation was. He took the chalk from Bud and gave them some rough figures. "We may have been able to take a bit from here, but if our agreement from Tuesday holds that will be going to wage raises."

"I emphasize with you Paul, but if that's where the raises are coming from then it's already spoken for," Kent reminded him.

Grimes took the chalk back, and Hamilton sat down. "Eric, let's say the final settlement is for ten cents an hour over three years. What happens after that?"

"The men vote on it. If they accept, it comes into effect."

"Not quite..."

"What do you mean, 'not quite'?"

"We still have to send the new contract to the regional office in Boston. It's subject to scrutiny by the Interstate Department of Trade and Commerce. I don't know if you have been following the papers, but no one is happy with increases in wages, while we're at war. Now I'm not saying they will find our settlement excessive, but it's a possibility."

Kent grit his teeth together, before continuing, "So what are you proposing Mr. Grimes?"

"All of us here would like to see you get what you deserve. After all, it has been since 1936. It would be a shame to see it questioned by some federal bureaucrat."

"I'm of the same mind, continue please."

"The company would like to help the men camouflage the raise."

"How?" one of the department Reps asked.

"We would put part of it into a capital replacement fund."

"You don't just put money into a fund," another Rep continued, "that's only accounting he showed us. Tell us exactly what you're talking about."

"What we are proposing is an employee bond contribution plan."

"A what?"

Hants 101

"It's simple," Bud continued, "during the first year of the contract each employee would be deducted one cent an hour, the second year two and a half cents an hour and during the final year five cents an hour. The money would be used to pay for capital bonds, which the company would sell to the employees."

"No!" the four of them exclaimed.

Grimes was not insulted. He merely sat down and began to talk to them one by one calling each person by his first name.

"Of course Harry, the office staff and management would be brought into the same plan. Even I would be in it."

Hamilton helped him several times by explaining the technicalities. They didn't get over the hump Thursday. Grimes continued again Friday morning. At noon, they stopped. They had been over it at least ten times. They were all seeing shiny new equipment. They were all seeing the raises, which could be demanded from the profitability that the new machinery would bring.

Kent leaned back in his chair and looked at the company men one by one. Not one of them was smirking. He thought back to when he had first moved to Manchester. He remembered the card dealers playing the thimble game for drinks, at a local bar, while they waited for a new game to start. The pea had been there. How had it moved?

These negotiations reminded him of the thimble game. Tuesday afternoon they left this room with ten cents an hour over three years. Now they would only be getting five. He tried to remember when the line had been crossed. They had said no, but now they were talking about five cents and some kind of bond plan. He knew he had tentatively agreed somewhere along the line. How had the pea moved?

True, they could possibly be knocked back by the Interstate Commerce Department. True, it wasn't patriotic to be getting a raise, while other men were going off to war. He decided to test them one last time.

"I know it's lunch time Brad, but there's one little matter we have not discussed."

"What's that Eric?"

"We haven't discussed the men who might be called up for military duty."

"What about them?" Austin drawled.

"What about their jobs?"

"I don't understand you."

"What happens when they come back?"

Riley looked at Austin.

"Yea, what happens to the men who get called up, when they come back?" the three, department Reps asked together.

Grimes looked at Austin as if to say; I did my job, don't blow it now.

"What do you want to happen to them?" the manager asked dryly.

"We want them to get their jobs back."

"Somebody else will be doing their job," Austin replied.

"Please Brad," Hamilton asked, his voice breaking for a second.

All the men in the room including Mr. Caldwell looked at Austin. It had been a long week. Don't let it have been for nothing, their looks were saying.

"What can I say?"

"Say they will get their jobs back," Kent answered.

The silence was total.

"Would you accept a job, not necessarily their former place?"

The ball was in Kent's court. The men were all looking at him now. It was a reasonable compromise. He looked at his three companions.

"We'll let the men decide, when they vote on the total package."

"Fine with us," one of them said.

Hants

It was over. Mr. Caldwell said he would have a proper draft of the agreement prepared over the weekend. Both parties would receive it on Monday.

The following week, seventy-nine percent of the plant voted in favor of accepting.

***

The Ring

4

It was June 1944. Ward was looking at Angeline with one eye and the water ahead and the sail with the other. The young woman was sitting in the bow of his sailboat, leaning back against the doubled up canvas sail bag, watching the shore of the Merrimack go past them in reverse. She wore a visor cap and sunglasses. Her nose was plastered with white cream. The straps of her halter were pushed out over the edges of her shoulders. Two lines of white ran down into the halter bust. He had never seen further than that, but one day he would.

She was wearing a pair of white shorts with large cuffs. Her stomach between the waist of the shorts and the bottom of the halter was flat and firm. How did she stay so slim he wondered and felt uncomfortable every time he noticed that she was looking at the waist he couldn't seem to control?

Still he wished the waiting would be over. Life would be so much more convenient for them, when they were Mr. and Mrs. He wouldn't need her autograph for every move he made regarding her inheritance. After all, what's mine will be hers and what's hers will be mine. I've got the brains, and she has the inheritance. What a successful couple they were going to make. Why, they might end up owning half of Nashua.

Ever since he had stopped talking about marriage, their relationship had improved. They seemed closer now than they had ever been before. He wondered how long her resistance would last. She had promised him she would make up her mind one way or the other, when the war ended. Then she would be ready. He would simply have to wait her out. If he pushed, she might find another mortgage broker. That had panicked him. He had almost lost it all.

Ward continued musing. He had been born into money, but it was mostly all on paper, which disappeared as quickly as the stock market changed. However, there was no law against marrying it, especially when it came so well packaged. His eyes drifted down to where the two stripes of white skin melted into the halter-top.

"A penny for your thoughts," Angeline said, noticing him looking at her.

"You should have pushed your straps aside weeks ago. You're going to have two peel marks across your tan."

"I'll be all right. I'll cream them up tonight, before I go to bed." Then she faked a pout. "Ward, you promised you would teach me to sail this year. I haven't had one lesson yet."

"I've only been waiting for you to ask," he replied, dodging her eyes.

"Well, I'm asking."

"Fine, we'll start today," he relented.

"You don't sound very enthusiastic. You don't have to if you don't want to. I heard there is a new sailing instructor at the Marina."

"You're imagining that I don't want to. I can hardly wait to sit where you are and watch the world go by. This is hard work you know. I mean; I have to keep my concentration on what I'm doing. That's what I do all week."

"Tell me what to do then."

"You can start by making your way down to this end. I'd like you to take the tiller from me."

She held the life line, which ran through eyelets on the ends of chrome plated supports with her left hand and the boom with the other hand. Gingerly, she stepped towards the rear of the boat along the teak floor.

When she was near enough to him, Ward held out his arm. "Let go of the boom and take hold of me to steady yourself."

She did as he said. His hand was strong and made her feel confident. Then she took hold of his arm with both hands. It was like the boom. He guided her into the seat, which he had occupied beside the tiller, removed her hands from his arm, placed them on the wooden handle that was attached to the rudder post and then squatted down. One of her feet brushed against his hairy leg. She didn't feel embarrassed and let it continue touching him.

"Okay, helmsman, here we go, lesson number one. You always have to keep the sail full, or you don't go anywhere and you lose control to the current."

"I understand."

"Look up to the top of the mast. Do you see that wind vane?"

"You mean that piece of metal?"

"Yup"

"All right, it's in the wind. You have to keep the tail perpendicular to the sail. Every time you see that piece of metal, or the weathercock, as it is properly called, starting to become parallel with the boom, you have to move the tiller, a bit until you get it back at a right angle to the sail. Once that is done, you can bring the tiller back to where it was."

"Why doesn't the sail stay in the correct place?" she asked naively.

"It's because the boat is in the water, and the current takes the boat and the sail is attached to the boat. When the hull shifts, so does the sail, but it's also in the wind."

"I see," she said, gripping the tiller more fiercely.

Ward stayed near her for a while watching the water ahead and following the wind above them as he told her to push the tiller to the right or pull it towards her.

"The Merrimack is not the most ideal place for sailing," he commented. "It's too shallow and too narrow. However, it's convenient. I'll take you over to the coast someday. Over there, the centreboard is down flush in its cradle, but here it's not deep enough to keep us upright."

"This isn't difficult. I should have taken up sailing a long time ago."

"Better late than never," he laughed with a smile. "There's a sand bar coming up soon. We'd better sail out into the middle of the river. After the sand bar it widens for about three quarters of a mile, before curving."

When they had passed the sand bar, Ward made his way up to the bow of the boat and leaned back against the sail bag.

"When we reach the bend in the river, I'll take the tiller back. We're going to be down wind, and it will take a lot of close tacking to get us back to the Marina at Thornton's Ferry.

"What's tacking mean?" she asked.

"It means going forward against the wind by weaving back and forth across the river. It's no easy trick. This river is narrow. You should try to come down to the Marina more often. Give me a call."

"I might just do that. But, I have to warn you, I may not be as available as I have been for the next couple of months."

"Oh," he inquired feeling a gnawing twinge of jealousy, "anything that I shouldn't know about?"

"No big secret, it's only golf. My father and mother left me two shares at the Hudson Golf and Country Club. I've been receiving their annual report for years now, but I've never gone near the club. In April, I was feeling a little sluggish sitting around not getting any exercise. I called the secretary at the Club. He put me in touch with the convener for the Ladies Golf Association. My first lesson is supposed to be Tuesday evening, barring rain."

"I've never been there, but I imagine that they have a good looking Golf Pro," he exclaimed warily.

"Actually the ladies have their own Pro. Have you heard of Collette Horn?"

"I know of the Horn's, but I didn't know she was the ladies Pro. He doesn't deal with our firm, but I am an off and on customer at his sporting goods store. As a matter of fact the life jacket, you're wearing came from Horn Sports."

Angeline smiled coquettishly at him. "I'd love to go out for another sailing lesson and I'll take you up on a day over on the coast. Just ask me, any weekend between now and September."

Shaw was taken back somewhat by her energy. "Don't get me wrong. I am not playing bait and switch, but rowing season started this week, and I am going to be quite busy too. We won't set a date until we get our new schedules worked out."

"You mean I have to fit your new schedule?"

"Are you trying to be difficult Angeline Sylvester?" he huffed.

"Not really, just funning with you Ward."

"In any case Angeline, you mentioned those shares you have in the Golf Club. For quite some time now, I've been thinking there might be something better you could do with your inheritance. It's just sitting in a vault, generating coupons."

"What were you thinking of?"

"Money is a tool. It should be made to earn its keep."

"How" she asked seriously?

"There are a lot of opportunities around. You take my summer cottage at Litchfield. I picked that up two years ago in an estate sale for next to nothing. I've cleaned it up and had the use of it. If the deal I'm working on this week goes through, I should end up doubling my money with 10% interest on the whole. Not bad, wouldn't you say?"

"Why that's fantastic Ward. You are certainly using your brains."

"It's simple Angeline. You could do the same thing."

"I'm not that smart, Ward."

"Sure you are. I'll help you."

"I am afraid I would lose my money," she said pushing the tiller away from her. "You talk about inheritance, but we both know it isn't all that much. My father worked so hard for it. It would be a terrible insult to his memory if I were simply to lose it."

"But you won't lose it. You'll have me advising you."

"Well, give me an example."

"We both can see that more and more industry is starting to call the Merrimack Valley home. It's bound to continue when the war is over. People are going to be moving into the valley between Manchester and Nashua. Property values are bound to go up. Anybody who buys now is sure to make a bundle."

"I don't know Ward. There are still a lot of abandoned farms in the area. Take my boss Mr. Austin; he has been paying taxes on a place west of Milford for the past ten or fifteen years. Every year the farm gets a little more run down. For the time being, I would rather invest my father's money in something safe and secure."

"I understand, Angeline," Ward assured her making

sure not to show any disappointment. "Some Sunday we'll go out to the Twilight Gardens Memorial Park and place some flowers. I never knew your parents, but Mr. Middleton, Norris and Fry always speak well of them."

"It's very considerate of you," Angeline said sincerely. "I'll tell my aunt Avis you offered. She and I usually go out once or twice during the summer to put a wreath on their headstones."

Austin strolled out of his office one morning with an envelope in one hand and several sheets of writing paper in the other. He stopped in front of Angeline's desk and waited until she finished what she was working on.

"What can I do for you fine sir?" she joked.

"Do you remember the ad I asked you to place in the Pulp & Paper Magazine last December?"

"I recall it vaguely."

"I guess there's a three month delay in publication so the ad wouldn't have been printed until probably March."

"So!"

"The so is, I received a reply this morning, my first reply. We're into July," he explained.

"I didn't know you hadn't heard from anybody."

"Qualified people are a scarce commodity with this war on."

"Is this one qualified?"

"He sounds all right to me."

"Maybe he's a draft dodger?" she joked.

"I doubt it. He'd be staying out of sight."

"Where's he from?"

"Oregon."

"That is awful far from New Hampshire. What would he want to come to a place like Nashua for?"

"It's a job Angeline. Maybe it sounds better to him than the one he has."

"You could be right," she replied then cocked her neck in an odd manner.

Hants

Roxanne burst out laughing, "Are you having trouble with your neck this morning, Missy?"
"I was out for one of those golf lessons last evening and I think I must have pulled something."

"Watch out you don't get hit by a golf ball," her boss joked. "I hear they smart more than pulled muscles."

"You two are ganging up on me."

"Never," Roxanne replied with a broad grin. "We're a team, remember."

"I would like one of you to reply to this gentleman today," Brad said seriously. "Tell him we would be delighted to meet with him. Tell him we'll pay his travel costs."

Ted Newton arrived two weeks later. If it weren't for the thick, wire-rimmed glasses perched on the bridge of his nose, his athletic movements would inspire a casual onlooker with admiration. His shoulders were big, like a ball player's. Angeline and Roxanne thought that the tri-striped worsted suit he was wearing, gave him an air of stylishness. Austin saw his tan and wondered if maybe he was a ski bum. He decided to reserve judgment, until they had spoken. Still, he hoped that he hadn't wasted a return plane ticket. After introducing the young man to his team, Brad showed him into his office and quietly closed the door behind them.

"I brought a copy of my school records with me, Mr. Austin."

The manager was impressed. His visitor had a B.Sc. Cum Laud in applied chemistry from North Western and a Masters in Econometrics from some school in California.

"You've done some very good research, Mr. Newton. Your letter mentioned degrees, but I had no idea that your marks were so high."

"Thank you. I spent a lot of time on my books in those days."

"And you don't anymore?"

"Now I have a wife and two children. Priorities change."

"You play any sports when you were in school?"

"No Sir, my eyes, I have cataracts."

"I suppose that's the reason you're not in uniform?"

"Right you are!"

"I know all about it. They said my feet were flat, when I tried to enlist."

"I've heard that it's more common than most people imagine."

"Well anyway, you mentioned that you had participated in efficiency tests. What exactly did they consist of?"

"After I finished school in Illinois, I hired on at the Chicago shunting and switching yard. It didn't have anything to do with chemistry, but it was a job. I did get a lot of exposure to scheduling, flow of goods and estimating. It was a decent basis for practical analysis, but I didn't have the analytical tools required for serious work situations."

"Two years later, I left and went to California for the Masters. It was excellent. I did my thesis on continuous flow systems. That was my passport to a place on a team of technical experts doing time and motion studies at one of the biggest paper mills on the West Coast. It is a huge complex just a little outside of Portland. Even with the war on, they employ six thousand people. That position lasted for twenty months.

"In the meantime, I'd married my girlfriend from Chicago. They refused me for military service at the recruiting depot in Portland. A child was born to us. As a bonus, I learned a heck of a lot about tests and research. When that contract was completed my wife, and I went to live with my parents in Tigard, Oregon where you contacted me.

"I ran into an old friend there who's in sales. He supplies pumps to a few mills on the West Coast. He gave me a stack of his trade magazines. That's how I saw your ad."

"Well, I'm glad you did. You are starting to sound better every minute. Tell me, what you know about production?"

Hants 113

An hour later, Ted stopped talking about production.

"I'll tell you what Ted. I'll offer you a six-month contract and match the salary you had when your last job finished. There will be a review, after six months. At that time, in all likelihood, we'll have a permanent place for you on staff. In addition, the company will pay to move your family. I'm sure you and your wife will find the price of accommodation in Nashua about the same as in Oregon."

"I'll take it."

"Just like that, you'll take the position?"

"Yes, just like that, I'll take it."

"You don't want to think about it?"

"I was thinking all the way here."

"How about your wife, do you want to discuss it with her?"

"She'll be closer to her family here. They're in Illinois."

"I'll have to make a call," the manager said picking up the phone. "It will only take a minute."

"Yes, may I speak to Mr. Caldwell please?"

"One moment please."

"Hello Robert, Brad Austin speaking."

"Hi there, what can I do for you?"

"I wonder if you would have time to see me this afternoon to draw up a short employment contract."

"Let me check my agenda. How about 2 p.m.?"

"See you then," he said hanging up.

Austin stood up. "Come on Ted. I'll show you around the mill. Afterwards, we'll have lunch. There's a five o'clock train coming down from Concord, which goes through to Boston. You might even be able to make flight connections this evening."

"By the way, what's your wife's name?"

"Fay," he replied with a warm smile.

In spite of the vote to accept the new contract in 1942, there had been some isolated discontent among the Local's rank and file. Bert Herrick was one of the more vocal dissenters. Many of the mill hands frequented a small bar housed on the main floor of an old run down hotel, which was located not far from the main gates of the plant. It was a favorite stop of Bert's on warm days.

After shift on the first payday in July, he was standing in line at the bar with other mill hands. They were waiting to get their cheques cashed. He scanned the room and spotted a table where three of the men from his department had taken a seat. When one of them looked his way, he motioned to save him a seat.

Once he was seated and had been served, he took the time to scrutinize his pay stub more closely.

"Damn deductions," he grunted, "pretty soon it won't be worth going to work."

"I know," agreed an individual named Ferris who sat beside him. "It's getting almost as bad as those socialist countries over in Europe. Those poor bastards don't even get pay cheques any more. The government deducts it all at the source."

"Well, that's not going to happen in the States," Bert said.

"I'll say," added one of the other men, "our boys are over there whipping them bastards, so their damn European Socialism doesn't spread to the States. Hitler and his National Socialists will never set foot in America."

"Hey Dan," Bert shouted over two tables to get the attention of their department Rep, "when is this Bond Deduction crap supposed to stop on our pay cheques?"

"I was against it from the beginning Bert," the Rep shouted back defending himself. "It was all Kent's doings."

"Could be Kent is getting a little too old for the game," Herrick growled back.

"Hey buddy," hollered a big fellow sitting at the table next to the Rep's, "don't go knocking Kent. He's good people. A lot of us wouldn't have got through some tight jams without his Cafeteria Office."

Hants

Herrick became mum. Several minutes later, Fred Boles, the person who had made the remark about Hitler endeavored to draw his shift buddy out of his brooding.

He signaled the waiter. "Bill, when you get a moment," he said nodding his head towards Bert, while gesturing with his right hand. "Bring us two more cold ones over here."

"No more for me Fred," Bert resisted. "It's pay day. I have to get some groceries."

"We all have to get some groceries Bert. Besides it's already ordered."

"Okay, but I gotta go after it."

"What's eating you?"

"It just burns me off, that's all. We go into the sweat box for eight hours every day, and then the company comes along and confiscates a part of our hard earned money. I mean there ought to be a law or something."

"You'll be getting it all back with interest, Bert. I think the work is getting to you. Why don't you ask for a transfer to another department? Rotating does a man well. You need a change. Now something ideal for you would be what Buddy landed himself. Have you seen him strolling around shooting the breeze with the new efficiency fella?"

"How did he land an easy touch job like that?"

Sam Snarkie sat beside Boles. He brought the index finger of his right hand up to his lips and said quietly, "Union takes care of its own."

On his way out, Lenny, the big fellow who had spoken up for Kent came up to their table. "Is there something on your mind Bert?"

"What's going on with all these studies?"

"I imagine they're going to install some new equipment where it's most needed."

"What happens if they replace five men with one man?"

"There's a guarantee, nobody will lose their employment."

"Perhaps not, but will the new job pay the rate of the five who were replaced?"

"How am I supposed to know?" Lenny argued. "Look Punk, if you don't like the way things are being run, why don't you do something about it? Nominations open next week for those who want to run for Local Rep. Elections are going to be held the first week in August. I hear Kent is going to try for another two year term."

Bert didn't like being called Punk by anybody. He started to rise. Snarkie's big hand settled onto his shoulder, and he could feel the man's strength pressing down.

"Let it ride Bert."

Lenny turned and left the bar. When he had passed through the door, Sam turned to Herrick.

"That wasn't such a bad idea of his. Why don't you run?"

"Are you kidding?"

"Seriously, I'll nominate you. Like I said a while ago, you need a change of scene. It would be the perfect position for you."

Herrick looked at Snarkie and Boles. They both stared back sympathetically.

"I'll give it some thought. Let you know in a few days."

"Don't wait too long," Ferris said, "nominations close soon."

Herrick was thoughtful for several minutes. "I guess maybe Lenny was right. Kent only does his job the best he can. If I remember right, it was the Hillbilly – Cracker managing the plant, who dreamed up the bond contribution scheme."

"You remember right."

"How did a fella like that get ahead of all us town boys?"

"I've asked myself the same question many times," Sam replied. "You know I made it through to first year of high school. Austin and I were in the same class. I can still remember him. He wore farm boy work clothes

Hants 117

to school and knew nothing about nothing. We all called him the Hick. He took a couple of beatings out in the schoolyard that year. Nobody expected him to pass. Everybody figured he would never come back to Nashua, after the first year of high school. I was as surprised as hell to see his picture in the paper along with the final year graduating class."

Boles came to life. "I remember him too. He was downright stupid. Country boys shouldn't be let into the management of big industrial complexes. They just don't have a broad enough understanding. I mean; there is nothing learned on a farm that can help them manage a paper mill. I agree Bert; it would take a stumble bum from the sticks to dream up the Bond Deduction Plan."

"Maybe it's time us town boys teach the Hick the lesson the he didn't learn at Nashua High."

"That's why we said not to wait too long. Nominations close next week," Ferris repeated.

"I'll give you my answer tomorrow."

It was near ten on the following day when the manager's car pulled up in front of the gatehouse at the plant entrance.

"Morning Baines," he greeted the old gateman, after rolling down the window. "Would you call my office and see if there are any messages please?"

"Won't take me a minute Sir," the guard replied picking up the receiver of his phone. After a few words, he stretched out through the booth's sliding window holding a phone and said, "Would you take this, please Mr. Austin? It's Miss Sylvester."

"Morning Angeline, what's up?"

"They have called twice for you from down on Number Three paper machine. It's Rod Nelson. I told him you were in a meeting. The wire broke during the night. They haven't been able to start up yet."

Brad eyed the gatekeeper who didn't seem to be listening. "Thanks for covering for me. I'm on my way."

He found Nelson and several grease, smeared individuals standing around the open end of a huge vacuum roller. Its function was to extract the water from the liquid pulp, as it is being spread across the revolving copper screen. The giant cast iron bracket housing the bearing which supported the end of the cylinder lay on the floor in front of them. It was split in two along a jagged break.

"Problems Rod," Austin asked, when he arrived within speaking distance.

The head of maintenance pointed to the crotch of the casting.

"The babbitt was worn away. When the wire broke, there was too much vibration. The casting of the roller mount split right down the middle."

"What's this?" his superior asked, indicating a similar piece of equipment in intact condition.

"We dug that up down in the yard. It's off an old machine. The serial numbers are the same, but it won't fit the old base plate."

"Why won't it fit?"

"The feet are cast differently. We could strap it down; however, the chances are very strong that it would only vibrate loose again. We'd be right back to where we started from."

"This old machinery is such a damn headache," Austin exclaimed with vexation.

"I checked with the suppliers. They don't have this bracket in stock. They said they couldn't promise anything, before three months." Nelson explained.

"Three months! Why so long?"

"It's the war. All the production facilities are overloaded pumping out equipment for the battlefields."

"Then we will have to make do. What's under this floor?"

"Right here there are about eighteen inches of concrete resting on gravel."

"You are certain?"

"Positive, see the light spot over there. We had to dig it up about three years ago, to replace a rusted out water line."

Hants

"We don't have much choice," Brad conceded. "Instruct the men to tear up the floor and have them pour a new base plate to match the feet of this bracket. You better have the machine shop make up some long tails for the mount bolts, which can be shoved in, under the old floor. If there are no spare parts, we don't want this one vibrating loose."

"It will take at least forty-eight hours for the concrete to set."

"It can't be helped. Two days down time are better than three months. I'll tell production to send the men home who work on this machine." Austin turned and walked into the plant.

"All right boys," the foreman ordered, "let's gather up all these tools. They won't be needing us, until the new base is set."

The remainder of the morning flew by unnoticed. It was a quarter to twelve, before Brad eventually crossed the threshold of his office. Angeline had already donned the jacket of her tweed suit.

"You're jumping the gun a little, aren't you?" her boss quipped, seeing her ready to leave.

"The early bird gets the worm."

"The worm?" he repeated with a puzzled expression.

"A Closing-Out Sale starts at twelve noon, on the dot, at Sterling Shoes."

"I see. The worm is the shoes." He commented while sorting through the paper in her in/out tray. "By the way, have I got anything scheduled for this afternoon?"

"Yes," she stammered, squashing a Watteau down over her pageboy, "it's all on your desk. His name is Brockton."

As the midday horn began to sound from the top of the water reservoir in the mill yard, the office door closed behind Angeline. At one twenty that afternoon, the buzz of the intercom forced Austin to leave off his paper work.

"There's a gentleman to see you."

"Send him in please."

A lanky blonde individual, wearing a porkpie hat and one of those horrible no cuffs, no pleats, no tuck suits, walked through the door. Austin came forward from behind his desk to meet the visitor.

"Good afternoon," he greeted, extending a hand. "It's Brockton, isn't it?"

"That's correct Sir," the man replied, presenting him with a business card.

Analog Devices Ltd.
John Brockton
R & D
Chicago, Illinois.

"Did you receive the literature I sent you?"

"I've only now finished reading it."

"And what do you think?"

"Frankly, John, I am slightly confused as to why you've come to us. After all, we're in the paper business."

"Precisely, how much do you know about computing devices, Mr. Austin?"

"Let me think," the manager reflected, "I must have used a slide rule and adding machine thousands of times."

"I'm sure you have," the man from Chicago smiled. "I was thinking more specifically about electromechanical computing devices."

"It's quite a new field, isn't it?"

"Yes."

"Of course I've read about them in the journals. However, I am afraid that my knowledge of electronics couldn't be written home about."

"Actually, their potential is fantastic. We've only touched the tip of the iceberg. Presently, they're being employed experimentally in design and production work. It's conceivable that one day they'll be operating a complete factory like this. But in any case, you're in

Hants 121

the paper business," he said, reaching into his briefcase. "That's why I am here. Have you any idea what this is?" Brockton asked, sliding a ribbon of paper across the desk.

Austin examined it. "Looks like a piece of ticker tape from a stock broker's office."

"How about the paper?" the R & D man pressed him.

Brad held it up to the window. "Same quality as our AC bleached."

"Congratulations!" Brockton beamed. "It's always a pleasure to talk to someone who knows his business. That piece of ticker tape is what led us to you." He reached into his case again. This time he withdrew a manila colored card. "Ever come across anything like this before?"

The sample was flexible yet resilient. The surface seemed to be coated. "It's very unusual Mr. Brockton."

"The item you're holding comes from a mill in Alabama, but not from one of the Alabama Paper Corporation's mills," the visitor explained. "We feed information into these new computers on cards like this. The quality is very high. Besides being a uniform thickness, they must be brittle enough to be punched with holes, yet pliant enough to run through turning rollers, without tearing or folding."

"Sort of a cross between a long and short fiber," the mill executive suggested.

"The future is with computers Mr. Austin. My company estimates the volume of our business will triple when the war is over. We must be able to guarantee our customers an uninterrupted supply of these cards. For this reason, we're looking for a mill, which can be our back-up supplier."

Austin was attracted by the Chicagoan's pragmatism. Suddenly, it all became clear. It was much deeper than Analog's representative could ever imagine.

"At the present time, Mr. Austin, my company's chief concern is to find a mill which is capable of producing this quality. Before I go any further, I wonder if you would tell me if the proposition would be of any interest to you."

Brad didn't want to sound too enthusiastic, yet he was already hoping that it would be true. "Our present development policy is to be partial towards profitable innovations."

"My firm is mindful of the fact that a product like this is not brewed up overnight." He set a thick file on the manager's desk. It was bulging with sheets of chemical formulas, charts and process instructions. "We're prepared to underwrite the laboratory costs, development costs and personnel costs of any research undertaken, to see if production is feasible at this mill."

Brad eyed the pile of data. "That's very generous of your company. When do you need an answer?"

"Not right away, it's understandable that you would need some time, but we would appreciate your promptness. There's another mill in Oregon, which is being considered."

Austin shifted his weight, crossed his legs and leaned back in the swivel chair. "You realize I will have to contact my head office."

"Of course, by all means that's very reasonable."

They continued to discuss the details until midafternoon. Subsequent to Mr. Brockton's departure, Angeline, breezed in with an arm full of reports. Her boss looked her straight in the eye and started to rub his hands together.

"You certainly seemed pleased."

"Good reason to be," he chuckled. "I think the needle in a haystack just found us. At least, I hope it did."

"Which needle?" she queried.

"The needle of rejuvenation!"

"What in the world are you talking about?"

"Oh, it doesn't matter," he laughed, "but how about celebrating with me? I'll take you to dinner."

Hants 123

"Now hold on," she objected, "you have a production meeting at six with the department heads. However, if you are offering, I'll settle for something a little more tangible."

"Like what?"

"A friend of mine has asked me to go to watch a rowing match at the Boat Club on Saturday. I don't want to sit in the bleachers all alone. My aunt said she wasn't up to it."

"Who is your friend?"

"Ward Shaw."

"I remember him. His dad was sort of a gentleman farmer. The boys at Nashua High were a bit rough on him, because of his father's money. "

"The money is all gone. What the crash didn't get, his father squandered travelling the world. He is a lawyer now over at Middleton, Norris and Fry."

"I take it he's in one of the races or he'd be sitting in the bleachers with you."

"Yes, he's in several."

"Are the races on all day Saturday?"

"No, they'll only be for a couple of hours after lunch."

"Okay, I'll accompany you Saturday p.m."

She set the reports down on his desk. "You'll need these for your meeting this evening. What rejuvenation were you talking about?"

"I'll tell you all about it Saturday. Should I meet you there or come to pick you up?"

"I could pick you up."

"No, I'll come to get you" he insisted. "What time?"

"Say about 12:30."

"By the way, is Mr. Shaw a special friend?"

"He takes care of my estate. That's how I met him. We go out from time to time. There's nothing definite between us. You have everything for the meeting. I'm on my way now."

"Thanks, I'll see you tomorrow."

The week rolled by quickly. At 12:30 pm Saturday she was still trying to decide what to wear when her Aunt Avis called out

"Hurry up slow poke. I see his car turning into the driveway."

There's a chill in the air she thought. Why be uncomfortable in a skirt? I'll wear my trousers.

Avis and Brad were talking in the parlor when Angeline came down. He stood up when she walked in. She felt her stomach contract. He looked the perfect country gentleman, standing there in a Norfolk jacket and roll neck navy sweater. For a second, the same feeling came over her that she had experienced when Lester Marshall had introduced them. They left immediately.

Brad felt awkward as they drove along in silence towards Thornton's Ferry.

"So, tell me more about this lawyer friend of yours?"

"He's only a Nashua boy who likes boats. Besides rowing canoes, he has a sailboat. I've been out in it with him on the Merrimack. He dabbles in real estate too. I think he would like to be rich. He thinks there's money to be made in housing, in this area."

"He could be right. There seems to be a lot of industry moving into the valley between Manchester and Nashua." He went on to tell her about the visit from the spokesperson from Analog Devices.

The parking lot was three quarters full, when they arrived. There were a lot of people milling about beside the Boat Club.

"Let's not take a seat just yet," she suggested, "I'd rather walk around to see whom we might bump into."

"That's fine with me."

It didn't take her long to spot Ward. He was near the boat house doing limbering up exercises with some of the other rowers.

"Come on over this way," she said, "there is someone I want you to meet."

Hants

Ward saw them approaching and moved away from the other racers to meet them.

"Hi Angeline, I'm glad you could make it. It's going to be a great event."

"Ward, I'd like you to meet Brad Austin. He's my boss at the mill."

The two men shook hands. "Good to see you again Brad. You've come a long way from high school."

"You're not doing so bad yourself, from what Angeline tells me," Austin commented. "How many races are you in?"

"Four. I'm in a big canoe with twenty paddlers for the inter club match. Then I'm in a two seater twice, and I finish the day off in the one mile rowing heat by myself."

One of the other men called out, "Come on Ward, we're ready."

"I have to go. Enjoy your races."

"Good luck!" she exclaimed.

"Thanks," Ward said then started to walk back to the other rowers who were in his team.

"Shall we go and find a seat then Brad?"

"Sure."

Ward was kneeling in the middle of the big club canoe with his paddle raised. His eyes searched the bleachers. The starter gun went off. He missed the first stroke but fell in with the others on the second. After that Angeline and Brad were gone from his thoughts.

The summer went by fast. During the third week of the autumn, Ted Newton's efficiency studies came to an end. He sat in front of Austin's desk in the late afternoon of October 26th looking at the thick file, which represented three months' work. His boss leaned forward placing his right hand on the manila cover. "So, what's in it, Ted? Is the prognosis good or bad?"

"A lot of data has been collected. I'll spend the next three months working it up into recommendations on implementation and monitoring."

"Not very encouraging then, of course, I knew that. Only, I needed it on paper from an independent source for the regional office in Boston."

"I don't mean to sound like a prophet of doom. Bandages can only do so much. Major surgery is desperately needed here."

"Oh, I know," his superior lamented, leaning back, "but that is easier said than done. I had a hard enough time trying to convince the Union to accept a few minor personnel changes. Can you imagine what their reaction would be if I said that I was shutting down a whole section to replace machinery? That is supposing I could get permission from regional and find the financing. But anyway, this report of yours is the first step. I've got something to build on."

"I hope it will be useful."

"I have no doubt. Now about you, your contract has 3 months left. Do you have anything lined up?"

"I have a few feelers out."

"You know I mentioned when you started there was a possibility you would be asked to stay on."

"Yes, I remember."

"I think I have a place for you, if you're interested."

"Actually, I kind of hoped you would. Our little girl has started school, and I'd rather not break up her year if possible."

"Tell me Ted, was there any particular reason why you didn't stay in chemistry? I recall you were a summa cum laude."

"I was a bit fed up with chemistry. It seemed as if I'd had my nose in a test tube, since the age of nine. I wanted to get my sleeves rolled up and to do something that was more applied. I wanted to understand what makes industry tick."

Austin began to explain the project he was taking on with Analog Devices.

"You've probably met our two staff chemists."

"Yes, both competent men."

"The fact of the matter is, we need the services of an experimental chemist. It has been twenty years since either came out of school. They're fine for quality control; however, I'm afraid research work would be going a little beyond their scope."

"It sounds very challenging."

"Can I take that as an acceptance?"

"I'm sure Fay will be very happy when I tell her. We are expecting a new baby in the spring."

It was not only the company that was laying plans for the future. Secret maneuvering was in progress on the Union side, which would drastically alter the company's strategy. At the same moment the two men were discussing the new project in the manager's office, Bert Herrick's came off shift. When he walked through the gates, a taxi whisked him away to the bus station in downtown Nashua. He only had time to buy a ticket and climb on a waiting bus, before the driver pulled on the swing lever and shut the door. The big coach backed out of its bay and headed in the direction of Boston.

Bert was on the train from Boston, when it pulled into the Chicago's Union Station the next morning. Being Saturday, most of the downtown Chicago offices were closed. At nine o'clock, he knocked on the outer doors of his Union's Headquarters. At first there was no answer. Eventually, he saw an overweight, balding individual in a wrinkled suit appear and approach the door.

Gordon Ruskin was the Union secretary. He supposed the person in front of the glass door was his visitor from New Hampshire. He was glad this man hadn't let him down.

The Secretary had little contact with the Nashua mill since Eric Kent took over. The man was very independent. He never asked for assistance. Everything was according to the regulations with him. He filed his monthly reports and forwarded a copy of the new contract at the conclusion of the negotiations.

While he was going over the minutes of the 1942 negotiations, Ruskin was surprised to find that one of the department Reps asked for the Local to be consulted prior to establishing a rate of pay on any new position, which would come out of reclassification. Upon cross checking, he learned the resolution had originated with one of the rank and file, a Bert Herrick. More recently the man's name came up again in a monthly report as a candidate for nomination to represent the Local. Ruskin contacted Herrick secretly. The man had been receptive. They had agreed upon a private meeting.

The secretary opened the door and showed in the visitor from New Hampshire. They went into his office.

"So you see Bert, we're interested in you. Kent seems to be getting a little too matter of fact. A more aggressive type of person is needed to sail through the troubled waters, which lay ahead. In fact, we're prepared to support you as the Union choice among the four who are seeking to represent the Local."

What a break Herricks thought. He had hoped for something, but not that much. Now he would show them all. He was about to thank Ruskin, but stopped short.

"What would you want from me in return?"

"Oh, nothing in particular, my motive is only the well-being of the Union and your Local."

"As I explained to you a few minutes ago, it was you who brought yourself to our attention. We would only hope you would show your appreciation by including us, here in Chicago, in the Local's business, on an ongoing basis, instead of after the fact in monthly reports. You know; I could be of great assistance to you. You don't have a lot of experience. I could coach you on a lot of issues."

"Well if it's only coaching, I could go along with that."

"Who is this Austin, anyway? He hasn't been there all that long. It used to be Marshall. I once spent a whole morning in his office. He invited me to have dinner with him, but I had to get back to Boston, to catch my train."

"Austin and I were in the same grade nine class together, before I dropped out. He was a real hick, who came into Nashua off some cracker farm, so he could continue his schooling. I don't know how he got to be manager. If it had been up to the town boys, he would never have got off the farm."

"Has he got a dark side? You know, sometimes a little bit of well-placed scandal is worth a month of negotiating."

"Nah, he is as clean as a whistle. You can't fault him personally. These days, you have to cut through a lot of layers to get through to the Hick. He dresses real well and is polite to everyone. It's just that he is all efficiency. We got along fine with Marshall. Sure the place is run down, but we are all earning a living. Who cares about what's fifteen or twenty years down the road? We might have the Hun in Portsmouth if they don't stop him in Europe."

"Let's not go that far Bert. There are a lot of people in our Union, who have German ancestry. You know Chicago always was and still is an immigrant-threshing floor. Most of them get through with their heads intact and they are good people. Anyway, we should get down to discussing your future as head of the Local in Nashua."

For the rest of the day, they outlined a preliminary strategy. Everything turned on Herricks being nominated. If he collected the necessary number of sponsors, the Union would come in during the ratification. When he returned to work on Monday morning, no one was any the wiser about his weekend activities.

When Ruskin found himself alone Saturday afternoon he mused at Herrick's comment about 'the Hun being in Portsmouth'. In this sheltered Great Lake city, it was easy to forget a war was going on. No battle ships came into the Chicago Harbor. It wasn't like

Portsmouth, which was bustling with Navy. Still he didn't think there was much threat. After all, during the same week in July, Rommel had been eliminated, and a conspiracy had been uncovered against Hitler. Added to that, Paris had been liberated in August.

By December, 1944, Newton had established a pilot project in the laboratory. From the beginning, it was one stumbling block after another.

"I just don't understand it," Ted declared when he noticed Austin approaching the apparatus one day. "We've tried everything. There is no way to bond the soda and sulphite fibers together with the uniform texture needed."

"Do you remember saying last week the composition of our wood fiber might not be the same as the sample from Alabama, which Analog Devices left us?"

"I recall that. New Hampshire pulp comes from jack and white pine."

"It was just a hunch, but I phoned the U.S. Department of Agriculture. They informed me only sash and long leaf pine grows in Alabama. I wired one of our mills outside of Montgomery to see if they could give me a chemical breakdown of their pulp. The response just came in," he said passing the telegram to the chemist.

Newton's eyebrows rose. "Two point three gallons of raw turpentine per batch of pulp," he exclaimed, "we've only got traces in ours."

Immediately, he began flipping through a compound dictionary.

"Hum, let me see. Kraft turpentine...Kraft turpentine...Here it is. It contains a large percentage of pinene. If pinene is heated to a high temperature isoprene is formed. Let's see what they say for isoprene..........That's what butyl-rubber is made from."

"Son of a B," Austin exclaimed, "we've found it. The pinene bonds those fibers to make a flexible yet resilient cardboard."

Hants

In spite of their initial enthusiasm, the succeeding experiments still failed to produce anything like the commercial samples. The manager had the shop construct and install a conical cyclone on the discharge tube of one of the huge digesters in which the wood chips were pressure-cooked. It condensed the turpentine that escaped along with the relief gases. Under the best of conditions, they only succeeded in achieving a turpentine count of a little over a gallon per batch of pulp. In March, Newton was at his wit's end. He took a week off and went away to consult a research laboratory.

Ted's departure coincided with Gordon Ruskin's arrival in Nashua. He had motored up from the Windy City in his Studebaker. A suite had been reserved for him at a quaint riverside motor court, south of town, near the Massachusetts State line. It had an adjoining meeting room. His presence and the meeting of a select group of the local members had been kept private.

A reflection of the last glimmerings of what had been a brilliant orange sunset was fading across the surface of the Merrimack. The men were washing down the end of their meal with strong New England beer.

"I'm sure glad the Eighteenth got repealed," one of the department Reps sighed, wiping a line of foam from his moustache.

Ruskin pushed back his chair and rose to his feet.

"Well now brothers, since everyone has been fed and watered, shall we bring this meeting to order."

"I'll second that."

"Under the circumstances, I think that it would be wise if we took an oath that the minutes of this evening's meeting won't be discussed with anybody, who is not now present."

"I'll second that."

The pledge being taken, Gordon glanced around the long rectangular table at the array of slightly intoxicated moon faces, staring back at him. This should be easier than falling down stairs, he thought.

"Brothers, you have been invited here this evening to discuss an important matter, Union spring cleaning. Every organized group of men like us needs a fresh infusion from time to time. In the past, a sincere and diligent man has represented this Local. However, he has been in the driver's seat for several terms. From what I understand the ball game is changing in Nashua."

"There is talk of modernizing the mill. It will be a trying period. The conciliation strategy of the past might not be appropriate in this new climate. For this reason, the Union has decided to add its sponsorship to one of the nominees who will soon be seeking ratification to represent this Local.

"Let me tell you. It was a hard choice. There are three good men running against Kent. We reviewed the histories of all three very carefully. One nominee came to our attention, as a result of his contributions to the last negotiations. Brothers, I would like to turn this meeting over to Bert Herrick."

At that moment, the loud scraping of a chair sounded from the far end of the table. A somewhat wobbly, David Cully gained his feet.

"Hold on there a minute, you two. I wondered why Eric hadn't been included. If we've been invited here for a private back stabbing party, you can count me out."

Ruskin's beady eyes leveled straight at him. "Have you asked permission to address this assembly?"

Several of the men looked at Cully smirking.

"Permission!" he mocked. "Look Mister Secretary or whoever you are. We don't need your kind coming around stirring things up. Come on boys, let's get out of here."

"Stop," Ruskin shrieked, bringing his open palm down hard on the conference table. "What do you think you are pulling off? There has been no motion for adjournment."

The assembled individuals knew the rules. Besides if Herrick was getting Union sponsorship, there was a good chance that he would get in. It would be convenient for them to be on the right side of the Local, when their department needed something. Not a sound was heard.

Cully stared at the immobile men. "All right, have it your way," he said with submission, "but I'll have no part of it." He started for the door.

"Let me remind you Mr. Cull," Ruskin sneered, "you've taken a pledge."

The defecting member stopped in mid-stride. "Just what's that supposed to mean?"

"Only that you've taken an oath of secrecy."

"I'm part of no oath," he hissed.

Ruskin came back wheedling, "Tell me Mr. Cully, are you a married man?"

"What's that got to do with anything?"

"Do you have any children?"

"Five."

"For their sake I hope you remember that breaking the confidence given to your brothers here tonight would be sufficient grounds to be expelled from the Union."

Cully started to walk towards Ruskin. Herrick stepped in between them.

"I think you should go home and sleep it off Dave."

"It's my money that keeps things like that growing fat," his shift buddy said pointing at Ruskin.

Four of the men stood up at the table. "Go on home David."

The defecting member lowered his eyes and headed for the door.

"Don't forget your pledge David," someone at the table called out.

When the door closed, Herrick began to talk slowly.

"All signs are that this war is soon to finish. There are lots of indications we're in for some big changes at the mill. We heard about it at the last contract talks. Now there's this new chemist. First it was studies. Then they started those lab experiments. The Local needs somebody who won't sit around holding management's hand."

"Excuse me, Bert," Ruskin interrupted, "I'd only like to add a few words. It was unfortunate about what happened a few minutes ago. As it was suggested, this is not an axing party. You were invited here to be informed that the Union is supporting Mr. Herrick's bid. We ask for your support. Anybody who helps won't be forgotten."

He surveyed their faces. There was nothing to read in their expression. He guessed Kent was on their minds. They had to be won over. It hadn't been in the strategy, but he decided to make an exception. After all, Cully hadn't been in the strategy either.

"As far as Kent goes, Chicago is sending him a notice to the effect that he has served the men well and that perhaps he should step back to his bench to give someone else a chance."

Their looks softened. Herrick noticed it. He was glad that he had accepted Ruskin's offer to coach him. Wiry little Jack Needham had always possessed a special knack for sniffing the winds of change. He requested and was granted permission to address the meeting.

"Fellow brothers, we would all agree there's a lot of sense in what we have been hearing. There probably isn't a man in this room who doesn't owe something to Eric Kent; however, the sweeping scythe of change stops for no one. He, who learns to jump, stays in the race. I think we as a group should ask Eric not to seek ratification from the membership."

"I second the motion."

"I propose we accept Jack's motion to send a notice to Eric."

"The motion is carried," Ruskin said with satisfaction.

"Thank you brothers," Herrick said, coming back to the head of the table to continue his speech.

Hants

When Newton returned to Nashua a week later, he brought back a solution to the bonding problem. In a matter of days, they were able to produce a laboratory prototype that was as flexible and as resilient as the samples. Analog's President contacted Austin directly, inviting him to Chicago to work out the details of a supplier contract at the soonest opportunity. It was beginning to look as if 1945 would be a good year.

Shortly after 10 a.m. on May 7th, Angeline was leaving the office to take some reports to Accounting, when the phone began to ring. She was going to leave it, but dutifully went back to her desk.

"Good morning, Mr. Austin's office, may I help you?"

"Hello Angeline."

"Oh, hi Ward."

"Have you heard the news?" he burst out.

"What news?"

"The war is over. The Germans have surrendered. Japan can't hold out alone."

"Are you sure?" she pleaded.

"Positive! It's official! I'm in the stock broker's office. It just came over the wire a few seconds ago."

"Oh Ward," she bubbled, "I have to hang up. Nobody knows here."

"Okay, I'll phone you back."

She almost ran to the Accounting department. From there, the word spread out to the plant. The steam whistle began to scream. The machines went down everywhere. The mill hands began leaving without even punching off. When Angeline got back to her office, Roxanne was standing at her desk with an open billfold in her hands.

"I know Angeline. I've heard. Did I ever show you my boyfriend's picture?"

"I didn't even know that you had a boyfriend."

"I didn't want to say anything in case he didn't come back. We met eighteen months ago in Portsmouth. He was on shore leave from his post as Navy Petty Officer

1st Class on the USS John Quincy Adams. Here, I have a picture."

Angeline took the billfold from her outstretched hand.

"He's...he's... very black Roxanne."

"Of course he's black honey. This is a real country boy from Alabama, not a watered down New England brown like me. I'm going to put Africa, back in my line with this fella. We're going to make babies."

"I'm so happy for you Roxanne."

The phone began to ring. It was Ward.

"Angeline, I'll pick you up after work. The Hudson Golf & Country Club is spreading the word that they will be sponsoring a victory dinner and dance tonight. Mr. Middleton and Mr. Norris are both members. They've reserved a big table."

"I have my car Ward. I'll meet you there."

"Okay, just ask for the Middleton table."

"And Ward."

"Yes."

"Can I bring Roxanne along?"

"You mean Roxanne who works in your office? She's..."

"I know."

"Sure Angeline. We've just won the war, and they were on our side. I'll let Mr. Middleton know."

She was glad that Roxanne had come with her. Ward was no company at all. He kept going from table to table visiting this one or that one. At the Middleton table, everyone talked about how business was going to boom. The two women started talking about babies. For the first time in Angeline's life, she realized that she too would like to have a baby.

When the dance music stopped playing at 10 p.m., she was in Ward's arms. He looked down into her eyes.

"Will you marry me?"

"Are you joking?"

He shook his head.

Hants

"Yes, I'll marry you," she said, starting to laugh and felt tears coming into her eyes.

He tightened his arms around her waist, lifted her off the floor and turned around before saying,

"Mrs. Shaw."

"Mr. Shaw," she enunciated in response.

"We have to get a ring. Take tomorrow off. We'll go shopping."

"Okay, I'll tell Roxanne now," she said, pulling away from him. "We really should be going too. I'll have to drive her home."

When the news broke that the hostilities had terminated, Brad had been sitting in the boardroom of the regional office of the Alabama Paper Company in Boston. He had been explaining the mill's requirements in plant and equipment for the new computer card process. The regional vice-president summarized the corporation's policy.

"You understand what I am saying is only preliminary. The company has a general policy with regards to these matters. A paper machine is not a fixed asset. Should any unforeseen difficulties arise, it can always be loaded onto a railway flatcar and shipped to another division. We would also underwrite the installation and start-up costs. The building, on the other hand, is very permanent. The local unit must demonstrate its sincerity by securing the financing for the plant requirements.

Before anything can start, you must be in possession of a notarized supply contract. It should contain maximum and minimum quantities, satisfactory prices and have a life of at least ten years, barring legal grounds for rupture with sufficient notice."

It took Brad three hours to get out of Boston. Traffic was bumper to bumper as far as Somerville. People were celebrating everywhere.

Several days later the Local's leadership campaign opened. Kent had rejected any suggestion of not running. It was not until Ruskin stepped out from behind the membership to congratulate Bert Herrick that Eric realized how he had paid for his long independence from the Chicago office.

When Angeline told Brad that Herrick was the new head of the Local, he shrugged and replied, "Guess we'll have to wait until Herrick makes his move. Would you stay for a second, please? I want you to take down a letter to Analog. I need to see them again about getting a contract."

Angeline reached across his desk to pick up a pencil and pad. He saw the ring.

"That's new isn't it?"

"What?"

"The ring, it's on your engagement finger."

"That's because it's an engagement ring. With all that has been going on, I forgot to tell you Ward asked me to marry him, on the evening of the Golf Club's victory supper."

Austin felt the strength go out of his legs and his arms went limp. She noticed how his expression changed. It took him several seconds to gain control. His voice was dry and breaking.

"I'm very happy for you Angeline, very happy for you both. Let's leave the letter for now. I need a minute to get my thoughts together."

She saw it and the joy dissolved in her. She wanted to run. Why hadn't he said something? All those times she thought maybe it was her clothes, or hair or make-up. Why had he been such a stupid man?

"Buzz me when you're ready," she said shyly, before backing out through the door.

When she returned from her coffee break there was a note propped up on her typewriter.

"I'll be back in a day or two. You can reach me at Analog."

She felt relieved. She didn't think she could bear to see him the way he had been.

***

The Spring

5

On June 18th, 1945, Local 93's working contract expired at the Nashua Mill. A week later Alabama Paper received a notice from Chicago. The old contract would not be automatically renewed.

Austin smiled, and laid the notice down on his desk. He remembered how he had naively sat down at Eric Kent's table several years earlier and asked him if he could stop by his office that afternoon and renew the old contract. Then the smile faded away. He didn't like negotiations. He wasn't green anymore, but he would still rather be out in a field than sitting at the bargaining table.

On October 1st, seven years would be behind him as the resident manager at Nashua. During that time, he had very little time for himself. The only personal interest permitted was a very private; never spoke of feeling for his secretary, Angeline Sylvester.

He could still remember the afternoon they had been introduced. There had been something shy, and half hidden in the look she gave him. For a long time, he had been coming to work to see Angeline, in the same way that most men go home at the end of the day to see their wives. Now it was over. She was getting married. Ever since the day the ring had been seen, he seemed to only be going through the motions of working. If it hadn't been for this computer card project, he probably would have started looking through the professional classifieds, in the back of the industry trade journals, a long time ago.

It was old Marshall who had laid this bundle of worries into his lap. He hadn't been stupid. Both he and his secretary had been aware of how small New England towns frown upon friendships between men and women in the workplace. They had kept it secret from everybody for years. Then at the end, they had bolted together. The only person who possibly could have known was Roxanne. She had never said a word. He wished that he had been braver.

There were new faces on both sides, which squared off against each other at the contract table. Kent was still there. His department had kept him on as their representative. Austin was saddened by the man's presence. It was like the beaten leader of a political party who comes back to serve under the new chief. Somehow, it lacked dignity. He thought of the sirens. They must have hold of Kent.

Brad looked from Kent to Herrick. The Local's new Rep's jaw was set firmly, and his lips were pressed together. He decided to test the water.

"If we can wrap this up before noon Mr. Herrick, I'll pay lunch for everybody."

No one laughed. Herrick's lips began to move. "We aren't interested in corn pone, Mr. Austin. We all have a big job ahead of us here. The sooner we start, the sooner we all find out where we're at."

"I second that," one of the department Reps said.

Mr. Coldwell, the company's legal counsel in Nashua was still acting as Chairman. Once the rules of procedure had been passed around, Brad cleared his throat and asked the Chairman to read the old contract. It was half way through the second day when the manager finally broke loose of all the false starts. He began to talk from the hip, instead of answering to some point of order.

"The plain fact of the matter is, if we don't take a definite direction now, one department after another will be closing in the not too distant future. At present, we're operating without a profit margin. A capital replacement program must be undertaken without delay."

One of the Reps talked out of order; "We've heard that one before. That's what was behind the Bond Deduction plan, which has been eating into our pay cheques, since the last time we were here. So, what's the problem? Why aren't you scraping some of these rust buckets that we are working on?"

"That's a very valid point, Harry."

"Please gentlemen," Mr. Coldwell insisted. "You must be recognized, before you speak. Just give me a look, and I'll give you a nod."

Austin continued, "The capital fund is just starting to get big enough to do something with it. Now the question is, what do we do with three shifts of men, if a whole section is shut down? An overhaul could take months. Besides that, we are in old product lines. Even if we do buy new machines, there is no guarantee that we will keep our share of the market.

"There are a lot of mills in this country producing exactly the same product line as we are. With the war, over, American producers will probably have to put up with more foreign competition, right here on our own turf. Think about it for a minute men. How did Nashua come to be one of the top paper producers in this country and stay there so long?"

The other side of the table stared back blankly at him. Finally Herrick spoke,

"You tell us, Mr. Austin."

"The competence of the local work force had something to do with it."

"That's flattery."

"All right, somebody long before Marshall had the courage and initiative to bring this mill into new areas of production that then came into high demand."

"So, what's on your mind, Mr. Austin?"

"Computer cards," he replied without hesitation.

"What?"

"They are rectangular cards in which holes are punched, so that information can be fed into computers."

"I've never heard of them," the new Local boss said.

"You gentlemen have all seen Mr. Ted Newton around the plant. At present he is busy on the computer card project. I'll get him to explain the whole thing to you."

Ted was uneasy just being here. He had never been a member of a union. He had never seen Austin talking to the mill hands as if they were all sitting on the back veranda. He cleared his throat and started to talk. Sweat was running down his sides. When he stopped, he couldn't remember what he had said.

Herrick's voice was low and deep. "That's a lot of fancy talking, but even I know that anything to do with computers costs a lot of money. Where is the financing supposed to come from? We haven't even raised enough cash to replace one of our rust buckets, let alone go in for all this high tech stuff. Besides that, who's going to run it? We're still passing the paper tail by hand, whenever there is a start up."

"The bank will lend us up to seventy-five percent of the cost of the building and Alabama Paper will cover the equipment. This unit will have to pay back head office. That only leaves twenty-five percent."

"If head office will kick in for the equipment, why don't they just replace one of the machines we have?"

"Corporate policy states that each division must be self-sustaining, except when it comes to research and development. Head office underwrites equipment and installation costs for development of new product lines."

Hants

"And where does the other twenty-five percent of the building come from?"

"We haven't been able to find a lender."

"Then we are talking about fiction. I think you fellas should get your feet back on the ground."

Everyone but Kent was smiling. "Do you have a suggestion?" he asked.

"Yes."

"Go ahead."

"The Local could revise the debenture that went along with the bonds the men are now subscribing to. If the Union would lend us the rest out of the pension fund, I think we could swing it."

Bert sat up straight, stretched his arms out on the table in front of himself then leaned forward-looking Austin straight in the eye.

"That's absolutely out of the question. We came here to seek a raise not to act as moneylenders for hair brained schemes, which even the banks won't go into. Do you realize that the men have been losing ground during the last six years? We all know the price of bread wasn't supposed to go up during the war; however, it did."

Brad felt deflated. It had been almost a year since Brockton had come to see him. It seemed as if they hadn't moved this thing an inch. It had all been uphill and they were still nowhere near to getting it off paper. Now it was the union.

He knew it was head office strategy. Of course, they had been in touch with the bank. Directors don't simply say no. Too many good people would leave. They had to keep the wheels turning, and that took managers. Headquarters had to let the managers hope they could change things, even believe they could, or they would never put their energies into just keeping the wheels turning.

He thought about the pension fund. The idea had come from the financial officer he had talked to over the phone down in Montgomery. He could still remember the man's words.

"Talk to the Union about borrowing from the pension fund. If you don't have their support, it will never work. They might even go on strike. Just see if they're in good faith. Ask them for the balance of what is needed from the pension fund."

Austin was tired. Why should he push for this? Neither the men nor the company was interested. After all, it wasn't him who was responsible for the condition of the plant. This was like rolling boulders up a mountain side. He would have to do it for himself. It would be his mark. Up to now he had done nothing but the routine. Maybe after it was over he would look elsewhere for a new challenge. However, if he wanted to leave his mark here, he would have to fight. He backed out of his thoughts and answered Herrick.

"It's true that we have been operating without a margin of profit. But maybe we could squeeze a bit of a raise out of somewhere for the men. The war is over. We could increase our prices by one percent."

"Our concern is our margin of livelihood, "Bert replied, "not your margin of profit. We're looking for ten percent across the board. A one percent price increase won't cover that."

"Be reasonable," Brad grunted.

"Fine, we'll be reasonable Mr. Austin. You're asking us to put the older member's retirement in jeopardy for some project that neither the banks nor the company will back fully. A venture which rests upon one customer who could go bankrupt and leave us with so many computer cards we could wallpaper every house in the United States with them. That's not being reasonable."

"This is preposterous. All we're asking is for the men show their good faith."

"Let me remind management that Local 93 is without a contract and is still on the job. All we are asking is that the company shows good faith and bargain with us reasonably."

Hants

Austin came back like a whip, "Unless we do something to turn this mill around; there might not be anything to negotiate about in a very short time."

"So you say," Bert sneered.

"Please gentlemen," interrupted the chairman, "I think both parties have sufficiently stated their positions for this preliminary session. I propose an adjournment until this time next week. All those in favor, raise your hands."

There were for and against on both sides; however, the majority was in favor of adjournment. As the men were leaving the room, Ted Newton heard one of them say, "He sure showed the Hick! That was good." Ted wondered whom they were talking about.

At the second and third session, the company offered two, then a three percent raise. The Union held fast. In spite of the fact that talks were officially broken off, plans went ahead for implementing the new process. The search began for an architectural firm. It came as little surprise when the Local announced a work stoppage for the twentieth of July. It was to be for one day, so that the combined membership could participate in a strike vote.

There was a large rectangular, clapboard building at the fair ground. Many of the towns' people had gone there to square dance or have their handicraft judged. Local 93 was called to this building on a stifling hot July twentieth. The chairs used during bingo games were arranged in four sections, and the long tables were piled along the walls.

An aisle up the middle was crossed by another at the half way mark. Five hundred chairs were in each bank, and there was a large open space at the back. The seats began to fill up a little after one o'clock, in anticipation of the 2 p.m. meeting. A series of speakers was to address the assembly before the vote.

At two twenty-five p.m. a black sedan pulled up in front of the gray clapboard building. Austin got out and approached the door. He was wearing black dress pants and a white dress shirt with the collar open and the cuffs rolled up. A burly individual wearing a peaked cap stopped him at the door.

"I've gotta see your membership card."

"I don't have one," the manager replied.

"You've gotta have one to go in."

"Do you know who I am?"

"All I know is that you are some smart Alec, who thinks he can just walk in without a card. What are you, some kind of nosy reporter?"

Brad took a step forward. The man blocked his way.

"Hey, Frank. Come on out. We've got a wise guy."

Frank stepped out into the sun. The manager was sure he had seen the man in the plant.

"Let him through Tom."

"But he doesn't have a card."

"He doesn't need one."

"What are you, some kind of Union official?" the man asked as Austin stepped around him and replied,

"Not quite."

There were men standing at the back and along the walls listening to someone speaking at a microphone up front on a small raised platform. He made his way up through the space between one of the banks of chairs and men standing along the wall. Nobody paid any attention to him. The man at the microphone opened the floor to anyone who wished to speak. Each person was limited to five minutes. Austin listened to them. There was a pause in the meeting.

"Does anybody else want to address the assembly?"

No one came forward. The question was repeated several times.

Brad stepped out from among the men and walked towards the platform. A murmur swept through the first few rows.

"Yes I would like to speak to them," he said approaching the microphone.

"I don't know," the man said. "You're not one of us."

Kent was sitting in the front row. He stood up. "Let him speak."

Several others repeated the same thing without bothering to stand up.

Austin started to speak. There were no dramatics.

"I would have failed in my responsibility towards you by standing by and watching you throw everything away, without making one final appeal to your reason."

Herrick and Ruskin hadn't noticed Austin. Bert muttered, "The son of a B...," and made a step forward. Ruskin caught him by the arm.

"Too late, let him talk, then go up and answer whatever he says."

"What I have to say won't take long," Brad said, stepping away from the microphone as he heard his voice coming back at him from the overhead speakers. "I'll try to be as clear as possible.

"In order to put a new crop in the ground each spring, a certain part of the previous year's harvest must be set aside for seed. But just that is not enough. Each year the seed must be rotated into a new field. There comes a time when the yield keeps falling. At that point, the smart farmer takes his portion of last year's harvest and trades it with somebody else for a new kind of crop.

"Gentlemen, we have passed the rotation stage at the Nashua mill. We need a new product. You have heard the men talking here today about the new process. I have seen the ballots, which you are going to cast before leaving. One question on the ballot is asking you to approve a loan from the pension fund to help finance the new process.

"It has unlimited potential. There are few competitors. The number of computers is going to double in the next ten years. We will have developed the expertise here. It could lead to a second machine.

"This mill risks dying," he emphasized, "if we don't do something soon. If it goes down, your son's may have to move elsewhere to look for work. It would affect the whole town."

Austin became calm. He shoved his two hands into his pockets, took a deep breath and said,

"That's all."

They watched him walk off the platform and go down the center aisle.

Herrick waited until he saw the white shirt disappear out the door, before stepping up to the microphone. He leaned forward casually towards the chrome instrument; then a deep throated mooing sound filled the building from the speakers in the rafters. He had caught the men's' attention. They rustled uneasily in their seats. Someone in the crowd started oinking. Bert took the microphone into his hands and went,

"Oink! Oink!"

The men fired back, "Oink! Oink!" then began to roar with laughter.

Outside, Austin was just opening his car door. The uproar inside pierced the clapboard building's shell and reached his ears. They're laughing at me. He flicked the key so that the motor would turn over. The automobile bolted forward leaving a cloud of dust, where it had been parked.

"Now that we've had our agriculture lesson for the day," Bert joked, "let's get back to reality. Seed corn doesn't buy cars and houses. That takes hard cash. If people like Austin had stayed on the farm, maybe mills like Nashua wouldn't be in such bad shape. It's not up to us to pay for their mistakes.

When it starts getting cold next January, I don't want you and your families to be rotating the heat from one room of your houses to another, because you can't afford to buy another cord of wood. When the machines really do break down, I want your money in the trust fund to be available for helping replace them, not squandered in some seed swapping fiasco. When you retire; I want you to be able to live with a little bit of dignity and not have to curse some Hick, who dreamed that he was holding a magic wand.

Hants 149

"There are three questions on the ballot. Say no, to all three of them, and you say yes to a strike."

Brad Austin was not a man who took much time out to have a drink, yet he did enjoy a cold beer on occasion. Today was one of those occasions. The black sedan pulled into the gas station that was halfway between his house and the town. The sign out front said Cold Beer. Once inside the store, he slid back the cover of a large metal floor chest. The long necks of brown bottles were sticking out of the chopped ice. He didn't have a brand. His fingers wrapped themselves around as many of them as they could hold, and he brought them over to the counter. The gas station attendant put them in a brown paper bag and handed him his change saying,

"Sure is a hot one."

"Upon reaching his dwelling, all of the bottles went into the ice chest except one. Then he flicked the radio on. The three thirty news was just coming over the air.

"Local 93 of the Pulp and Sulphite Union is voting this afternoon to decide whether they will take strike action to back their demands for higher wages. Our on the spot reporter has phoned in that the balloting has begun. We should have the results for you on our 5:30 p.m. news cast."

Brad removed his shirt, sank back into an armchair and prepared to wait until the five thirty news. Over the next hour or so, several empty bottles appeared on the kitchen table. Eventually, he lost interest in the Sox game, which was being broadcast from Fenway Park. At a quarter to five, there was a loud knocking at the back door. He got up from the chair, walked through the parlor and into the kitchen.

The outline of a police officer was visible through the screen door. The officer was wearing a tight tunic, high leather boots and a visor cap. Brad felt awkward standing in front of the man without his shirt on and with a bottle of beer in his hand. However, he quickly found his voice.

"May I help you?"

"I hope you can," the officer replied from the other side of the screen.

Brad took his shirt from the back of the chair and buttoned two or three of the buttons, before taking the hook from the eye to let the officer in.

"Excuse my appearance, I wasn't expecting anybody."

"I'd have one with you, but I am on duty. My wife said she would have a cold one waiting when I get home. Anyway, I'll get down to the point. Are you Brad Austin?"

"Yes."

"There's been an accident. Before noon, the Coast Guard found a capsized boat floating just beyond the surf line at Rye Beach. When they brought it on board, there was a man's body inside the hull. They said that it looked as if his foot had got tangled in the anchor line. Whatever happened, he's drowned now.

"There was enough ID on him to lead the Police to where he lived. We found a letter from you on the dresser. The captain asked me if I would stop by and see if you would mind coming to make a positive identification for us."

"I am not really sure that I should be driving. I've had a few this afternoon."

"That's no problem. I'll take you in the cruiser and bring you back."

"Okay, I'll just straighten myself up a little."

"I'll wait in the car for you," the officer declared.

"By the way, whom did I write the letter to?"

"I'm sorry, I'm not at liberty to say until we have a positive identification. I'll be outside." At that, the officer turned and left the kitchen.

The policeman didn't go into Nashua to cross the Merrimack. Instead, he drove a little south along the Boston road, then down a dirt road towards the river. It came out at a one lane wooden bridge, which was little known and even less used. After crossing the river, the cruiser took one gravel country road after another, always heading northeast, towards the coast.

"Where's the body being held?" Austin asked the officer.

"There's nothing at Rye. It's just a summer spot. The Coast Guard brought it into Hampton. That's the closest coroner. They needed a death certificate. The Coroner needs a name, before he will issue a certificate."

"You certainly know these back roads well."

"I should, all this area has been my beat for the last six years. There are a lot of comings and goings that most people never see. That kind of comings and goings likes to stick to the back roads. A fella robbed the Savings and Loans over at Haverhill in Massachusetts back in February. He came over the state line and the Mass. Police couldn't follow him. I was on duty. Someone reported seeing his car go down a certain road. I knew where it came out. We nabbed him."

"Where are we going to in Hampton?"

"There's a small morgue at the Hampton Hospital. The body is being held there. It costs the State a bit, but in this heat, bodies deteriorate quickly. Besides, they're accustomed to handling the dead."

"The cruiser arrived at the hospital at 6 p.m. The policeman led the way down into the basement of the building. They stopped in front of two steel doors over which was written the word, Morgue. The officer rang a bell for the attendant. A balding man wearing a white hospital smock let them in.

"I've been expecting you. Your Captain called to say you had gone to get someone who might be able to identify that one the Coast Guard fished out this morning. Is this the gentleman here?"

"This is him."

"The Coroner hasn't been in yet, so we haven't touched the body. It's over there on that table, under the sheet. Step this way, please sir."

Brad followed them without actually being conscious of his own movements. He saw the form of the body under the sheet. He saw the attendant's hands taking hold of the corners of the sheet and start to fold it back. The dead man's face came into view. It was very bloated.

The skin was turning blue. The corpse's mouth hung open. One eye was closed, and the other looked directly at him.

Brad felt the beer start to churn in his stomach. A wave of dizziness came over him. The Morgue attendant noticed him swaying.

"If you are going to be sick, there's a sink over there."

"I'm okay," he replied, holding tight onto the railing which ran around the edge of the table, "it's just the heat and the smell in here."

"Ever see this man before?" the officer asked.

"Yes."

"Who is he?"

"He's my brother."

"What's his name?"

"Shane.... Shane Austin. The same as mine.

"Don, you can cover him up now. Give the Coroner a call. Tell him that he can come in to examine the body as soon as he is able. Tell him that the man's name is Shane Austin.

I'll take you back to your place Mr. Austin, but first we'll stop at the Station. There are some papers that have to be filled out. Your brother can stay here for a few days, while you make funeral arrangements. I'm sorry about all this. Were you close?

"We had our differences, but there was nothing serious in it. What was in the letter I wrote him?"

"It was something about Hants."

"That's what our differences were about. Hants is our old family farm."

"That happens in a lot of families," the officer said, pushing open the Morgue door.

Hants

It was late, when he said good night to the policeman. The alcohol had worn off. He was feeling depressed and went to sleep straight away.

At ten o'clock Sunday morning, Brad began to wake. An insect was buzzing somewhere in the room. He had been dreaming and was feeling good. It had been somewhere out in the country. Somebody had been calling, and there was the smell of lilac.

He rolled over in the big double bed to look at the window. A huge black fly was batting itself against the screen. After watching the insect for several minutes, everything started to come back to him. He remembered the ride to Hampton, the beer and the fair grounds. He wondered what they had decided.

Slowly, his refreshed body uncoiled and got out of the bed. It was a four poster made of a dark red maple, which may have come from the furniture factory at Hudson which had been formerly owned by Angie Sylvester's father. He thought of Shane and became sad. After a cup of coffee, he drew a lukewarm tub of water and soaked in it for half an hour.

Brad suspected that the vote on the previous day hadn't gone his way. It was their laughing, when he was driving off. Still, he had to know for sure. When dressed, he went to the wall, took the telephone earpiece off its hook and turned the crank.

"Good morning, may I help you?"

"Yes, operator I'd like to call Milford."

"Number please."

"I don't have it."

"Name please."

"I think it's Neville."

"Thank you sir ...I have an A. Neville and a W. Neville."

"A."

"One moment sir, I'll connect you."

The ring sounded three times.

"Hello!"

"Hello, may I speak to Angeline please?"

"Angeline... oh, Brad it's you ...this is me."

"Sorry to disturb you on a Sunday."
"No bother, I was just reading."
"What were you reading?" Brad asked.
"The 'Great Gatsby', it's quite new."
"I haven't heard of it. Angeline, I had to go out of town yesterday afternoon," he explained. "I didn't hear how the vote went."
"They're on strike," she replied with sadness.
"I suspected as much, but I had to be sure."
"The newscaster said that it was close."
"Well, I guess that's that."
"Where were you yesterday?" she asked.
"Hampton."
"Why Hampton?"
"There was a boating accident," he clarified. "The Police thought I might know the victim."
"Did you?"
"Yes."
"Who was it?" She wanted to know.
"My brother," he replied.
"Oh Brad, I'm sorry. I wish I hadn't asked."
"That's all right. We were both big boys."
"How are you feeling?"
"I'm okay, just a little sad, and now a strike too."
"Oh, you poor dear, what are you going to do today Brad?"
"I don't know."
"You shouldn't stay there all alone musing about what you can't change."
"Maybe I'll go up to Hants." He thought out loud. "I guess I should say my farm. It was left to Shane and me, but now that he is gone, I guess it's my farm."
"That's a good idea. It's nice out this way now. The lilacs are in bloom."
"Yea, I guess that's what I will do."
"Why don't you pick me up on you way through Milford? You shouldn't be alone. I'm seeing Wade for supper. There's a function at the Boat Club, but he's not coming

until six to get me. As long as I'm back by four, I'll have plenty of time to get ready."

"All right, Angeline, I'll do that," he agreed.

"I'll pack a basket. We'll have a picnic."

"I'll pick up some soft drinks."

"Don't bother, I remember you saying that there was a spring back there. I'd much rather spring water any day than a soft drink."

They had to leave the car at the beginning of the lane up to the old Austin house. It being the height of the season; the hay and weeds had grown up and choked off the entrance. She was wearing a pair of baggy shorts, low soft shoes and a white sleeveless blouse. He took the basket and blanket from her and said,

"I'm wearing long pants, so I'll go forward and try to make a path through the tall grass."

When they reached the house, Brad led her around to the side, past where the kitchen garden had been and on to the edge of what had been the beginning of the apple orchard. A rusty cast iron fence stuck up out of the overgrown vegetation. The fence enclosed a square area. Several headstones were visible in the hay.

"This is our family burial plot."

"Who's in it?" she enquired.

"Both my parents and a baby who died as an infant. I think I'll bring Shane back here," he replied.

"It's very overgrown with hay and weeds."

"I'll see if I get someone with a mowing machine to clean out the lane this week. I'll ask them to run a scythe through here, while they are at it. It will have to be cleaned up, so that a grave can be dug."

They went back around the house and walked to the creek, which ran down from the spring. Brad held her hand while she stepped on the big round stones that formed a natural bridge over the creek. As they made their way up through the back pasture, the outside world seemed to fade away. They began to talk, as if they were old friends.

Angeline was glad she hadn't left him alone today. She just let him talk. She could see the stress falling away. He seemed a lot younger to her out here.

"I don't know why you don't resign," she said finally. "They don't appreciate you there. After all you've done, to go on strike like that. It's ungrateful. I wouldn't stay where I'm not appreciated."

"But the new process."

"If Herrick has anything to do with it, the new process will never see the light of day."

"Oh yes it will. I have a meeting with architects this week in Manchester. Also, there are other ways to finish the financing, besides borrowing from the Union pension fund. That was just a suggestion from somebody at the head office in Montgomery."

"Haven't you seen enough of mills yet? I mean; you started out from this farm, and you've risen to the top. Do you know how many people in Nashua would give everything to be manager of that mill?"

"You're right Angeline. I am getting tired of mills. I was thinking that the other day. When I get this new process through, I'm going to use it to ante up my bid for a spot at head office in Alabama. If there are no openings, I'd like to try for something similar, somewhere else."

Angeline felt a pang of regret hearing him say that.

"But, you have the farm now. You could do something with it."

"I know," he said and became silent.

By then they had reached the spring. A large oak tree growing about fifty feet to the right of it, was casting a huge round shadow, which blocked out the noon day sun. They spread the blanket out in the shade. While she unpacked the basket, he went to the spring and filled up a two-quart earthen pitcher that she handed him. When he came back with the ice cold water, she had already set out two places.

"Hungry?" she asked, smiling at him.

"I'm starving!"

Hants 157

"Good," she laughed stripping the waxed paper away from a tray of quartered sandwiches; "there are two, tomato and mayonnaise, two cucumbers and mayonnaise and two chopped egg."

"These are delicious," Brad gasped, poking a piece of tomato into the corner of his mouth. "Did you make them?"

"Uh, huh," she laughed.

"I'll have to make arrangements for a funeral this week."

"Maybe, I could handle it for you. If you're going into Manchester, you'll be quite busy."

"You wouldn't mind."

"No, I'll ask my aunt about everything I have to do."

"I would appreciate it, just something simple. I'll probably be the only one there.

"I don't know who his friends were. I'll run a notice in the Nashua and Exeter papers."

"Here, have a piece of celery," she said, holding a branch out. "There are carrot strips in that piece of waxed paper too. Just take off the elastic."

When they had finished eating, Angeline began to gather up the plates and the tray.

"I'm going to take these dishes over to the spring and rinse them off a little. There's fruit for dessert, but let's wait a while."

Long ago Albert Austin had built a basin from field stones and mortar to contain the water that bubbled up from the ground. He had inserted a piece of clay drain tile into the stones and lined it with cement so that it would act as a spout. It was still in place.

Angeline lay the dishes on the edge of the basin, wiggled off her engagement ring and set it on the stone ledge, before rubbing her hands under the water flowing from the spout. It was freezing. She rinsed the dishes one by one, shook them in the air, and then they went back to the blanket.

"Would you like to walk up to the top of that ridge?" Brad asked. "We could see the Appalachian hills over in Vermont, from there."

"Sure."

When they reached the top of the bluff, Angeline could see the mountains.

"This is a great spot. I can see why you held onto it. You'll have to show me the house, when we go back to the car."

"It's quite a wreck now, but it was a very fine house when my mother lived in it. My father might have been a sodbuster, but he provided well. They entertained visitors regularly. My mother had my father lay an oak strip floor in the parlor. I can still see her waxing it."

"You know, if you fixed it up, you could live out here and commute into Nashua. It's not that much further than Milford, and I go in every day."

"The thought has crossed my mind more than once."

On the way back down to the spring, they started to run. Angeline had to grab onto his arm to keep from losing her balance.

When they got back to the blanket, she asked him if he felt like some grapes. There were strawberries too.

"If I were to come out here to live, I think I'd rather stay out here, instead of going into town to work."

"It would be nice," she agreed, "but it's hard to make a living off farming around here. There are a lot of abandoned properties. You told me your own father died from overwork."

"You forget, I'm a mechanical engineer. I'd mechanize the whole place," he said seriously, snipping a grape seed off into the grass.

"It would cost a lot of money."

"Angeline, I'm not rich, but I am not poor by any means. I've been working since I finished university at Dartmouth. A lot of what I earned is in the bank. There are other things besides agriculture that I could do out here."

"Like what?" she asked, holding him out a strawberry.

"Fattening cattle."

Hants

"What?" she asked.

"It's called feed lotting."

"I've never heard of that."

"It's really quite simple. Instead of letting beef cattle roam over a pasture and feed on natural growth, you keep them confined in a limited space, like the lower pasture we just walked through to get here. Then you bring the hay and grain to them. They fatten twice as fast."

Angeline forgot herself and went into the idea with him.

"I've got lots of money. That would be a good investment for me. We could go into business together. I'll buy a herd, and you can run the fattening operation. We'll split the profit fifty-fifty."

Brad stopped hearing her talking. He leaned over and kissed her on the lips. She was so surprised she didn't move. He felt himself blushing.

"Excuse me. I shouldn't have done that."

"You don't have to excuse yourself. It was a perfectly natural reaction. After all, I'm a girl."

He looked at her smiling.

"You can do it again, if you want," she urged.

He moved closer to her and put his arms around her waist. Her hands went up onto his shoulders. She felt his lips closing against hers. She relaxed, and her mouth meet his lips. Her tongue brushed against his. She lost all desire to resist the emotion she was feeling. Her body came up against his, and they fell back on the blanket. It was a full fifteen minutes, before she pulled herself off of him.

I'm afraid that I am not used to this. My lips are starting to hurt," she laughed. "Could we just lay here together without kissing?"

"I don't mind at all," he replied.

She rearranged herself and let her head rest on his chest. He held her with one arm and stroked her hair with his other hand. They stayed like that for the better part of an hour. Eventually, it was Brad who thought of the time.

"I hate to disturb you ...I mean us, but I did promise you that I'd have you back by four."

She pushed herself up onto her elbows and looked down into his eyes.

"I know. I've been thinking about that too, but I didn't want to mention it. It's nice just being here like this. I've never done this with anybody before, not ever with Ward. He has just kissed me good night. I probably shouldn't be telling you, but I am. I've only read about doing this in novels. It's so much better when it's real. Have you kissed a lot of women in your life?"

"Not a lot."

"A few?" she pried.

"A few."

"Have you been like this with a few?"

"A couple. ......Angeline"

"Yes?"

"I shouldn't really say this, but ....I think that I am in love with you."

"I think that I know that you are," she replied with impudence.

"How long have you known?"

"I wasn't sure. I suspected it a couple of times, but I knew for sure the day you found out that I was engaged."

"I should have said something."

"I wish you had said something," she declared.

"Come on. I'll take you back home."

"Okay, Brad," she said, lifting herself up off him, "I'll help you gather these things up."

On the way back to the car, he showed her the inside of the house.

Before she got out of the car to go into her aunt's house, Brad placed his hand on her forearm and said,

"Angeline."

"Uh, huh."

"About today that won't happen again."

She smiled at him saying, "Now we're friends, Brad." At that, she got out of the car, waved bye and added, "Today will be our secret."

***

Angie

6

When Austin arrived back at his place, there was a car parked in his driveway. He pulled up behind it and got out. A man sat at the wheel and didn't look up until he was beside the car door. Brad got the surprise of his life.

"Kent, Eric Kent, what are you doing here?"

The car door opened, and the Union man stepped out.

"I came to see you."

"Well, come on in."

"I've been here awhile. My wife will be expecting me soon for supper. I only want to have a word with you. Let's go in the back yard. I'd hate to be spotted by someone driving by."

"Whatever you like Eric," he agreed somewhat amazed.

They went behind the house.

"You have a nice view of the river from here."

Hants

"I'm afraid that I don't take very much notice of it."

"For what it's worth, I didn't vote for the strike."

"I heard that it was close. There are probably quite a few like you. What's on your mind?"

"I didn't see them do it to me, but I saw them do it to you."

"Who are they?"

"They're Herrick and Ruskin."

"Who is Ruskin?"

"He's the Union secretary from Chicago."

"That's interesting, thanks Eric. What did they do to you?"

"They turned the men against me, because I'm from out of State."

"But you've been in New Hampshire so long. Surely, you are one of them?"

"I thought so, but what I'm hearing from a few old friends, is they really worked up a hostile feeling against me during the election for the Local leadership. I was an outsider. They had to purify their ranks."

"That's going a little far."

"I've been told those were Herrick's exact words."

"It was probably Ruskin who put them in his mouth. Herrick doesn't strike me as having much on the ball."

"You could be right."

"I'm afraid you're wrong about me though Eric. I'm a New Hampshire man. It couldn't have been the outsider with me."

"But you're not a Nashua man."

"They call you the Hick. They laugh at the fact that you come off a farm. Herrick got them roaring, after you walked out yesterday afternoon."

"I heard them."

"You really want the new process, don't you?"

"Yes."

"How much do you want it?" Kent inquired.

"I want it, as much as I've ever wanted anything."

"I figured so. It would be a nice note to leave here on."

Austin looked at him seriously. "You're a very smart man, Eric. What else do you think about this situation?"

"You know, Mr. Austin."

"Call me Brad," the manager urged, softening towards him.

"Brad, I grew up in Vermont. As a kid, I watched the water race around saw mills. There are a lot of them there. Just about every stream has a small dam and mill pond on it. When I started working, I worked in sawmills. I remember how the sluice gates operated. If we walked out onto the dam and closed the sluice gate, the saw mill would come to a halt.

We closed them while repairs were going on, to be sure there were no accidents. Nothing moved because there was no water in the mill race. When the repairs were over we would lift the sluice. The water would then rush through the race, instead of the sluice and turn the saw mill gears."

"This is all very interesting Eric, but I don't see what it has to do with what we are facing."

"Only this Brad, Herrick is nobody. His only power comes from pushing against you. You are the sluice gate. As long as you're there Herrick will turn forever. It's you personally that he's against, not the new project. To him, you're the Hick, the outsider. He's the town boy. He's going to teach you a lesson. Take you away, and Mr. Bert Herrick stops turning."

"What do you suggest I do, Eric?"

"That all depends upon how much you want the new process to come in. I have to go now. My wife will be holding supper."

"Thanks for waiting until I got back Eric. I'll move my car so you can get out."

Angeline was still upstairs when Ward arrived.

"My, aren't we spiffy tonight," Avis Neville said letting the young lawyer in. He was wearing striped gray trousers and a pale beige cutaway jacket. "Business must be picking up?"

"I guess you could say so."

Hants

"Come along into the parlor. She won't be long. I'll just go tell her you're here."

When Angeline's gamin figure appeared in the doorway clothed in a long black dress and elbow length white gloves, Ward Shaw stood up and stared.

"You look elegant, Angeline."

"You aren't exactly a disgrace yourself, Ward."

"Now you two enjoy yourselves," Avis chirped, straightening her niece's bangs. "I'll leave the veranda light burning."

All the way to the Club Ward bubbled over with his new business venture.

"I tell you Angeline, I'll make a hundred thousand if I make a dollar."

"You'll be rich."

"We will be rich," he assured her.

"But how on earth are you going to make so much money?"

"I just finished telling you," he replied with irritation.

"Excuse me Ward. My thoughts were somewhere else. Explain it again."

"Are you feeling all right this evening?"

"I'm feeling fine. Tell me again."

"Have you ever heard of the old Ivy place, south west of town along the Nashua River?"

"Can't say that I have, but that's not saying much. There are lots of old mansions in Nashua that I have never heard of."

"The Ivy's had seven boys. It was a big name around the turn of the century. One son went to the State Capital; another went up high in the Marines. What they were most known for was their annual Bar-B-Q. Three or four hundred people were invited.

"Whatever happened to them?"

"The girls whom the boys married, forgot you have to have sons to carry on the name. The last male died off last year. Their place has been on the market since then. The house and barns aren't much. They will have to be torn down. But the land is high and flat with lots of trees."

"What do you mean; the house and barn will have to be torn down?"

"I bought the property. The buildings are too run down."

"I didn't know that you were interested in agriculture, Ward."

"You don't make a hundred thousand farming, Angeline."

"What do you want the land for?"

"I'm going to develop a suburb to Nashua, called Wardberg. With the war, over, everybody and his cousin will be getting married. Just think of all those babies. They will have to house them some place. Now that I have the property, I'm looking for a partner to divide the farm up into serviced lots and another partner who will build modest priced houses on the lots."

"It's a lot of risk. Are you sure that you will be able to sell that many houses?"

"It's official, Angeline. Last week, the State Legislature, declared the Merrimack Valley between Manchester and Nashua an industrial development zone. People will be buying houses."

"That must have cost you quite a sum."

"There were two others bidding against me. It wasn't cheap."

"Did your father or uncle lend you the money?"

"No, I borrowed it from the bank."

"I thought that you had trouble borrowing for that cottage which you bought and sold last year?"

"That was last year. This is this year."

"I don't understand."

"It's all too complicated to explain, Angeline."

By then they had arrived at the Club. The lounge was full. People were spilling out onto the back terrace, which overlooked the river. Ward and Angeline took a glass off the tray that a young man in a tight white jacket carried through the guests. Ward began talking to a man whom she recognized as another lawyer. She had been introduced to him before.

Hants

They are probably talking about Wardberg she thought, wandering over to the floor length window. Outside, she could see two of the waiters maneuvering a step ladder among the people walking about on the terrace. They were lighting the kerosene pots, which were attached to long stands. Beyond lay the marina. Most of the berths were occupied by small motor or sail craft.

She glanced back at Ward. His glass went up, and his head nodded to her. She nodded in return. At that moment, Angeline spotted Collette Horn among a group which had gathered around the piano. They were joining in with the words to the music. When Collette saw her approaching, she stepped away from the others and came to meet her.

"As usual, you are disgustingly well tanned," Angeline said when they reached each other.

"The tan goes with the job. You can't be a golf pro without going out into the sun."

"Some people have all the luck."

"What's happened to you, Angeline? Collette pushed. "We never see you out on the course anymore."

"I don't know. It is six of laziness and half a dozen of business."

"I heard you and Ward got engaged."

"As a matter of fact, he popped the question at the Golf Club. It was the night of the victory supper."

"I am very happy for you both."

"Thank you."

"Come and join us at the piano."

"I will in a minute. I just want to go to see Ward for a second. It doesn't look as if they are going to close the French doors out onto the terrace. It's bound to get a little chilly later on. I want him to get my shawl out of the car, before we start to eat."

"See you later then."

At seven o'clock, one of the waiters started walking around the terrace, holding up a small chrome triangle and turning a striking bar around inside of it. He worked his way into the dining room. Slowly, people began to fill up the tables. Ward and Angeline ended up sitting at a table for six.

One of the couples was Ward's younger brother and girlfriend. She was a small dark haired girl who went to school in Boston during the winter and worked as a lifeguard during the summer. The other couple was Dr. and Mrs. Alex and Susan Cook. They were a little older than the others were.

"Excuse me but haven't we met before?" Susan said after they were introduced.

"I can't say that I recall your face," Angeline replied.

"I'm sure that I've seen you some place before. Maybe you were a patient of mine."

"Patient?"

"Yes, I was a nurse, before Dr. Alex and I were married."

"Where were you a nurse?"

"In Manchester, but not exactly in the city, I was at the TB Sanatorium just outside of town.

"It's a small world. I was a patient there for sixteen years. They declared me a total cure, six or seven years ago. You have a good memory for faces to have placed me after all this time. We must meet for coffee."

How fortunate for you. What have you been doing to make up for lost time?"

"Actually, I have been living a quiet existence. The whole time I was in there, I regretted I couldn't have a regular life and work like other people. I took a business and office practice course by correspondence. When I was released, I found I had inherited a small fortune. Everybody said travel. If I had gone traveling, I still wouldn't have been integrated in normal everyday life. That was what I wanted most. I work in an office, in a plant, in Nashua. I'm the resident-manger's personal secretary."

"I think I would have liked to work in industry, but it is too late now. Have you and Mr. Shaw known each other very long?"

Hants

"Actually, he manages my estate. That's how we met."

"We're soon to be married," Ward added.

"That calls for a drink," Dr. Alex exclaimed, taking up the bottle of wine, which was already on the table and poured a little into everyone's glass.

While the small town socialites dined on orange duck, creamed asparagus and sweet beet salad, a local band played hushed tones from some of Tommy Dorsey's favorite numbers. After dinner, many of the couples went up front to dance on the small polished hardwood floor, which was between tables and the band.

The Shaw table went out to dance on the terrace under the light of the kerosene torches. Ward was a good dancer. He led her through all the movements effortlessly.

A heavy dew ran from the clubhouse down to the river. Angeline was glad she had her shawl. The Cooks were the first to say that they were returning inside. The newly engaged couple followed them. As soon as they went through the French doors, a heavy man smoking a cigar hailed Ward from the far side of the room. Angeline followed.

"Howdy, Ward."

"Hi Art. I don't believe you've met my fiancée Miss Sylvester, Angeline Sylvester."

"Can't say that I have," the cigar smoker replied, extending his hand towards her, "my congratulations to you both."

She stretched out her gloved right hand to meet his firm handshake. Like most of the other women, she hadn't removed her white gloves during the dinner.

"You're a mighty smart girl."

"I beg your pardon, Mr. ...?"

"Howe."

"Smart Mr. Howe?" she inquired.

"Yes you're a smart girl to have said yes to Ward."

Angeline blushed then asked, "Why?"

"Your husband to be is a rising star in this town. Has he told you about the development?"

"As a matter of fact, yes, on the way here this evening."

"I have some good news for you Ward."

"You've decided to come in?"

"I have."

"Great, I assure you that you won't regret it."

"I know I won't. I have a bit of experience with this sort of venture. My men will survey the farm. We'll find out where it would be best to put streets through and then cut out lots. I'll also cover the cost of servicing each lot with water and a septic tank. We'll only open up twenty-five to start with. I'll fund the work and get paid as each lot is sold. Come to my office tomorrow. We'll work it all out. You can draw up a contract."

"I'll come by in the morning."

Just then an attractive woman with blond hair and a plunging neckline came over to them.

"Art will you be a dear and get me a refill? There are too many people for me to make my way through to the bar."

"Sure Hon. I was just going that way myself. Lorna, these are the Shaw's or at least soon to be. Angeline is Ward's fiancée. Ward and I are going to do some business together."

"How very nice to meet you, you'll have to come over for dinner. I'll tell Art when."

"We'd be glad to," Ward replied. Angeline only smiled politely.

Since the next morning was a work day for most of the people at the Club, the room began to thin out early. Ward and Angeline left at nine. They were half way between Thornton's Ferry and Milford when Ward's hand slipped down off the steering wheel and onto his fiancée's thigh. She took hold of his wrist firmly with her left hand and placed his hand back on the steering wheel.

"We're not married yet."

Hants

"Okay, I'll behave. Here give me your hand," he said holding out his upturned palm.

She placed her left hand into it. His fingers closed around hers.

"Am I mistaken Angeline, or are you not wearing your ring? I don't feel it."

She took her hand back from him and felt her third finger through the glove. "My ring, where is it?"

"You tell me," he replied continuing to drive towards her place.

"It can't be at the Club, I didn't take my gloves off all evening."

"Maybe you left it on your dressing table?"

"I don't think so."

"When you were washing?"

"Oh my, the spring."

"What?"

"Nothing."

"You said spring?"

"Just a spring, you know, the kind that water comes out of."

"I know what a spring is, but what does that have to do with your ring?"

"I left it there, when I was washing dishes."

"Angeline, you're not making sense."

"Brad Austin phoned me this morning to find out what the Union had decided. He had to go over to Hampton yesterday afternoon. His brother was drown in a boating mishap. He didn't get to hear how the Union members voted.

"I had to be the bearer of the bad news. That was two blows in twelve hours. He sounded depressed. I suggested that he get out of town. He said that he thought that he would go to his family's old farm. It is on the other side of Milford along the Souhegan River Road. I told him if he would stop to get me; I'd pack a picnic lunch."

"That was kind of you. I should let you know when I lose in court."

"The man was distraught. I couldn't leave him like that."

"What would people think, if they knew you were alone on a deserted farm with a man?" he joked.

"Nothing happened."

"I know, but that is not the point."

"Ward you are raising your voice."

"I am not raising my voice." he exclaimed defensively. "It's just that we are supposed to be engaged."

"That doesn't mean that you own me Ward. He was like an injured bird. I couldn't have just ignored him."

"Well, where is your engagement ring?"

"You sound as if you are interrogating me."

"I am not interrogating you."

"I went to wash off the lunch dishes at a spring in the field. I took my ring off so that it wouldn't get wet. I must have left it on the rocks."

"You must have?"

"Ward stop acting stupidly."

"I'm not acting rash." he blustered with exasperation. "Was that the first time you were at this farm?"

"I am not answering that. It's too ridiculous."

"Fine, don't then," he blurted out.

"Ward, stop squeezing my hand. You're hurting me."

He had to let go of her anyway at this moment in order to turn the steering wheel. They had just arrived at her aunt's house. He pulled the car up to a stop a short way from the house. She got out quickly without saying a word. He followed her and caught up to her half way between the house and the car.

"Angeline stop."

She stopped and wheeled about briskly.

"Say you are sorry."

"Sorry for what?"

"You hurt my hand."

"I was jealous."

Hants

"I told you, you're being stupid."

"You didn't answer my question."

"I've had enough of this. I'm going in the house. I want you to go home right now," she said with agitation and turned towards the house.

His hand shot out to catch her by the arm, but he missed, and his fingers caught in the shoulder strap of her dress. The light chiffon gave way easily under her thrust forward and his tug. The air was filled with the sound of tearing cloth. She stopped and turned to face him. He let go. The top panel of the front of her dress was torn away exposing a black silk slip.

"I'm sorry Angeline," he stammered. "It was an accident. I didn't mean to ......"

"Get out of here Ward!" she shrieked. "I'll call my aunt."

At that moment, the door opened behind them. The elder Neville stood in the light.

"Is that you, Angie?"

"I'll be right in, Aunty."

"Will you go home Ward?"

"Is everything all right?"

"I'll be in a second," her niece said turning towards the front veranda.

"Angie!" the older woman exclaimed. "What has happened to your dress?"

"It was an accident, Mrs. Neville," the young lawyer said defensively.

"Are you responsible for this young man?"

"Yes."

"I don't know what has been going on here, but I suggest that you leave these premises."

"You see what you have done now," his fiancée hissed.

"I only wanted an explanation."

"Angie come up here onto the veranda."

The young woman obeyed, holding up the front of her dress with her left hand.

Avis's voice was stern. "Ward, I want you to leave."

She put her arm around her niece's shoulder, and the two of them went in. The door closed behind them. The heavy case bolt slid into place. He rammed his hands into his pockets with disgust, hung his head and scuffed his way back to the idling vehicle. Inside the house, his fiancée settled down on the carpeted stairs and began to sob. Her aunt sat beside her and asked sympathetically.

"What happened out there?"

"It was just stupidity," she sobbed.

"Did he hurt you?"

"He squeezed my hand."

"Is that all?"

"He was jealous, because I went for a picnic with Mr. Austin."

"What nonsense."

"That's what I told him."

"And the dress?"

"Just more stupidity," she sobbed.

"Come on, let's go to bed. We'll talk more about this in the morning."

The following morning, Angeline, was returning to her room to begin dressing, when the telephone began ringing in the kitchen. She hurried down stairs and took the ear piece from its hook on the side of the wall phone.

"Hello."

"Hello Angeline, this is Ward."

"Oh, hi Ward."

"I want to apologize for what happened last night. I think maybe I had a little too much to drink after dinner."

"Your apology is accepted. We're engaged. I'll just have to get used to the fact that I have to think about someone else now before I act."

"Not really, I want you to be exactly how you are. I know there's nothing between you and Brad Austin. He's your boss, and you work closely together. It's only natural you should emphasize with him."

"Okay, Ward, we're friends again."

"Angeline, I'll call you again during the week. I have to hang up now and get moving. I'm not going to the office this morning. I have to go to Manchester to see about something for the development. On top of that, I promised Art Howe that I would see him today."

"Call me Wednesday."

"It's a deal. Bye."

"Bye."

When she hung up, Avis came into the kitchen wearing a quilted housecoat.

"Who was that?"

"Ward."

"And?"

"We made up."

"Stay and have breakfast now. You can get dressed afterwards."

During the breakfast, Angeline explained what had led up to the torn dress the evening before.

"I'd say it was six of one and half a dozen of another."

"That's why I accepted his apology. I'm going to go up to the spring on my way to work and see if my ring is still there."

"No reason why it shouldn't be."

"You know Aunt Avis, even before last night I have been finding Ward acting strangely."

"What do you mean?"

"Well, it's little things, but there is something of significant importance."

"Which is?"

"You know he doesn't have much money. What he does have, he has gone and tied up in some kind of real estate development, which involves a considerable amount of risk."

"Don't you trust his judgment?"

"I don't know. It seemed to happen so all of a sudden. I find it strange the bank will lend money for a housing development, when there are no definite buyers in sight. They won't lend the paper company the full amount needed to build a new building. It's to house the machine that will make computer cards. The computer cards are already sold ten years into the future."

"You can't understand business dear. Your mother never could figure out what your father was doing. I can remember her wanting him to save, and he would only reply. 'You must spend money to make money'."

"I suppose you're right."

"If you're really concerned about his judgment, why don't we go see how he is managing your inheritance? It would give you a chance to ask Mr. Middleton what he thinks about this real estate deal."

"It's an idea."

"George Middleton and I became good friends, while you were in the hospital. I'll give him a call. He should still be at home."

"Sure, why not," her niece agreed.

The senior lawyer gave them an appointment for 11 a.m. that same morning.

"I should call the office."

"Go ahead while I clean up these dishes."

"Nobody will have arrived yet. I'll get dressed first."

Angeline waited until after eight, before calling.

"Hello, Roxanne."

"Yes, Angeline. Did you oversleep?"

"No, I've been up for a long time. I have an appointment at 11 a.m. this morning. I won't be in until after lunch."

"I'll tell Mr. Austin. I can't chat right now."

"I understand Monday morning. Bye then."

"Bye."

At that moment, Brad came out of his office and headed towards the staff lunch room to get a cup of coffee.

"Mr. Austin."

"Yes Roxanne."

"Angeline called in. She has an appointment this morning. She won't be in until after lunch."

Hants

In a way, the manager was glad. He was still feeling a little awkward about what had happened the previous day at Hants.

"Then you'll have to fill in for her. I had a busy morning planned."

"Fill in how?"

"We've got to get Ted Newton installed in this office and find him a secretary. See if you can get hold of him while I'm gone for coffee. Also get Jerry Riley to come up from Personnel."

"I'll try them both, but it may take a little time. Most of the men from the office are down in the plant helping the department heads shut everything down or getting schedules for who is to do what that must be done. This strike left them a little unprepared."

"They haven't set up pickets yet."

"They will probably be there by noon."

"See you in a bit," he added, before going for his coffee.

When Brad returned, Riley was sitting in his office.

"Hi, Jerry."

"Morning Brad, what's on your mind, the strike?"

"I need a girl Jerry."

"What kind of girl."

"I need someone who knows office work, who is responsible and who doesn't talk about her work outside of work."

"For, yourself?"

"No, I've got Angeline Sylvester. This girl will be for Ted Newton."

"You mean Ted from the lab?"

"You mean, Ted who worked in the lab."

"I don't get you."

"I'm bringing him into the office here. He is going to be in my old office on the other side of Roxanne."

"What's the matter with Roxanne?"

"She's already over worked. This is a new spot. Ted is going to be chief cook and bottle washer for this process. I want somebody in the office here who can grow with him."

"I though you couldn't get the money for the building. Isn't that what this strike is all about?"

"We'll worry about the strike later. Who do you have for me, or who can you get? I'd rather someone who is already on staff, but if you have to bring someone in...."

"I've got the perfect person for your Mr. Newton."

"Who?"

"A young woman named Grace Bailey."

"What does she do?"

"She's in Personnel with me. She came down from Accounting about a year ago. Before that, she was in Marketing for about eighteen months, very keen. She types fifty-five per minute and does shorthand too, very responsible. She and her husband decided to stop at two boys. They're paying down a mortgage. I've never heard a mean word said about her."

"When can I have her?"

"Today if you want."

"I'll let you work out the details. Have her come in this afternoon. Roxanne and Angeline can start to show her around."

Just then Ted Newton's head appeared in the doorway.

"You wanted to see me?"

"Yes Ted."

Jerry Riley stood up. "Here Ted take my seat. It's already warmed up."

"I'll see you later, Brad."

"See you Jerry."

When the Personnel Manager had left, Austin turned his attention to the young chemist.

"Do you feel ready to move up Ted?'

"Depends on where up is."

"Up, is setting up shop in the vacant office over there. It also means taking over this new computer card process from the starting line. I've got too much work. I'll stay in it until the financing gets worked out, but after that it'll be your baby. I'll be here as a resource person for you. You're a natural for it."

"Those efficiency studies have familiarized you with the mill. You're the one who broke the bonding problem. I'm giving you first crack at the project, but I'm warning you, it's a lot of responsibility."

"I'm not afraid of responsibility."

"Good, move your things up to the office this morning. Here's a file. It contains all what I've discussed with the architects. Read it. Give them a call. They are in Manchester. Set up an appointment. Their telephone number is in there. The contact person with them is Terry MacDonald. They just finished the new jail in Concord, and now they're doing a cement block plant in Manchester. I'll leave it to you," he said passing him the file.

Avis Neville and her niece arrived at the neighborhood where Middleton, Norris and Fry were located about 10:45 a.m. It was an old street. Both sides of it were lined with trees. There were many period and family homes in this part of town. The former owners had employed domestics. The women pulled up near a large, black, shingled house. There was a tower in the front. The entrance door went through the base of it. The building housed five lawyers and three support staff. The two women made their way towards the entrance. Once inside, a middle aged woman with her hair pulled back in a bun greeted them.

"Mr. Middleton told me to expect you. Have a seat. I'll let him know that you're here." She disappeared down the corridor for a few minutes and reappeared with a tall-distinguished man who had a thick white moustache.

"Avis!" he exclaimed.

"George," Mrs. Neville beamed, taking his outstretched hand, "it's so good of you to see us on such short notice."

"Not at all, I've been meaning to call you anyway. It's just that I'm always so busy."

"Mrs. Henderson, would you bring me in the Sylvester file."

"Right away, Mr. Middleton."

"And this is my niece, Angie Sylvester."

"Of course, I remember Miss. Sylvester telling me she was also a member of the Golf Club the evening of the victory supper. You and Ward have become engaged."

The young woman pulled off her glove and showed him her engagement ring. "There's the proof."

"Come into my office ladies."

Mrs. Henderson followed them and left, after leaving a large manila file on the oak desk. Once they were settled in two-padded armchairs, Mrs. Neville started the conversation,

"Tell me George, what you know about this real estate development your younger partner has got himself involved in."

"To tell you the truth, Avis, I haven't really been keeping up with it too much. He's always buying or selling something. As a matter of fact, most of us here in this office engage in a bit of real estate on the side. It seems to go with the trade. A lot of our business comes from property transactions.

"As for this new deal, I don't really think it's much of a development yet. It's only a vacant, dilapidated house and some overgrown fields. Frankly, I don't see where he got the money, but I never pry, if it's not client business. Every lawyer in this office is entitled to make a buck on the side, as long as it doesn't interfere with client business."

"In a word, what do you think of it, Mr. Middleton?" Angeline asked.

"A bit risky, it's a long way to building houses. Even then, they have to be sold. Personally, I prefer to buy something that is already built, fix it up a bit and then resell it. There's a small profit, but I do it with such regularity that it proves to be a good sideline."

"I think it's risky too," the young woman added.

Hants

"In a way George, that's why we wanted to see you. We thought we'd like you to take a look at how Mr. Shaw has been managing Angie's estate. It all looks the same to us, but you have a better eye. Who knows maybe he is doing a better job than you did, when you were looking after it."

"He probably has been," the old lawyer said, picking up the manila case. "I had too many things on my hands at the time. That's why I gave it to Ward to look after."

He undid the tie string, flipped back the top, turned the case upside down and shook it over his desk. A single sheet of paper floated out. Mr. Middleton picked up the sheet of paper and read it from beginning to end, before looking back at the two women.

"Miss Sylvester, it should be you who is telling me about this project."

"Me?" she squeaked.

"Yes, this is your Power of Attorney. It's all in here."

"I beg your pardon?"

"It's all here. You authorized him to use the securities we were holding here as collateral for a loan from the Nashua Savings and Loans. The proceeds were to be used to buy a farm out along the Nashua River west of town."

"I what?" Angeline stuttered.

"That's what it says here."

"May I see that please?"

"Certainly," he said, passing her the piece of paper. He watched her face turn pale.

"Mr. Middleton, this is not my signature. I never signed this. This is the first time in my life I've seen this document."

The old lawyer felt a dull pain begin to grow somewhere deep inside his head.

"May I see it again, please Angeline."

He let the whole page sink in, before speaking, "Avis, did you witness this?"

"I don't know," she replied, stretching out her hand for the document.

"I'm sorry, George. This is not my signature."

Middleton felt a throb between his temples. He picked up the phone on his desk.

"Mrs. Henderson, would you have Ward come to see me."

"He won't be back until this afternoon."

"In that case, would you get me the lending officer over at Nashua Saving and Loans?"

"I'll put it through on your line."

"George, this is some kind of fraud," Avis exclaimed.

"Let me try to work it out, please, before we start into that."

The desk phone rang.

"Good morning, Howard White speaking. How may I help you?"

"Mr. White, this is George Middleton from Middleton, Norris & Fry."

"Good morning sir, what may I do for you?"

"I'm doing a routine inquiry with regards to a member of our firm, a Mr. Ward Shaw."

"Oh, yes Mr. Shaw. How may I help you?"

"It's with regards to a loan he has with your institution."

"I'm familiar with it. One of the largest I've signed all year."

"Then everything went through all right."

"There were a few hitches at the beginning. It was a question of collateral. His fiancée came through with it, and we were able to close."

"Has he been making his payments on time?"

"No problem yet."

Howard White was a credit man. He had a lot of experience in it and had developed a sixth sense. He thought he caught something in the caller's tone.

"Tell me, Mr. Middleton, is there some irregularity that I should know about?"

George Middleton was also experienced. The tone and the choice of words the bank officer used sounded

Hants 183

somewhat familiar. It was the quiet underside of the town talking. He had heard it before. It sifted everything. It let nothing get through. It knew all. It fed on irregularities. Especially indiscretions committed by the supposedly more respectable members of the community. For a quick second, the senior partner saw a threat. It could involve the practice. He had Norris and Fry to think about.

"No, nothing in particular it's just routine."

"Call again anytime."

"Thank you."

For a long minute, the elderly gentleman looked at the young woman.

"Do you love him Angeline?"

"I don't know anymore? I'm too confused for the moment."

Then the man of law looked at Mrs. Neville and in his best courtroom voice asked,

"Do you trust me Avis?"

"Yes."

"Will you let me handle this?"

"On one condition."

"What is that?" George queried.

"If he has hurt my niece, then he must pay. And if he must pay, then I trust it to your discretion that he pays in a way, which will not bring further pain to my niece. It must not just be swept under the carpet to protect the name of Middleton, Norris and Fry. I'll let you chose the time and the means."

"It will be done as you say."

"I know you lawyers have your own law by which you protect your profession, but let me warn you George, I follow a different law."

"Which law is that Avis?"

"The law of property."

"And what law is that?" The lawyer asked with a slight cringe

"It's the law, which says the only law is the law, which helps accumulate, protect and transmit property."

"I understand you. There won't be any sweeping under the carpet."

"Angie, I think we can leave everything in the capable hands of Mr. Middleton. Let's go have lunch somewhere."

Ward Shaw came in at three thirty that afternoon. Mrs. Henderson waited until he had checked his memos.

"Mr. Middleton said he would like to see you, when you arrived. He's in his office with Mr. Norris and Mr. Fry. You can go right in."

When Ward opened the door, the three partners looked up from their conversation.

"You wanted to see me."

"Yes Ward come in. Leave your things on the table there. Pull up a chair."

They waited until he was comfortable. Mr. Fry began to speak.

"So how are things Ward? You busy these days?"

"As a matter of fact yes."

"I suppose it's this new real estate venture of yours?" Norris added.

"As a matter of fact, it is. I was in Manchester speaking with a builder this morning, and I've just come from a meeting with Art Howe, the surveyor here in town."

"It must be going to be quite big?"

"All told, it could involve a hundred units."

"A hundred houses," Norris whistled, "I've never heard of anything like it in this town. That is going to involve a substantial amount of money."

"Not really, it'll be in stages, with the early stages financing the later."

"Still, it's a lot of funding for one person."

"I have a couple of partners."

"Anyone that we know?"

"They prefer to remain silent partners."

"One of your partners has chosen not to remain silent," Middleton said. "Tell me Ward, have you ever seen this document?" He passed the young man the Power of Attorney.

Ward took one look and became panic stricken. He looked at the three of them. They were expressionless. He didn't let down his bluff.

"What's this supposed to mean?"

"It means the ladies claim they never signed this document. In fact, they're quite worried about Miss Sylvester's property."

"We're engaged to be married. She's my fiancée. I can explain everything."

"I hope you can," Fry snorted. "She's a charming young woman. It would be a shame to see her get hurt."

"Ward," George Middleton said dryly, "on the odd chance you can't explain everything, I'm going to tell you what is going to happen."

"But I can. She loves me," Ward protested.

"In the event she doesn't see eye to eye with you, you're going to acquire three new silent partners, we three. We will buy out Miss Sylvester and her property will be returned to its file case."

"But you can't do this. I've been working up to this for years."

"Ward, if Angeline Sylvester doesn't go along with you, there is a word for what happened here."

"What word is that?" Ward exclaimed.

"Theft."

"No, not that," the younger partner insisted.

"I'm afraid so."

Norris spoke up; "We've never had any theft in this firm Ward. We don't intend to start now. Do you understand?"

"All I understand is that everybody is jumping to conclusions."

"Nobody is jumping. You've got all the time you need. Why don't you advance your wedding date? Some things are more easily understood in community of property. Anyway Ward, we won't hold you any longer for now. We only wanted to let you know, if you should have to refinance the mortgage in a hurry, the firm won't let you down."

Shaw rose, gathered up his things and left the senior partner's office. He took the staircase up on the left and went up to where he worked. The first telephone call went to Milford. There was no answer. The second went to the strike bound plant.

"Hello, Angeline Sylvester speaking, may I help you?"

"Angeline, it's Ward speaking."

"Oh, Ward! What a surprise, I thought you were out of town all day?"

"And I'm surprised to find you there. Isn't there a strike going on?"

"That doesn't affect us. The office isn't Union. We still have heaps of backlog. As a matter of fact, we're breaking in a new girl"

"I'd like to see you this evening."

"I'm a bit tired. I didn't sleep very well last night. But let's not talk about last night. We got past it this morning."

"How about Wednesday evening then?"

"Let me think on it Ward. I'll give you a call back."

"I'll wait to hear from you then. Bye."

"Bye."

Brad Austin came up to her desk just as she was hanging up.

"Are you working?"

"There's nothing that can't wait."

"Do you think you can handle the details for a funeral?"

"I'm sure I could," she replied without hesitation.

"I would like to have Shane buried this Saturday. I'd like you to run an ad in our paper and the Exeter paper, if they have one. Just a simple church service some place, then back to Hants for burial."

When he said Hants, she lowered her eyes and blushed. As she looked back up, she saw him smiling.

Hants

He looked over at Roxanne, who was busy with the new woman, then turned and winked. At that, she smiled.

"My aunt can probably arrange something at one of the churches in Milford. It would be convenient for you."

"I'll leave everything to you. Roxanne had someone cut the hay in the lane and clean up around the headstones. If you need any help, get her to give you a hand."

Neither woman saw very much of the manager during the rest of the week. The strike vote on the previous Saturday was the straw that broke the camel's back. There was a series of mini conferences during the week. Things went from bad to worse. It began to look as if the collective agreement had served its useful life. Every time a section was examined, it seemed to be nothing but a patchwork of past compromises, which were no longer relevant. At least this was the Union point of view.

The company was opposed to rewriting the whole agreement. Experience had shown, in other industries that once this road was embarked upon, many companies never came back. After months and sometimes years of haggling the two sides would come to an agreement. By then, many key employees had drifted away, suppliers had found new outlets and customers had been won over by the competition.

Angeline was drying the supper dishes Thursday sundown when the phone rang. It was Ward.

"You were going to get back to me."

"I've had a headache all week."

"Are you avoiding me?"

"Not at all."

"Who is it?" Avis asked.

"Ward," she said, putting her hand over the mouthpiece, "he wants to see me."

"Haven't you told him yet?"

"I don't know how to say it."

"Just tell him you know how he got the loan. See what he says."

"I can't."

"Then give me the phone and I will."
"No!"
"Then invite him for Sunday night dinner."
"No."
"Listen niece, you can't hide from it. If it is a big fire, a little wind won't blow it out."
"I'm afraid it might be a big wind."
"Invite him to dinner. Now that is the end of it."
"Ward, are you still there?"
"Yes, where were you?"
"I was talking to my aunt Avis. She's inviting you for dinner on Sunday."
"Sunday dinner, I wanted to see you alone."
"We can sit out on the veranda afterwards."
"I didn't mean alone like that."
"Well, come for dinner. We'll go for a ride, when we've finished eating."
"Angeline I can't make it Sunday. I have to see somebody."

At this point, the young woman stopped sliding. She knew he was lying. Angeline began to feel confidence coming back into her. If he couldn't face them, maybe there was something.

"Ward, I'm busy right now. We're doing the dishes. If you are tied up Sunday, we'll have to make it some evening next week. Give me a call."
"Fine Angeline, we'll take a weekend off. I did apologize about last Sunday."
"And I accepted it."
"Good, I'll get in touch with you next week, bye for now."
"See you, Ward."

Brad reached his sister Dora on Thursday night about nine o'clock. With regrets, she couldn't make the funeral. It was her third month and not going well. There had been no answer at the other sister Wendy all week because she and her husband had taken a vacation. They were somewhere near Alexander Bay in New York. There was no telephone.

Hants

It was quite a surprise when the hearse pulled up in front of the small church. Half a dozen individuals stood about near the door smoking and talking. Austin followed the pallbearers in through the double doors. There were at least another twenty-five people in the pews. Now he was glad he had gone through with it. A front pew was reserved for him. Two or three of the faces looked familiar. He wondered if it was he who was in the coffin, would there be this many at the funeral.

The religious ceremony was short. The man of God knew all the words by heart. When it was over, he led the procession out to where the hearse was waiting. Everyone got into theirs or someone's automobile and followed the black wagon as it made its way out of Milford and along the Souhegan River Rd.

Angeline had not gone to the church. She didn't know Shane Austin and didn't think that it would look proper to be there with Brad. About the same time the pallbearers carried the coffin into the little church, the young woman got in her car went out along the North River Rd. passed the farmhouse and up to the crest of the hill.

There was an opening in the fence at this point. She pulled into it and parked the car behind a growth of bushes. There was shade in under the trees. It was very peaceful. The bees droned in the flowers. There were lots of perfume scents floating through the air. She waited about an hour, before hearing the cavalcade of cars approaching along the flats.

From her spot in the bushes at the top of what used to be the apple orchard, Angeline could see everything. The man of God put something on the headstone. Several of the pallbearers began to shovel the fresh earth back into the hole. It looked eerie from her vantage point. The burial didn't take long. Soon everyone began to make their way back to the line of cars in the lane. At last, the hearse pulled away. Brad stood all alone looking at the grave.

He didn't notice her come out of hiding and walk down the slope. She was about ten feet from him, before she spoke. He turned around looking very surprised.

"I saw it all from up top there," she said pointing back to where the car was parked. "It wouldn't have looked proper for me to go to the church. I didn't think that you should be alone here, after everybody went."

"That was very thoughtful of you."

"What were you thinking about, when I came up."

"I was thinking, I was thinking........You know; a part of me just went underground. We weren't too close today, but the first fifteen years of my life was with Shane. I don't bear him any malice for what he did to this place. It's all mine now. My mother left it to us jointly, with the stipulation that should one of us die, the other's half would go to the survivor."

"It was a good day for a funeral. I hate it when it rains," she commented.

"I don't go to many of them."

"I've been to quite a few," she said, dropping a small bouquet of buttercups and daisies on to the fresh ground.

"I'm glad you came."

"Are you?"

He looked at her squinting against the sun. "Yes, I am. I was going to invite you, but I didn't think I should. You know how people talk."

"Let them talk."

"I beg your pardon."

"Brad."

"Yes?"

"Would you kiss me please?"

He approached her, took hold of her left elbow with his right hand and drew her in towards him, before putting his lips on hers. She swung her arms up around his neck and let the full weight of her body fall against his chest. They didn't stay together long. When she pulled away from him, she was crying.

"What is it Angeline?"

"He didn't love me. It was only the money. Oh, I just want to die."

He took her back into his arms and held her until she was quiet.

"Do you want to tell me about it?"

It was as if a hypnotist had snapped his fingers and said now you will wake up. She had gone into shock Monday morning and stayed in it all week. The bubble was broken. She told him everything. When she had finished, she looked at him sheepishly and asked,

"Is there something so terribly wrong with me that someone couldn't love me for myself?"

"No, you're a loveable person. As a matter of fact, if you think back to our picnic last weekend, you should recall I said exactly that to you."

The young woman thought for a minute then asked timidly, "Would you say it again?"

"Last weekend I thought I was falling in love with you, now I know I have fallen in love with you."

She sighed and laughed, "I guess I know what I have to do."

"What'?"

"Talk to Ward."

"What are you going to say? My boss has fallen in love with me."

"He'd only laugh and say that you are some Hilly Billy upstart whom the town boys are giving a good whipping, down at the mill."

"He wouldn't say that."

"He already has," she assured him.

"Then what will you say?"

"I'll tell him when a woman makes friends with a man, there are no spaces. They are one until he does something to separate them. I'll say that he has driven a wedge between us, and now I can't trust him. If he did this thing, he is liable to do something again in the future. I can't bring myself to trust him anymore."

"Do you think you and I will be friends one day?"

"I've already started to become your friend. I told you so last Sunday."

"I'm glad."

"So am I. You know Brad; you should move out here to live. We could see each other more often. It's so hard at work. We're always so busy, and there are always other people around."

"As a matter of fact, I decided to move this morning, while I was in church for the funeral. I'm going to see a contractor this week about renovating the house, putting in wiring and indoor plumbing."

"He'll probably tell you to tear it down and start over from scratch," she warned.

"Then he won't get the job."

"Do you think you'll be all right here alone? I shouldn't stay too long. My aunt wanted to go shopping this afternoon. She will be wondering where I am."

"It was nice of you to come." He was sincere. "I've been running from myself all week. What I have to do is going to be very difficult. I had to talk to somebody. I didn't know whom to turn to. Before last Sunday, I wouldn't have thought that it would be you."

He paused feeling a bit embarrassed and then continued, "Angeline."

"Yes."

"Do you think I am an upstart Hilly Billy?"

She stood up on her tiptoes and kissed him softly on the lips. "Does that answer your question? Now I must go. I'll see you Monday morning."

He held out his hand saying, "I'll walk you back to your car Angeline."

"Angie," she said, taking his hand and starting back up the hill.

"What do you mean Angie?"

"Call me Angie!"

"Isn't that what everybody calls you?"

"Only my aunt Avis calls me Angie."

***

Going Home

7

Early Monday morning, Brad made an appointment to visit the Regional Vice President, in Boston.

"I'd like to try to find the remaining balance for the building from a source, other than the men's pension fund." Austin said to the executive.

"Didn't you talk to Finance in Montgomery?" the Vice-President asked.

"Yes."

"Didn't they tell you that the balance, I think twenty-five percent, had to be raised from the local employees? In your case, it's less, since your mill has been operating this bond program all during the War."

"I thought that it was only a suggestion."

"It was no suggestion," the executive assured him. "That is company policy, when it comes to the type of project, which you're contemplating."

"I don't understand."

"Let me put it this way Mr. Austin. This is a very big corporation. We have divisions all over North America. We have a planning department that incubates too many projects as it is, for the number of people we have available to achieve them. We'd like to see our resident-managers implement corporate projects.

Every now and then we have resident-managers like you who come up with a good idea. We've had a fair amount of experience with this, and there is a corporate policy to cover it. That policy says projects that don't originate in corporate planning must have the backing of the local work force to reduce chances of failure to a minimum. You understand our point of view. The best laid plans of mice and men can't do much against a hostile Local."

"They're afraid that they'll lose their pension fund."
"Impossible."
"I don't understand."
"Didn't Finance tell you?"
"Tell me what?"
"That the loan is one hundred per cent guaranteed. We take out an insurance policy on it."
"You're kidding me," Austin exclaimed in disbelief.
"No, I'm very serious."
"That's great news," the Nashua manager said with relief. "I shouldn't take up any more of your time with this. What you have just told me sheds a whole new light on the issue."

He stood up and shook hands across the desk with the Boston man.

"Good luck to you Austin. There are lots of openings up top for men like you. You could go far in Alabama Paper."

"Things are looking better already," the resident-manager said, before leaving the thickly carpeted office.

Ward Shaw's fiancée had left a message for him, while he was out Tuesday afternoon. When he came in, Mrs. Henderson told him that Miss Sylvester would

Hants

be pleased, if he could meet her at The Blue Sword. It was a small coffee shop, one door back from the main street in downtown Nashua. Ward was elated. It was the best news he had for a week. He could hardly wait for 5:15 pm and arrived at the coffee shop before her.

Ward took a table for two near the back window. There was a planter overgrown with ivy between that table and the next. It had the effect of isolating the table from the rest of the room. He stood up and waved, when he saw her coming in.

"I'm so glad to see you," he bubbled.

"Are you?" she said smiling.

"Yes, I've had this wonderful idea all weekend."

She didn't respond.

"Angeline, why don't we get married in September?"

"Isn't that a little fast?"

"We've been engaged since May and have been seeing each other for several years."

"But we don't really know each other all that well yet," she remarked.

"What's there to know?" he exclaimed hoping that his bluff would see him through.

"Ward, let's stop playing games," she said solemnly. "I want to know why you forged my and my aunt's signature on a Power of Attorney. I want to know why you used it to secure a loan at the Nashua Savings and Loan, by putting up a good part of my inheritance as collateral."

"I did it for us Angeline."

"You could have asked me."

"I wanted to surprise you."

"You certainly did surprise me. I was beginning to have doubts about my own self-worth. I can't believe that someone whom I had so trusted could have done a thing like that to me."

"Angeline you're making a mountain out of nothing. All your property is safe and sound in the bank. Now let's talk about our wedding this September."

"I'm afraid I can't Ward."

"Oh, Angeline, don't say what you don't mean. You'll only regret it."

"Ward, I'm not trying to hurt you. I'm trying to protect me from being further hurt. I trusted you without limits."

"Give me a little time, please. You'll see. We'll be the richest couple in this town. We'll have the biggest house and throw the most sought after parties."

"There's more to life than that. I want to be loved."

"I do love you. That's why I did it."

"I'm sorry Ward. I don't believe you."

"What do I have to do, get down on my knees here in the cafe?"

"Ward, I want you to listen to me. Look at what I'm doing. I'm taking off your engagement ring."

He grabbed her by the hands, "Don't do that."

"Don't hurt my hands again, please."

He released his grip, and she finished sliding the band over her knuckle. She lay the ring down on the white tablecloth in front of him.

"I don't want it," he said dryly.

"It's yours. You paid for it."

"It's you I want."

"I'm sorry. I can't believe you, after what has happened."

"Please stop this foolishness Angeline."

"What's done is done Ward. We can't undo it."

"There's someone else," he jabbed. "A woman in her thirties doesn't drop a winning horse, unless she has another."

"Don't talk like that Ward."

"You'll end up being an old maid Angeline."

"I'll have to take my chances."

"We could have it all Angeline."

"Ward, you're wasting your breath. I can't stay any longer. I've done what I came here to do." She gathered up her purse and stood up.

He was dumbfounded and sat and watched her go.

Hants 197

Angeline Sylvester didn't look back. She was half way to her car, when her eyes began to fill with tears. Why did it have to turn out like this she asked herself putting the key in the ignition? Hadn't she eaten her share during sixteen years in the hospital?

The following morning about ten, the telephone on George Middleton's desk disturbed him while reading a file.

"Good morning George, it's Avis Neville."

"What can I do so early in the day for you Avis?"

"I'm calling for my niece. She asked me to talk to you about having the management of her inheritance taken out of Ward Shaw's hands. In fact, she requested that you see to its administration, if you can spare the time."

"Then something has happened?"

"Yes, she broke off their engagement."

"I am very sorry all this happened, Avis."

"It's not your fault George. We all remember Ward's father. He was such an exemplary man. But like they say, you can't tell a book by its cover. What you can do though is help us get her property back."

"I've already seen to that."

"Thank you George, I knew that we could rely on you."

That afternoon, Mr. Middleton, Norris and Fry drew up a contract, before they asked Ward to come in to join them.

"I'm sorry it had to come to this Ward, but we must protect the firm."

"Where do I sign?"

"Aren't you going to read it?"

"I'd have to sign whether I read or not, right?"

"I'm afraid so."

"Then there's not much sense in reading."

"As you wish."

When the three men had left his office, he put the documents into his briefcase. He told Mrs. Henderson that he was going for a little walk but that he wouldn't be long. Howard White at the Nashua Savings and Loan saw him right away. He was glad to see that Mr. Shaw had won the partners over to his development idea. Certainly, he would be glad to replace the Sylvester securities with these new and as he said, much more substantial guarantees. Yes, he understood Mr. Middleton, Norris and Fry wished to be silent partners in this project. No, he wouldn't mention a word to anybody in town.

Back in his office, George Middleton opened the vault, which was in the closet behind his desk. He made a place for the cardboard case that contained Angeline's securities, then closed the steel door and gave the dial a whirl, until he heard the tumblers drop in place. There was a bottle of bourbon on top of the vault. He poured a coffee mug full, then went to sit at his desk. The gulp of whisky burned as it trickled down to his stomach.

He selected a straight pen from his pen tray and unscrewed a bottle of ink. It took a bit of shuffling among the papers in the bottom right hand drawer of his desk, but eventually he found what he was looking for. He lay the seventeen by eleven-inch sheet of paper on the blotter in front to him. It was folded in the middle, to make four writing surfaces. The cover had a letterhead printed on it. It said, "New Hampshire State Bar" under that in smaller type was written, Discipline Committee: The old lawyer picked up the straight pen and began to write. When he was finished, the coffee mug of bourbon was empty. He put the complaint in an envelope and mailed it personally on the way home.

On the other side of town, negotiations at the mill dragged on and then broke off. Austin had stayed out of the sessions as much as possible letting the same team as before, along with Ted Newton, represent the company. He observed his presence only antagonized the Union. The last day of September the manager had put in a grueling afternoon doing paperwork. He went to the staff cafeteria for a break and found Angeline sitting there all alone.

"What are you going to do Brad?"

"About what?"

"The strike."

"Oh, that."

"What did you think I was talking about?"

"About us."

"That's important too, but you will have to get the strike settled first."

"I have a plan."

"Care to let me in on it."

"Suppose I could, but this doesn't go any further than you and me."

"It won't. Nobody even knows I have been seeing you at your farm."

"Talking about that, I should be moving out there to live about the middle of October. It looks as if the work will all be finished. But the plan, you wanted to know what it is. I don't think that you are going to like it."

"Try me."

"You won't like it."

"Why not?"

"There's a chance that I will be leaving here."

Her jaw dropped, "What?"

He smiled at her. "Well, either way I will be leaving here. If I drop the computer card process and settle, there is a good possibility that head office will offer me something higher up in the company."

"You didn't tell me anything about that."

"You were going through enough with Ward. I didn't want to add to it."

"Where would that put you and me?

"Let's not even discuss it, because I'm not interested in dropping the new process. It's my baby. That's what I leave for posterity."

"I don't understand. You said either way you would be leaving."

He looked at her introspectively. "You understand

this is very hush, hush."

"Brad, do you want me to throw this salt shaker at you?" She flashed a wide grin.

"All right Angie. It's a little bit of throwing a set of dice, which have chess games being played on them. Let's say tactical strategy."

"Go on."

"Do you remember the day after my brother's accident? We had a picnic?"

"Yes," she replied, feeling her cheeks warming momentarily.

"I never told you this. When I got back home, I found Eric Kent sitting in his car in the lane."

"That's odd."

"We had a long talk," he explained Kent's dam and sluice gate analogy. "He thinks that Herrick got the leadership because he was one of the boys who went against the guy from out of state. Mind you, there's no proof. It's just his gut feeling."

"I can understand why he doesn't talk about it," she said quickly. "The men would only say he is paranoid. Then they wouldn't want him to represent the department."

"I never thought of that."

"So he has taken his gut feeling and looked at your case and thinks Herrick is scoring points by leading the town boys against the Hick."

"That's about it."

"Just for the record Brad, I don't find anything back woods about you. In fact, I think that you are an intelligent, refined man who dresses well and has good social manners."

This time it was Austin's cheeks, which began to warm. "Well, thank you Miss Sylvester." Then he too mockingly flashed a wide grin.

"If I were you, I wouldn't repeat Kent's theory about Herrick and you. Somebody might think you're paranoid also. However, I do think that he's a very observant person and there might be a lot of truth in what he is saying."

The door to the staff cafeteria opened, and two women from Personnel came in and went to the urn of coffee.

"I have to get back," Angeline said, "I still have scads to do, before I go home. Stay and finish your coffee. I'll come to visit you at the farm on Sunday. You can tell me all about your plan then. Go and sit with them when I leave. I don't want any whispering going on about you and me. Just talk to them about the strike."

On the way back to his office, the manager stopped at the desk near the door leading into Ted Newton's office. Grace Bailey was busy building files for the flow of paper, which was starting to come in from the architects who were preparing the new building. A general contractor had also been engaged.

"Is Mr. Newton in, Mrs. Bailey?"

"No, he had a meeting this afternoon."

"Does he have anything scheduled for tomorrow morning?"

She checked the agenda. "No."

"Tell him I would like to see him first thing in the morning."

She wrote it in the 9 a.m. block on her pad then went and put a memo on his desk.

Ward Shaw had been in court all morning. He was late getting back to his office from lunch. On the way in, he picked up his mail from Mrs. Henderson. There were seven or eight envelopes. One had New Hampshire State Bar written in the top left-hand corner. They probably want money he thought, putting it aside for the last, while he opened the others.

There were cheques from clients, a bill from the process servers and a confirmation of service. When he unfolded the letter from the Bar, his eyes scanned the printed page then came back to reread it. He felt his legs and arms go weak. A cold perspiration trickle down over his ribs. The last paragraph stated,

"You are to appear before the Discipline Committee at 10 a.m. on the 12th of October 1945 to hear the complaint which has been lodged against you and to present such defenses which you may have. The hearing will be held in Room 204 of the new Concord Legal Complex at #14 State St. If you have any questions or have a prior engagement which can't be broken, please contact the committee secretary who will assign you a new hearing date."

Shaw got up and went to the window. A lane ran between the properties, which came together. He stared vacantly out onto the back yards of houses on the street. There were still coach houses to be seen. No one used them anymore.

His thoughts swam away through the law, back to law school and then beyond. Even as a little boy he remembered that he had wanted to be rich, richer than his father. When he came back to his desk, he was feeling angry. He picked up the notice and went to find Middleton.

George told him to come in. He knew what it was about. He had received a similar notice that same day as had Mr. Norris and Mr. Fry.

"I thought we had settled this," Ward stammered shaking the piece of paper in the air. "We agreed it was over. She got her property back and you three are getting a cut of my action."

"We had no choice, Ward."

"No choice, no choice be damn, I'm going to fight you. If I go down, I'll take you three with me. The law is my livelihood. It's how I pay my bills. Without my license, I'm done. You didn't have to do this."

"Settle down, Ward," Mr. Middleton exclaimed angrily. "You should have thought of all this, before you did it. Actually, you are getting off easy."

"How's that?"

"It's Avis Neville. She wants your hide. It was this or a Court of Law. We would have been called in for third party responsibility. All of that would be public, right here in Nashua. This Discipline Committee is private, and it takes place in Concord. Which would you have preferred?"

The young lawyer dropped his arms to his sides and stared at the senior partner.

"I see."

"I'm glad."

"I don't think that I have to tell you I'll be vacating these premises as of today."

"I expected as much."

Shaw left without another word.

When Ted Newton knocked on the manager's door at a little after nine a.m. on Friday, the latter had been working hard for over an hour.

"Sit down Ted. Shut the door too please." He waited until the young chemist was settled, before continuing, "How are the negotiations going?"

"They stalled again yesterday. It's like they're throwing sand in the gears. They keep asking why you aren't there."

"Who asks?"

"The head of the Local, Mr. Herrick is asking."

"What do you think of Mr. Herrick?"

"Well, he is a union type and I haven't had a lot of experience with unions."

"But you are learning."

"Yes, I'm learning and I can talk to Mr. Herrick without getting tongue tied."

"That's a big first step. I was even greener than you were the first time I met them. So, what is your assessment of the situation?"

"I'd say it's this new process. I think they're crazy though. It's like biting the hand that will feed you next year and for a good many years after."

"Exactly, you know we can't lose it."

"I understand, without the process, I don't have a place here."

"Exactly, tell me Ted, are you willing to fight for your

place here?"

"That all depends, I wouldn't kill anybody for it."

"You wouldn't be asked too."

"What then?"

"Let me explain the situation. You have said Mr. Herrick keeps asking for me."

"He does."

"Now I don't want you to misunderstand me Ted. What I am going to tell you might sound like paranoia to a stranger, but it's just small town life. You see, a lot of these men, Herrick included, know me from way back when."

"When was that?"

"Some of them knew me in high school. I grew up on a farm out along the Souhegan River Rd. At the time, if you wanted to go past the eighth grade, it meant coming into Nashua. I arrived for grade nine, and most of the boys had all gone through primary school together. They had their group, and it didn't include me. On top of that, my mannerisms were a little rusty. They nicknamed me the Hick.

To make a long story short, I stayed in school, and most of them didn't. Today the tables are switched. I sit up here in this office, and they're out there on the machines. A few of them resent the fact I got ahead of them. Bert Herrick resents it a lot."

"They're being stupid. It's what America is all about. A man can be born on a farm and get to be President."

"I know, and I appreciate your observation, but we don't live in a perfect world and what is supposed to be isn't always what is, especially in small towns. There are a lot of dark cracks. I suppose it's one reason many people leave them and go to the bigger cities."

"I understand what you mean. I grew up in one on the West Coast. Oregon isn't much different from New Hampshire. I've always had a problem with my eyes and have had to wear these thick glasses. The guys called me Four Eyes. I couldn't get a girlfriend. You've seen my wife."

Hants

"She's a very pretty woman."

"When I took her back to my home town on a visit, I heard a couple of the old boys cracking snide remarks like, 'How did Four Eyes ever get a doll like her?', when we were walking down the street."

"Then you understand what I am up against," Austin continued. "Now what I am going to say to you is completely off the record. If you think it's not for you, just say so. I'll understand, and there won't be any hard feelings."

"It's a deal."

"I think if I were not here for Mr. Herrick to butt his head against, he would lose credibility with the men, if he continued to prolong the strike. However, there's little possibility of me not being here, unless there's someone who can take over and taking over means going ahead with the computer card process. What I need is someone who knows the mill and who knows the process. Am I getting through?"

"I think that you're talking about me."

"I am."

"I don't have much management experience."

"True, but you have a lot of valuable work experience, a good education, and you have a good idea of the workings of this outfit. I know it's a big step, but I think you can handle it. I'd still be here to help you over the rough spots."

"But if you're still here, they aren't likely to end the strike."

"I don't mean here in this office. I mean on the other end of a telephone line. Nobody would know about it. You'd be luckier than I was, when I took over here. I replaced a man named Marshall. Within a month, he left town and went to live in New Mexico. It isn't all that hard. It just takes time. Pick up the thread. Follow it through until it leads you into the action and then simply fly by the seat of your pants. You're not alone. There are lots of department heads. They all know their jobs."

"Maybe they would resent my going ahead of them and the same thing would happen as with you."

"They don't know anything about the new process and you have to be willing to see it through or there is no deal."

"But even without you to oppose, the Union is very against the loan from the pension fund to cover part of the building costs. You said yourself; corporate policy requires them to show their support by financing 25% of the construction costs. They're afraid. If something happens, they will lose their pension fund."

Austin leaned back smiling. "Even that is no longer a real obstacle Ted. The company is willing to insure the loan, so there is no chance the men will lose their money. Nobody knows about this Ted. You're not to mention it to anybody. It will be your trump card. You will be able to close your negotiations with it. What do you say?"

"I'm very flattered!"

"I don't care whether you're flattered. Will you do it? There's a good raise in it for you. A couple of years as resident-manager here and you could be on your way. There's lots of room to grow in Alabama Paper."

"You want me to answer just like that?"

"You said it."

"But will the company go along with it."

"That's another hump to get over. Before they will let me off the hook at short notice, I have to have someone to take over. The replacement must be able to do the work, even if it's just for an interim period. Leave me the job of selling you to them."

"Okay," Ted said, reaching across the desk with an outstretched hand, "if you can convince them that I can handle it, then you are off the hook. But what will you do afterwards?"

"Oh, there are a number of options open. One of them is a hint from head office. It involves leaving operations and going into corporate administration."

"What do we do now?"

"First I try to get us an emergency meeting with the regional Vice-President in Boston and then we start to do our homework."

"Homework?"

"That's right. You have to be able to make those fellas in Boston think that you can carry the ball. Alabama runs about fifty mills all over North America, out of regional offices, and they're very good at what they do. They're liable to ask you questions on any part of the operations and not out right. It'll be a word in a comment, and they will know what you understand by your reaction."

"Where do we begin?"

"Tell your secretary to cancel everything you had on for today. Then get in touch with your wife and let her know what's happening. Tell her you'll only be home to sleep this weekend. We're going to go over as much of the operation as we can Saturday and Sunday. Come back here at 1:30 p.m. this afternoon."

When Newton left, Austin picked up the phone and asked Angeline to get him the regional office in Boston. He also told her he was going to be busy on Sunday. She understood. It took about fifteen minutes to get through the exchanges at that hour of the day.

The regional Vice-President, Mr. Hershey, found the request irregular. In addition, he had to leave early Monday morning to go to Montgomery for a briefing. It took a lot of wrangling and explaining, but finally he did give in. He would see them at 3 p.m. Sunday afternoon. There would be other regional executives present.

The meeting would be held in the boardroom at the office on Washington St. near E. Berkeley St. The security guard at the Berkeley St. door would have instructions to let them in. If a majority of the executives at the meeting didn't agree to accept the proposal, then Austin had to agree to settle with the Local, even if it meant abandoning the computer card process. He accepted the condition.

It was a quiet Sunday afternoon in Boston. Not

many people were moving about. Being the first of October, it was still warm. The two men looked out of place walking along Washington St. in business suits. The westward bound sun cast medium length shadows behind them.

"I feel like I've been cramming all night for an exam," Ted said, squinting against the sun.

"It's probably the most important exam you'll ever have in your life. For my sake, I hope you pass."

"I won't let you down."

"Don't worry about not letting me down. Don't let yourself down."

They entered the ten-storey brownstone building, which housed the regional offices. A husky black man, wearing a white shirt and tie and carrying a revolver on his hip, got up from a chair where he had been sitting. A huge key ring jingled at this side. As he approached them, he unsnapped the small leather strap which held the revolver in place and let his hand rest gently on the gun's butt. They stopped where they were. The security guard's voice echoed through the empty lobby,

"How can I help you gentlemen?"

Austin spoke, "We have a meeting with Mr. Hershey at three o'clock."

"What are your names please?"

They gave them one after another.

"I'll have to see some identification."

They each produced their billfold and pulled out what ID they had. The guard kept his hand on his gun, while he looked at it.

"That will be fine, sirs. I'll just go and lock the door you came in, then I'll take you up."

He had to unlock the elevator. When they got up to the ninth floor, the elevator car stopped, and the guard opened the door.

"This door locks again, when I close it. You'll have to get them to call me, when you're ready to leave. I'll come up and get you."

Hants

The elevator door closed behind them. Newton felt uneasy but followed Austin down the long hallway. It was exactly three o'clock. Austin knocked on the twelve-foot high reddish wooden door. A person whom he had never seen before opened it.
"Come in gentlemen, we've been expecting you."

The Nashua resident manager recognized the Vice-President, Mr. Cecil Hershey, sitting at the head of the long board room table. He stood up as the door closed softly behind them.

"Good afternoon Brad. It hasn't been too long since we last saw each other. If my memory serves, it was August."

"You have a good memory."

"This must be your, how shall I say it, your prospect."

"That is correct, Sir."

Austin introduced them, and Ted went forward to shake his hand.

The regional Vice-President went around the table introducing the five men who were in the leather armchairs.

The first two individuals wore golf clothes.

"This is Dunstan Morgan who heads up the Operations division of the administration here in New England and beside him is Clyde Houston who is the same in Finance and Accounting."

"Pleased to meet you boys," Clyde said with a broad grin. "Don't mind the clothes. Dunstan and I shot a quick eighteen, before coming in here. There wasn't enough time to change."

Next was Ralph Watson from Marketing, Denis Baines from Personnel and Stan Wodsworth from Corporate Counsel. They all shook hands, and then the new arrivals took up the places, which had been reserved for them. Morgan opened,

"I understand you boys want to play switch with the other side up in New Hampshire."

"You could say that," Brad replied.

"I've seen it done before. One of our boys in upper Michigan ran fowl of the Union. They hated him. He even got some anonymous letters. We were sure that it was going to finish in trench warfare, but they pulled a switch with a peaches and cream fella from our mill in Alabama. Everybody went back to work. It turned out to be nothing but a personality conflict between our boy and their boy."

"As you can see Brad," Cecil explained, "I have briefed them. I'll turn the meeting over to you and Mr. Newton. Explain everything from A to Z. When you've finished, we'll move in and punch you up a little just to see how solid, what you've said, really is."

The two men from New Hampshire talked for two and half-hours non-stop. One would take a run at a topic then bring the other in to comment and vice-versa. Austin drank three glasses of water. When they were done, the other six men took them on. The interrogation continued for another two and half hours. Newton began to feel like a school kid. They knew four times as much as he did. They laughed at his mistakes. At one point, Watson told him not to be stupid. Even Austin's self-esteem took a tarnishing. At eight o'clock, they stopped. The Vice-President asked them to wait out in the corridor,

"There's an alcove a bit further down from this room with several couches and some magazines. One of us will come to get you when we're ready."

They didn't talk while they were waiting. Both men were drained. They hadn't eaten since noon. When they thought back, it seemed as if their presentation and answers had been all wrong. About twenty minutes later Clyde Houston appeared in front of them. His soft sole shoes hadn't made any noise.

"You boys can come back now."

They took up the seats, which they had occupied previously. Cecil Hershey addressed them,

"I'll let Denis Baines do the talking."

Hants

Baines took a fountain pen from his shirt pocket, clipped it to a piece of writing paper and slid it across the table towards Brad.

"Mr. Austin I would like you to give me a written resignation effective immediately. Give whatever reason you wish."

The personnel man waited until he had the resignation in his hands and had read it.

"Mr. Newton, we are offering you the position of acting interim resident-manager of the Nashua mill. The contract has been written up by Mr. Wodsworth. It's for thirty days. If at the end of thirty days you don't have the place up and running, just clear out your things on the way home. One of our people will replace you the following morning. If the mill is operating, give me a call. We'll have you come in to sign a permanent arrangement. Your salary will be the same for the next thirty days. If we sign a new contract, when this one expires, you'll get a thirty percent raise to start. Are you interested?"

"Yes."

Stan Wodsworth took a fountain pen from his shirt pocket clipped it onto the hand-written contract and slid it across the table.

"Please sign at the bottom and have Mr. Austin witness it."

When they had both signed, Hershey picked up the phone near his right hand.

"Charles, those two gentlemen whom you let up are ready to leave now. Would you please come up and show them out?" When he had hung up he looked down at Austin, "Well, Brad I guess that about does it. If the place is up and running in thirty days, you will probably be hearing from me. There is a spot in administration in Montgomery, which would suit you just fine."

Both men stood up.

Clyde gave them a broad grin; "Good luck to you two boys now."

"Brad," Cecil added, "either way, Denis will be in touch with you to straighten up whatever we owe you."

"Thank you, Cecil and thank you gentlemen for your vote of confidence and your time on this day off."

Stan looked at him and said, "We never have any days off Mr. Austin. This goes on seven days a week. We just steal a few hours for ourselves here and there."

The following day the Nashua newspaper printed the press release that it had received by special delivery at nine o'clock that morning, from the regional office of the Alabama Paper Corp. in Boston.

"Sunday, October 01st at a top level corporate conference Mr. Brad Austin turned in his official resignation as resident-manager of the Nashua division of Alabama Paper, when asked to do by top executives. Effective immediately, Mr. Austin will be replaced by Mr. Ted Newton. Mr. Newton accepted to act as interim resident-manager, when requested to do so by corporate executives. The regional office is looking for an early settlement to the labor dispute, which has interrupted production at the Nashua plant for quite some time."

The strike was over by Friday. Ted Newton led the negotiation team from the company. He held back letting the Union know the loan would be insured until Thursday morning. It took Herrick by surprise. He was at a loss with Austin gone. He had planned to use the loan from the men's pension fund as his beachhead. Once he had battered his way through; he would do the same with Newton as he had done with Austin. Newton would be just another outsider. A second vote was held Friday morning on the new contract proposal. It was accepted by eighty-four percent of the membership. The men got their raise and the new process went in.

After the vote was counted, Bert Herrick made an undignified speech to the Local. He took the member's choice as a personal rejection. It degenerated into a yelling match between himself and half a dozen of those present. When it finished, Herrick announced that he was resigning as leader of the Local and that he was leaving the Nashua mill. Once he stomped out; the Local secretary came forward. A motion was presented. The floor was asked to invite Eric Kent to resume his former functions on, an interim basis. The Local would open a nominations call for the now vacant position, as soon as possible. Kent waited to see if there was any opposition to the motion. When there wasn't, he accepted.

Brad hardly set foot out of his residence during the two weeks, which followed the end of the strike. Newton would phone him at least a dozen times a day. During the third week of October, he called a moving company to take all his furnishings and belongings out to the renovated farm house, which he would now occupy.

Mr. Hershey communicated with him during the second week in November. The offer was extremely interesting, but Brad resisted. He thanked the regional Vice-President but declined the new position. After he explained about the farm, the newly renovated house and beef herd he was contemplating, Hershey empathized with him and admitted he had a similar idea about ten years earlier. He was going to build a pond on a piece of land which he owned and raise trout.

Near the end of November, Avis Neville received a call from George Middleton. He told her of his complaint to the Bar, about the hearing and that he had received the committee's decision. Ward Shaw's license to practice law in the State of New Hampshire had been suspended for two years from the date of the decision. At the end of twenty-four months, he could apply for readmission to the Bar and would be required to show just cause why he should be re-licensed in the State. He was free to appeal the committee's decision in a Court of Law. Mrs. Neville said that she was satisfied and she would let the matter lie unless Mr. Shaw should appeal the decision.

Angeline stayed on at the office until the 1st of April. Then she resigned, as she needed the time to prepare for her upcoming wedding. Mr. and Mrs. Austin officially took up residence along the Souhegan River Rd. on May 1, 1946. A baby daughter was born to the Austin's during the fall of 1948. The girl was named Virginia Austin.

***

The Wind

8

It was the Fourth of July long weekend, in 1973. The waiting room at Logan International airport was overcrowded to the point of being uncomfortable. Watergate was fresh in the nation's mind. Many of the people, who were waiting, voiced their opinion on the subject, to total strangers. Like the others, Brad and Angeline Austin, sat on the vinyl padded benches waiting for an announcement on the public address system that would send them to one of the loading gates. An older couple sat in the section of the waiting room from which domestic flights were loading and unloading. She appeared to be in her late fifties. He looked to be near seventy.

He wore a straw hat, open neck, short-sleeve, olive colored shirt along with light-brown, cotton pants and a pair of canvas shoes. His eyes were shaded by dark-green, wire-rim, sunglasses. He was of medium build, lean and still muscular for his age. The woman's hair was blond. It was cut short and combed back on the sides. She wore a paisley sundress and sandals. One arm was looped through the handles of a large straw bag.

A young woman sat between them who seemed to be about twenty-five. Her hair was blond and long. She was well tanned. Her crisp white blouse was tucked into the waist of a short, cotton summer skirt. She was wearing white tennis shoes.

A woman's voice came over the public address system,

"Seaboard Air, Flight 66, Boston to San Francisco is now loading at Gate 14. Will passenger's holding tickets for this flight, please report to the attendant at Gate 14."

"That's me mum," Virginia Austin said.

"I had a feeling it was yours."

"So did I," the man said slowly.

"Well, I guess this is it dad."

"Come on," he added picking up her flight bag and standing up, "we'll walk you to the gate."

When Virginia Austin had finished high school, she had done two years at New Hampshire State and then applied to her father's Alma Mater. That was three years ago. In her last semester, she had answered an ad on the Law Student's bulletin board from a big office in San Francisco, which was offering several positions to graduating students wanting to do their practical.

The rest was now history. She started July 5th. Today she was on her way to San Francisco to start a new life. She kissed both of her parents, before going through the turnstile.

"Don't forget to write," Angeline said, feeling her eyes beginning to water.

"I won't mum, promise," she vowed, pressing her lips against her mother's cheek.

"And your prayers."

"I won't forget them either."

Hants 217

"Give us a call every now and then," her father added in a scratchy voice, "call collect."

"It's a deal, dad," she agreed and threw her arms around his neck.

The Austin's stood at the glass, overlooking the runway, until Flight 66 had become a dot in the sky out over Boston Bay. The old man took his wife by the arm and said,

"Come on Hon, we should go now."

"I suppose you're right," the woman replied, grasping a bit of his shirt between her fingers. "I sort of wish we were going with her."

"I do too, but who is going to feed all those cattle."

"That reminds me, I am baking you a 4th of July surprise. We should be getting back."

They were almost at their house, driving along the North River Rd., when the old man exclaimed,

"Will you look at that?"

"Will I look at what?" his mate asked irascibly, annoyed at having the tranquility of her reflections upset.

"The fields are coming up green over there," he replied, pointing to the south bank of the river. "The Oberton's and the Sky's must not have planted this year."

"Honestly, dear," she chided, "you are hopeless. Here our baby is gone off to, you may as well say, the other end of the earth and all you can think about, is fields coming up green."

"Now you know I am going to miss her just as much as you, but I think we would be better off keeping our minds on other things. After all, it's not as if this was the first time she was going to be gone. She's been away at school for a couple of years now."

"I know, but it seems so far."

"To tell you the truth, I'm kind of proud of her. One of the things, which gives America its strength is the fact that an American citizen from Maryland is an American citizen in North Dakota and someone from Louisiana is a full citizen in Maine. We have to move about all over this country to exercise our citizenship, or it is just dead words in law books."

"I know Brad, but I only had one and that's the way I feel."

"When she takes her Bar, we'll go out for her swearing in, okay?"

"Yes, I'd like to see it." Then she also took a good look at the farmland on the other side of the Souhegan. "Maybe those two just got tired of scratching the dirt for a living. They probably started a lot younger than you did. They haven't only been flicking switches and pushing buttons to feed and water beef cattle. I've seen both of them in Milford shopping. They have a permanent stoop in their backs. That comes from heavy labor. Sometimes I wish we hadn't stayed so close knit, after we set up housekeeping. We'd probably know about what's going on in the neighborhood today, if we had mixed a bit with the neighbors."

"I guess we'll have to mend our ways," he replied smiling and then winked when she looked at him.

"You're making fun of me Brad Austin," she exclaimed.

"I wouldn't do that Angie."

"Yes you would," she continued, swatting at his arm.

This was the first time the cattleman had really become conscious of an almost imperceptible change, which was occurring in the district. Over the course of the next year, one farm after another fell fallow on the south bank. It was not until the malady crossed the river and struck the neighboring Hudson place to the west of them that the retired engineer actually got the full story on the development, which was in progress. He was up on the bluff, above the house, repairing the fence, which runs along the road, when his neighbor slowed down to say hello.

Hants

"Hi, Don! I noticed you didn't do any plowing or seeding this year, and now your place is all coming up in hay. Are you laying up your land for a year?"

"It's not my land no more."

"Not your land?" his friend queried with a puzzled look. "You're still living on it."

"Yea but it isn't me who is paying the taxes no more. I'm only renting the house from the new owners, until me and the missus get us fixed up someplace else."

"I didn't see a For Sale sign."

"That's because there weren't one," Don explained. "Skinny little fella from Manchester came in here last fall offering me twice what the place was worth. Course I grabbed at it."

"That's rather odd."

"I'd say lucky!" Hudson exclaimed.

"He must be somebody who doesn't know anything about land, somebody like a gentleman farmer."

"Oh, no, this gang got lots of smarts. They'll probably be around to see you one of these days."

"I'm afraid I wouldn't be interested."

"They'll offer you double what it's worth. With that, you could pick up a piece of scrub land anywhere and set up another feed lot, if you have a mind to. Course, you're getting to the age now when a man doesn't want to be having all the headaches of fattening beefers. You and the missus could take a trip. Buy a nice little house in Milford. That's what we're going to do."

"It's not the money, Don. I've spent the last twenty-five years bringing this property back. The apple trees are giving Grade A fruit. I replanted the maple bush and now every spring there is a steady run during the sugar season. It's a real charm to operate too, using plastic tubing."

"Obie Norton on the other side of me said the same as you last fall, but the other day I heard he decided to take their offer. His son DeWayne isn't interested in farming. He's making twice as much as his father ever made even on a good year, just working on a machine that makes photocopier paper, at Alabama."

"It sounds strange to me Don. Why would anybody want to pay double what a piece of land is worth?"

"I must confess it beats me. When they're paying that kind of money, nobody asks too many questions. However, there is a rumor going around. According to the rumor, this group out of Manchester is putting in a recreational retreat for big wigs. You know golf club, pheasant shooting, private cabins, the works."

"They must be a gang of lunatics. You can't have a recreational area without water. By mid-August, we'll be able to walk across the Souhegan without getting our ankles wet."

"I know that, and you know that, but if they want to go chucking their money around without checking things out first, well it's there tough luck. I am not giving it back. Besides, I also heard they're going to build some sort of a retaining dam across the river to make a sort of artificial lake. I can see their point," Don explained.

"Those city fellas like to come back from a weekend with, something to show their missus. They could keep their lake stocked up and under feed the critters. That way, they'd bite at anything. It would be a great way to hook them executives in Boston."

"Any how Brad, I gotta get moving. I got butter in here. It'll be running all over the seat in this heat, if I stick around talking."

During the summer four more landowners upstream from Hudson yielded to the smell of quick cash. During the first week of September, the Austin's started taking in what was left in their kitchen garden, at the side of the house. Brad went ahead with a three-prong fork sifting the earth along the potato rows. Angeline came after him, breaking the potatoes off their roots, brushing them off and putting them in a bushel basket. Rather unexpectedly, a voice hailed them from behind,

"Good afternoon folks!"

Hants

"Oh!" exclaimed Angeline, standing up and tuning around quickly, "you nearly scared the life out of me, young man."

"Excuse me madam," apologized the slight stranger who wore a striped jacket. "I didn't mean to startle you."

"She's all right," Brad assured the visitor as he propped the fork upright into the ground with a forceful shove of his foot. "What can we do for you son? Car broke down?"

"No, as a matter of fact, I came here to see you. My name is Ed McGillis."

"Not the same Ed McGillis, all our neighbors are talking about?"

"I had no idea," preened the stranger.

"A body who goes around buying things up for twice their value is bound to become a curiosity," Brad explained.

"Then you have an idea of why I stopped around?"

"I could hazard a pretty fair guess."

Angeline intervened, "I assure you Mr. McGillis; you're wasting your time. The Austin farm is not for sale."

"Just like that, without even hearing my offer."

"This is our home."

"I understand how you feel, Mrs. Austin," the real estate agent sympathized. "Your place is most agreeable. I was here one day when nobody was home and walked up through the pasture. There's a spring back there and a very nice maple bush. But times change and it's a lot of work for an older couple, without a son, to keep this place going."

"I am sorry, but the answer is no," the white-haired man said emphatically.

"That's quite all right. But, I'll leave you my business card, just in case you would like to get in touch with me, at a later date."

Douse Enterprise
Ed McGillis
Appraiser / Agent

101 - 203 Winnipesaukee St.
Manchester, N. H.
Tel: 249-4426

Angeline accepted the card and passed it along to Brad. He slipped it into his shirt pocket and said,

"I'll hold onto it, but I don't think you'll hear from me."

"I must be running along anyway. This was only a social call to introduce myself. I won't hold you good people from your gardening."

When the stranger had gone, Brad came over to Angie and slipped one arm about her middle. "What's the matter, Hon? Doesn't the idea of a nice new house in town appeal to you?"

"Quite the contrary," she laughed, pushing herself up on her toes to kiss him softly on the corner of his mouth, "it frightens me to death. What would I do with myself?" At that, she slipped out of his embrace and went back to picking up potatoes.

He pulled the fork out of the ground and returned to turn the soil over.

They continued to talk as they moved along the row.

"Douse is an odd name for a recreation business," she conjectured.

"There's nothing in these business names dear," he assured her. "The last time I was in Nashua shopping, I noticed a new store. The name on the awning was "Windfish". Do you know what they were selling?"

"Sea food or sailing gear?"

"Not at all, it was art."

"Well, regardless of their name, they must be doing all right to be paying so much for farm land."

"It's probably a lot by the Hudson's or the Sky's standards, but don't forget, they're just dirt farmers." She continued. "My aunt called people like them, New England crackers. When you take a dirt farm and use it in another kind of business, it has another value. Look at us. We aren't dirt farming, but it's a dirt farm. What do you think Hudson would say if he knew your feed lot operation paid four times as much as his farm, even in its best years?"

"He'd be jealous, I know it."

"Sure he would be, but we've never shown it to them,"

"What are we going to do with all the money we have socked away?"

"Virginia will probably squander it on something silly, after we're dead," she assured him."The idea of it makes me boil."

"We could always build some kind of a monument with it, or send it to Africa or even wall paper the house," he suggested.

"I think that I would just as soon leave it to her," his wife laughed.

"Let's hope she'll have a better idea of the value of money by then."

"Anyway, this Douse outfit must be doing fine. It has kind of pricked my curiosity. I've been wondering about them since the day I talked to Don, when I was mending the upper fence. After seen their agent, I'm really starting to wonder."

"Why don't you do a little bit of investigating, spend a little of your money?"

"That is not such a bad idea. In fact, I know just the person whom I am going to contact."

"Who's that?"

"Did you ever hear me talk of somebody called Bert Hampstead?"

"I recall hearing his name."

"Bert was my roommate, during my last year at Dartmouth. He was born and raised in Concord. His father did something in the State Administration. Bert started off in Science and then switched into Law. I heard he set up practice in Concord. I guess the family name was well known, and people started to come to him. Even in those days you needed a lot of connections to make a go of it in the practice. Many law students ended up working in the State Administration."

"I suppose the competition is pretty stiff in the Capital. Once Ward told me he would never have made it in Concord. He said that there were five lawyers for every client."

"Yea, lawyers are like bees. They like to be near the honey pot."

"I wouldn't exactly call the State House, a honey pot."

"Maybe not, but a lot of contracts come out of there."

"So are you going to call your lawyer friend? What do you think he will be able to find out? Douse is just a business. If there were anything illegal, their license would have been taken away."

"Oh, I'm not talking about illegal. I just want to know who they are. Bert has stopped practicing now. I was reading an article in the Manchester paper last year and noticed that he has been called to the Governor's Special Advisory Committee on Business Development. If he knows enough to be named to that, he could probably tell me who's in Douse. Instead of calling, I might take a drive upstate and pay him a visit. I'll write first to say I have some business to take care of there and if I have time, I'll stop by to say hello."

"It's a great idea. While you're catching up, I'll browse a bit. There are some nice stores in Concord." Then she straightened up and stretched backwards before continuing, "I'm getting a stiff back from all this bending, time for a break. I'm going in now. Come, in about ten minutes. I'll have the water boiled and a snack ready for you."

The thin, strong, white-haired man continued sifting the soil and thought about his new project. There can't be anything illegal, he thought, but there might be something in the wind that Bert can sniff out. Those people have been buying up places on both sides of the river for over a year now. I'm going to get to the bottom of this, even if it kills me.

Hants

Several miles upstream from Nashua, there was an ordinary red brick building on the West Bank of the Merrimack River. It housed the district offices of the State Water Resources Department. The district officer's headquarters was located on the second floor. There was a view of the Merrimack from his window.

Owen Bickle was not a man of great stature. However, what he lacked in height was more than made up for in corpulence. He sat in his office with his feet propped up on the windowsill looking out at the river. His tight fitting jacket and vest made him look like a football, bursting at the seams. It mattered very little to him if he occupied only a minor post in one of the far reaches of the State bureaucracy. In his mind, he was a great public servant. He had always avoided party affiliation and had survived many changes which others had not. His sole philosophy had been to serve the people of New Hampshire.

In a few years, he would be retiring. It had been a long, but eventless career. After a number of clerk positions, he decided that he would like to be outdoors. He had taken the water testers training and received his first assignment in the northern part of the state, stationed out of Berlin. He had been squeezed out by someone who had seniority. His replacement had requested a transfer, after having gone through a divorce. Around the time, several isolated cases of typhoid had emanated in the drinking water in the southern part of the State, during spring runoff.

Owen had reluctantly accepted a position in the troubled area. It turned out to be the one lucky break of his career. Being a bacteriological tester in the district, he had firsthand knowledge of the area's watershed. When the Merrimack Valley Industrial Commission requested that a local office of the Water Resources Department be opened on the Lower Merrimack, Concord had responded by building the red brick building.

They named someone from Concord to be the District Officer to whom a political favor was due. The man knew nothing about the area. Owen Bickle not only knew the area; he also had a fair amount of experience. He became the new officer's assistant at a higher rate of pay. When the man retired, Owen had simply become the District Officer.

Today he was feeling good. There was even cause to celebrate. Maybe he would take his wife to dinner.

"Well, I'll be," he said out loud to himself, picking up the report, which he had received from the State Water Resources Department that very day, "The Bickle Reservoir. I couldn't have thought of a better name for it myself."

It had all started during the spring run-off, last year. Every year he had received complaints of spring flooding. Somebody would lose several yards of their property to the swirling water, and he would get a very nasty call or letter from an irate taxpayer. The State would end up footing the bill for yet another retaining wall. It didn't make sense. There shouldn't trouble with flood waters in the Lower Merrimack Valley.

After all, most of the small estuaries, which fed into the river in the northern part of the valley, had flood control dams built into them. They could be closed in the spring, to control the run off and then opened later in the season to keep a constant water level at all times. By the time the Merrimack left Manchester, it was well under control. Why did it suddenly swell its banks when it got to Nashua?

He had spent a week measuring the current as it left Manchester and entered Nashua. There was an appreciable difference. The only thing he could attribute it to was the Souhegan. It was the only new water emptying into the Merrimack between Manchester and Nashua. He was amazed at the force, which the current measured at the mouth of the Souhegan. It meant the volume of water coming downstream during run off was twice what it was during the regular season.

Hants 227

It had been many years since he had spent much time in the country around the Upper Souhegan. Another week of driving the back roads had revealed many woodlots, which had been cut and not replanted. This meant the area's natural watershed had been greatly reduced. The State had a program to encourage private woodlot owners to replant their land, after it had been cut, but it was no quick solution. In his report to Concord, he had suggested some sort of flood control on the lower Souhegan similar to the upper valley. The report had predated the purchase of the Sky farm by Douse Enterprises, by approximately three months.

A year and a half had passed. Now today, it looked as if the recommendation in his report was going to become reality. However, it was beyond anything he had imagined. He had supposed that if his suggestion was acted upon, one or maybe two small dams might be built on the river with sluice gates. They could be opened or closed to control the flow of water going down stream. Now they were talking of a reservoir. A permanent, year round body of water would be created. In fact, it would be an artificial lake. He was flattered. All these long years of service would be recognized in the Bickle Reservoir. Oh yes, 1973 had been a very good year. He wondered where they would build it.

It was late October and New England had an Indian summer. Angeline and Brad Austin were sitting outside one evening reading a letter from their daughter Virginia.

"Can you make out this word, dear? My eyes aren't too good in this light."

"Pebble."

"She and her friend spent the first weekend of October camping near a pebble beach north of San Francisco."

"Sounds like a great life."

"She says one of the girls who works with her has asked her to spend Christmas at her parents place in

Carmel. She wonders whether we would mind her not coming home."

"I think we can get by Christmas on our own for one year. Maybe we'll take a little trip ourselves some place. Anyway, we'll be seeing her in June, when she takes her oath."

"I think she said June 21st."

"See if you can think of some place for us to go over Christmas. In the meantime, we'll take a day trip to Concord. I wrote to Bert Hamstead, to say we would be in Concord November 15th on business. I told him that if he had a free slot during the day, I'd stop in to visit for old time sakes."

"You didn't tell me anything about writing to him."

"I got a note back from him this morning. He's looking forward to seeing me, after so long a time. He said he'd be thrilled to meet my missus. Now I guess we'll have to go."

"Ooh!" she exclaimed, shaking her shoulders. "I just got a shiver up my spine."

"I'll go in and get your shawl, if you want?"

"Don't need it. I've got you."

"What?"

"Don't you know yet the finest shawl a woman can have about her shoulders is a man's arm?"

He laughed and slid across the step.

"Alright, shivers, let's read this letter together," he said, putting his arm around her.

The season was over. All the hay that grew on the Austin farm had been cut, bailed and stored away in the barn, which he had specially designed and built so that it would accommodate the automatic equipment. All he did was go in once a day and operate the tiny control panel that activated an overhead bale grabber. The bales were picked off the piles, set on a conveyor belt and then sent outside into the shelter where the cattle would come to eat. Another set of buttons would activate an auger that filled troughs with grain and feed mix. It was a completely mechanized operation.

Hants

The apples had been harvested. As in other years, he had let a harvest contract to an independent contractor. The man came as arranged with a full crew. The trees were picked clean. The bushel baskets of fruit were delivered to a wholesale broker in Manchester to be graded and bought. He and the contractor had split the sale fifty-fifty.

All that remained to do, before the fall rains came was a bit of clean up. There were steel stakes in a pile at one spot, bobbins of barbed wire elsewhere and bushel baskets and ladders in the orchard. The old man hitched the flat wagon to the back of the tractor and started out to make his rounds.

Brad was at the top of the bluff, on the edge of the orchard loading the flat wagon when the late morning sun reflected off something shiny and caught his eye. He found it strange, but didn't go to investigate immediately. Once everything was loaded at the stop, he climbed up into the tractor seat and moved the throttle forward. Instead of heading to where the barbed wire had been left, he nosed the tractor up towards the road to see what the sun had been reflecting off.

A small crew cabin truck was pulled up into the grass near his fence. On the other side of the road, on the top of the bluff which overlooked the river, he saw a man bending over a surveror's transit. When the stranger heard the tractor motor stop, he looked around. An old man with white hair, wearing a gray corduroy windbreaker was stepping between the strands of fence. The surveyor waited until the farmer was almost beside him, before saying,

"Hi."

"Hi yourself," Brad replied. "What are you up to son?"

"Oh, I'm just taking a sighting off the top of the bluff on the south side of the river."

"That's what it looked like you were doing."

"They're the same elevation."

"I know son. I've surveyed every inch of this area. My training was in engineering. They taught us how to use a transit. Why you are taking a sighting?"

"I can't say for sure. My firm got a call from a construction company to come out here and take a measurement at this spot."

"That might be so, but it's my land you are standing on. I own everything from the river back to the maple bush, with the exception of the roadway. It seems that if there were to be some surveying to be done, somebody should have let me in on it."

"It never even occurred to me."

"Well, you can't just go around surveying on other people's property without their permission. Now why don't you tell me what this is all about?"

"I'm sorry Mr. ....."

"Austin."

"Austin, but I'm not at liberty to say so."

"Well, I'm sorry son, but if you don't want to cooperate you leave me no choice."

"What do you mean?"

"I mean I'm going to have to call the Police and lay trespassing charges against you."

"Oh, you don't have to Mr. Austin. It's just a little sighting."

"That is not the point. Something is happening with relation to my property, and I haven't been informed of it. Now if you want to let me in, I'll let you through."

"Oh, yea sure, it's just a construction company. They want a little feasibility study done for a dam which is supposed to go in around here."

"Dam?" he startled.

"That's all I know."

"You're the second person who has mentioned a dam, in the last year or so."

"I heard it has something to do with flood control," the surveyor replied.

"I think you better gather up your gear and move along. Tell your office not to send anybody else around here, unless they talk to me first."

"I was just leaving."

The Austin's left early the next day to drive into Concord. The arrangement was for lunch in the dining room of a small, but quaint hotel. It was not far from the State Buildings and was called, The White Mountain Inn. The dining room was frequented by state Representatives, when they had to meet a visiting constituent or lobbyist.

The building was made of red, white and gray granite, which came from the state's quarries. The lobby was carpeted in a deep, thick, powder-blue carpet. There were a lot of polished wood and upholstered armchairs scattered here and there, alone and in groups. Angeline took a deep breath. She could smell plants and cloth and perfume all mixed together. It smelt good. She was glad she had come.

A black velvet cord crossed the entrance to the dining room. A small sign in a polished brass frame on a stand said,

"Please wait for the Host to seat you."

A tall gray haired man with a thick moustache appeared in a black dinner jacket carrying several menus under his arm.

"Hello," he said with a smile. "Do you have reservations?"

"We are reserved under the name Bert Hampstead," Brad replied.

The Host scanned a book which lay open on a pedestal, beside the sign.

"Oh yes, Mr. and Mrs. Austin," he said pleasantly, unhooking the black velvet cord, "I'll show you to your table."

When they arrived, Bert Hamstead stood up and grabbed his college friend's hand.

"Brad Austin, you old son of a b," he exclaimed, pumping his arm up and down, "I never thought I'd see this day. It's like stepping back in time. There aren't many of us still walking around. Where have you been keeping yourself?" Then he looked at Angeline. "Excuse me, I'm forgetting my manners, this must be .....?"

"Bert, I'd like you to meet my wife Angeline."

The Concord man let go of his hand and turned his attention to the woman.

"My, my Brad what a lovely lady you have."

His right hand took her right hand, and his left hand cupped her elbow. He drew up close and pressed his lips against her cheek, before saying,

"I'm very pleased to meet you Angeline."

The Host was waiting to seat them. As they sat down, he pushed their chairs in towards the table. Menus were placed before them. A waiter came who wore a tight black vest. She ordered white wine and the men high balls. As they talked about their university days, Angeline looked about the restaurant.

Bert laughed and raised his glass,

"I think the high point of my career at Dartmouth was the annual Winter Carnival."

"To winter carnivals," Angeline said adding her glass to theirs.

The entrée arrived. There was stuffed artichokes; a shrimp cocktail and a third had ordered New England oyster chowder.

"Brad is a very lucky man, Mrs. Austin."

"That is what I've been telling him for years."

"It's so comforting to have a companion in old age, someone who has lived through it with us, someone to remember with. I miss my wife a great deal. She passed away about several years ago. We were married for thirty years and never had any children. Now my life is peopled with strangers, except for when someone like your husband pops up."

"Surely you have friends."

"Oh, yes to be sure, but it is not the same."

"I understand."

The waiter came back assisted by a young blonde woman dressed the same as he was. They cleared away the spent dishes and served the main course. When the young woman asked, "The rack of lamb," Angeline held up her finger.

The scallops went to Bert and the New York steak to Brad. The waitress uncorked a bottle of Chablis and poured a small quantity into Bert's glass.

"That will be fine," he said with a wave of his hand.

Over the main course the two men started to talk about Douse Enterprises. Brad showed his old friend the business card that Ed McGillis had left on the day of his visit.

"The name sounds slightly familiar. It could only be a shell or a holding company. As soon as I get something, I'll let you know."

Bert wanted to know all about the feedlot operation. He admitted that he would have liked to do something like that himself.

"Being born in Concord into a well-known and established family had its drawbacks. It was too easy to make it. I never really became what I may have been. Oh, I'm not complaining, but you know sometimes people who are born outside the system are freer than those born into it. Those who are born into it lack personal choice. They know what is expected of them. Do you know, the only time I rebelled was when I went to study Science?

"Eventually I knuckled under and switched into Law as my family had always wanted. It's too bad you people hadn't looked me up earlier. I could have found your daughter a place to do her practical here in Concord. There aren't many openings, but I'm owed a lot of favors, and I never had any children."

"That's very thoughtful of you. If she gets tired of California, we'll certainly keep it in mind," Angeline declared.

When the main course was finished, the waitress came to take away their dishes. She was followed by the waiter who pushed a dessert and coffee trolley. Bert had a two o'clock meeting, so they didn't stay long after lunch.

"I'll get back to you Brad, as soon as I have something on this Douse outfit."

Concord was blessed with more than its share of stores and small shops. The Austin's made their way from one to the other during the afternoon. Brad acted like a living mirror, giving his opinion on everything, which took her eye. Then he paid the clerk, once she had decided.

The afternoon's shopping added three pieces to her wardrobe and one to his. With the cooler weather in mind, she had bought a mocha colored, soft thermal knit tunic with matching stretch thermal knit stirrups, a heather-gray, lamb's wool, jewel-neck sweater and a pair of classic-tailored, lightweight, worsted-wool trousers with cuffed ankles and side pockets. For him, there was a pair of tailored pajamas, rich navy, with a notch collar, one pocket and drawstring pants.

It wasn't until between Christmas and New Year's when Austin heard back from his old friend in Concord. Quite a bit of snow had fallen over night, and everyone along the Souhegan had been out early to open up lane ways and paths. The mail man had gone along the North River Rd. stuffing the country peoples' tin mailboxes with end of the month bills and a few late Christmas cards.

Brad had a blade hooked onto the front of his small 35-hp tractor, which he used to clean the yard and the lane, when it snowed. After his chores and the plowing were finished, he went to check the mailbox. There was one letter. It was post marked Concord. He knew who it was from. His hands were too cold to open the envelope. It was almost 11 a.m., time for a break and a warm up.

Angeline had seen him coming. By the time his clothes were off, and he had come into the kitchen, there was a steaming mug of hot liquid at his place on the table. The old man took a knife from the drawer and opened the envelope. Looking at the letter, two black spots appeared on the page. It would take some time for his eyes to adjust to the inside light, after coming in from the bright sun, which was reflecting off the crystal white snow.

"Hon, would you read me what Bert says? I can't see anything. There are sun spots in front of my eyes."

"Give me the letter," she instructed, "then, go and sit down. There's something hot there, which will warm you up."

When he was seated, she started to read,

**

"You've ventured into a strange nest with this Douse Enterprises. As I suspected, it's only a holding company. It owns or has interests in half a dozen companies. Two out of state companies own interests in it.

The principals in Douse are Bruce Adams, Donald Scott, Jack Strong and Phil Roberts. Adams is an incorporated Civil Engineer in Chicago. At present, his company is doing some consulting work for the New Hampshire, Department of Water Resources. Scott is a Philadelphia based financier who has many business interests in New England. Strong is a former New Hampshire congressman. Roberts lives in Portsmouth. He is President of Roberts Construction. The last big contract completed by his company was a quarter mile breakwater in Portsmouth. Apparently he is under contract to another construction company in Manchester called, Ivy Construction. They were involved in residential housing, but lately have been moving into heavier things like retaining walls and bridges.

There's absolutely nothing on any of the companies or the principles. There never has been an encumbrance registered on any of the corporations. Only one thing pricked my curiosity. They are a damn lucky bunch. One of their companies, Franconia Notch Developments owned a side of a mountain in the White Mountain National Forest.

There are a number of private owners in the forest, but they are heavily regulated, as far as logging and timber cutting goes. The State didn't expropriate them, but stands ready to buy them out at fair market value, whenever they want to sell.

Franconia's mountain side was accidentally cut a few years back. A group of amateurs took a contract to put through the right of way for a new line of high-tension power line pylons. When the mistake was discovered, Franconia was given permission to develop the land as they saw fit. There is a very nice ski resort there today. They didn't even have to clear the mountain side to put it in. The mistake saved them a substantial amount of money. If it hadn't been cut by accident, the State probably never would have issued the resort permit.

The same thing happened in Portsmouth. One of their companies owned the shore, which became enclosed, when a breakwater was built. Overnight it became a natural harbor. They built a five hundred-berth marina there. Today there is a waiting list to get in.

What they're doing in the Souhegan Valley is a mystery to me. They seem to be in the recreation field. You mentioned a golf club and a pheasant farm. It all seems very legitimate to me.

I hope this helps you out. There is no charge. I'm glad I could be of some service. However, if you would like to pay me, you and your lady friend could join me at the Boston Gardens on February 14th when the Black Hawks meet the Bruins. I am enclosing two tickets.
Happy New Year.
Sincerely,
Bert Hamstead."

**

"I knew there was something I forgot to mention that day we ate together."

"What's that dear?"

"The dam."

"Oh, you don't really think they are going to build a dam? It's only Don Hudson's hot air."

Then he told her about the surveyor he had caught up on the bluff shooting a line across the river.

"Maybe there is something in it," she agreed.

"I should let him know."

"Why don't you do it on February 14th?"

"Are you interested in going? I know you aren't a hockey fan."

"It's not every woman near sixty who gets to have a boy on each arm on Cupid's day. Besides, you didn't take me away some place over Christmas."

"Maybe I'll be jealous," he laughed.

"Then you can send your ticket back. We won't force you to come with us."

He let his hand fall over hers and caressed it softly, before saying,

"I'll take the letter thank you. We'll meet him in the Gardens, after our dinner for two."

Almost a month to the day past Valentines, the spring thaw began. The water in the Souhegan came over its banks in many places. The river flats which Shane Austin had permitted to be scrapped bare of their top soil were under water. The North River Rd was high, so it stayed open. In Milford, there was flooding of basements in low laying houses. It was in the Merrimack Valley, just above Nashua, where real havoc reigned.

As many as fifty houses had to be evacuated. The flood waters cut off access to the roads except by rowboat. Even the red brick building housing the local branch of the Department of Water Resources suffered some damage on the ground floor, when water seeped into files. Owen Bickle was seething. The papers were full of articles. A reporter from the Nashua newspaper came to see the District Officer for an exclusive interview.

"Isn't it normal policy to have some sort of sluice gate dam on the smaller waterways in this State, Sir?"

"It is, and I might add that they are a very permanent part of the landscape in the northern part of the State."

"Then why are we experiencing this flooding in the southern Merrimack Valley?"

Bickle remembered whom he worked for and chose his words very carefully.

"This is a relatively recent phenomenon in this area. There aren't many high regions in this district from which melting snows run down. What we are experiencing here is a change in the countryside. Continuous wood cutting and land clearing over the years has eliminated the natural watershed. What was once retained in the woodlands and soil now runs directly into the drainage system, as soon as it melts or as soon as the spring rains start. The most significant contribution to flooding in the Nashua area comes from the Souhegan River whose mouth is located just a few miles north of here."

"Isn't there something that can be done, Mr. Bickle?"

"Something is being done."

"Would I be asking too much, to ask you what is being done?"

"You understand, I can't talk about what I have not been authorized to talk about. However, I think it has now become common knowledge that Concord has adopted an official policy with regard to flood control on the Souhegan. The particulars will have to come from the government. This is all that I can tell you."

Within days, several articles appeared in the papers speculating about flood control along the Souhegan. Brad Austin was watching a news special on television the Sunday after this interview with the District Officer, when the telephone rang. Angeline called him.

"Brad, it's Don Hudson on the phone. He wants to talk to you."

"Coming!"

Hants 239

"Hello Don. What can I do for you?

"Hi, Brad. Have you read yesterday's paper from Nashua?

"Sure!"

"What do you think?"

"From what the paper says, this spring run-off sure is causing a mess."

"And?"

"And what?"

"How about the legal notices? Did you read them?"

"No, I didn't."

"Have you got your paper handy?"

"Yea, it's on the counter here in the kitchen."

"Why don't you pull it out?"

"Just a sec, I'll move over onto the table." He picked up the phone and went to the table.

"Allright Don, I've got the Legal Section. What was it you were talking about?"

"Take a gander at the 'NOTICE TO EXPROPRIATE' at the bottom of the third column."

**

"NOTICE OF EXPROPRIATE - Notice is hereby given that the State of New Hampshire intends to expropriate the north-west corner of Lot 16 Plan 22 in the District of Greenvale being in the County of Temple south from the Souhegan River 1000' at the boundary between lot 16 and 17, then west of there 500' and the south-west corner of lot 4, plan 65 in the District of Hillsboro in the County of Wilton, 2000' north of the Souhegan River along the boundary between lot 4 and 5 and then east 1000'.

**

The State also makes known at this time its intent to expropriate upstream of this spot at a later date, along the river banks when the exact area of the Bickle Reservoir has been decided.

**

"All parties wishing to submit an objection to the said design, must do so within 30 days by registered mail.

Registered owners of the properties affected at this date will receive an official notice of this intent within 7 days of this publication.
Department of Appropriations
State of New Hampshire"

**

"When I first read that I thought it was me. Then I got out an old copy of the title for this farm and found that I am living on lot 5. It's your place that is lot 4."

"I know, I know, I know!" Brad replied dumbfounded.

"What are you going to do?"

"There must be some kind of mistake."

"There is no mistake Brad. It says lot 4."

"A thousand feet! That will cut off the top of my orchard. Those trees are just now starting to bear a respectable fruit. Do you know how long it has taken me to bring that orchard back?"

"I understand. I've been watching it twenty-five years."

"They can't do this."

"They're going to do it, unless you and a lot of other people file an objection."

"I'll wait, until I get their written notice, then I'll object. I have to hang up now, Don. I want to explain it to Angie. Thanks for calling."

The notice arrived Wednesday. It was the same as what had been published in the newspaper. Within a week, public meetings were held in Greenville, Milford and Ponemah. Residents of Milford and Ponemah were opposed to the construction of a dam, which would create a permanent reservoir, because it would reduce the river to a trickle as it passed through their towns. People from Greenville and other upstream residents opposed the reservoir, because it would reduce the flow of the river and cause stagnation in their communities. About the only landowners not to object to the planned dam and reservoir were the new owners of five farms west of the proposed dam on both sides of the river, Douse Enterprises. They didn't even object to the fact that they were subject to future expropriation, when the exact bed of the reservoir would be determined.

The State Appropriations Department received the objections through until the middle of April. They were counted and reviewed summarily. The Expropriation Law said a public hearing must be held, if fifty per cent or more of the registered voters in the affected area objected to the intent to expropriate. The hearing would be presided over by a Judge. On May 1st a second notice appeared in the Saturday paper, in Nashua.

**

"Public Notice - Notice is hereby given that the State Appropriations Authority will hold a public hearing in the community Centre in the Town of Milford on June 21st. The hearing will be presided over by Judge Henry C. Gains. The subject of the hearing will be the intended expropriations, dam and reservoir along the Souhegan River. All parties wishing to make an oral presentation before Judge Henry C. Gains are asked to notify this Authority within ten days of this publication, by registered mail.
Appropriations Authority
State of New Hampshire"

**

It meant having to cancel their attendance at Virginia's swearing in for the California Bar. There was no way out. Angeline refused to go alone. Virginia said she would send them a video.

The public hearing started on June 21st and finished on the 24th. Many people in both the Souhegan and Lower Merrimack Valley had registered to address the hearing. Those who came from the Lower Merrimack Valley all were in favor of the Bickle Reservoir. Many people from Nashua came and supported the project. They were all heard first.

Brad and Angeline Austin sat through the whole thing without saying a word. They knew many people had suffered losses in the spring floods and were justified in expressing their opinion. When the pro Bickle side had finished, the Judge began to hear those who were opposed to the dam and reservoir.

Minnie Yeats was the last to speak from Milford. She was an eighty-seven year old widow who lived in her own house, which had been built by her husband.

"As I understand it your Honor, they're going to build an artificial lake a few miles upstream from us. In other words, they're going to transfer the mill pond out of Milford and move it up river. We'll have to change our name Judge. The cotton mill in Milford has closed, but the mill pond is still there. Milford owes its name to that mill pond. When they built the pond to turn the mill, they built a road across the dam. Without that pond, Milford is nothing.

"My husband Tom courted me on the pond in a row boat, in the evenings during three summers, after he finished his daily work. There are many other women in this town who were wooed on warm summer evenings out on the pond. If you build a reservoir, you will take away our mill pond, because there won't be enough water to keep it filled. If you take away the mill pond, you will tear the heart and soul out of Milford."

When she sat down there were a few winks and sly smiles. There were even some snickers from those who supported the reservoir.

The Mayor of Greenville spoke on behalf of the ratepayers as a group.

"Judge, I have a report which was prepared by the municipality with the help of two professors from the Biology Department at New Hampshire State University. The reservoir, which is proposed, will change the fundamental nature of the Souhegan. As Mrs. Yeats said, the river is already dammed. The dam has a sluice gate in the middle, which can be lowered and raised. In effect, this means there is always movement in the river no matter how low the water level gets.

Hants

"The reservoir which is being proposed has no moving parts in the retention barrier. It is what is known as a spill-over-dam. The water will be held at a steady level in an artificial lake year round and only during the spring run-off will there be much of a current. During the rest of the year, movement in the waterway will be sluggish, as it will depend upon surpassing the lake level, before anything will go over the top of the dam. At the height of the dry season, nothing will go over the dam.

"A consequence of this will be a permanent stagnation in the river above the dam. According to the report I have, the oxygen count will be so low that most of the aquatic life will die off. This includes a very special variety of speckled trout, which the area is renowned for. This stagnation will provide a ready breeding ground for various varieties of algae. In the Greenville area, the river will become a floating mass of green pulp. The whole town of Greenville is opposed to the Bickle Reservoir."

Once again there were many comments among those who were seated.

"That is only a hypothesis from two ivory tower types," yelled one man.

"There's no proof that it will be like that," hollered another

"I don't see why our taxes are going to pay the salaries of people who go around writing silly reports. Maybe we should send those two professors a couple of gallons of the water we had to drink during the floods and see if they survive the bacteria that was in it," cried out a woman from Nashua.

Austin sat quietly listening to it all. He had intended to speak both about the disappearance of the mill pond in Milford and the stagnation that would occur in the river. Both points had been covered. He could see that they weren't strong points. They were too emotional. He didn't know the law, but he understood how it worked. There had to be something solid. When his name was called, Angeline squeezed him by the hand and smiled.

"Tell them the truth."

He went up front and cleared his throat.

"Your Honor, I am the owner of one of the properties which is being expropriated to build the abutments for the dam and to relocate the North River Rd. What I have to say concerns the spot, which the State has chosen for the dam. That farm has been in my family for three generations. I know it very well. The State is proposing to abut the Bickle Dam up against a bluff or ridge, which runs through my farm. The ridge is cut in two by the river and continues again on the south bank.

"Judge, that ridge is nothing but a mound of gravel with a thin layer of topsoil on it. When my father farmed it, sometimes the plough-share would turn over gravel. Now I am not a civil engineer; however, I was trained as a mechanical engineer. I know enough about forces and soil mechanics to understand what the lack of a solid base against which to abut will do.

"There will surely be a problem of seepage around the dam. Since the ridge runs through the river, quite probably there will be seepage under the dam. The seepage added to the force of the water at the height of the spring run-off could cause the dam to shift. It could even topple or break. The result would be a twenty-foot high wall of water bearing down on Milford. If such a mishap occurred, quite probably there would be loss of life and serious property damage."

Judge Gains thanked him, and the next person was heard.

At the end of the third day, the Judge retired to an office in the Community Centre for an hour. When he returned, a hush fell over the people seated in the room.

Judge Henry C. Gains spoke slowly and clearly, "First, let me explain to you the powers which are granted to me by the State Expropriation Law. I have the power to issue a Temporary Injunction against any contemplated project. It's only effective for thirty days. At the end of that time, it may be renewed in a proper Court of Law, if sufficient reason is presented to do so.

"In order to grant a Temporary Injunction one of several conditions must exist:

1) it must be obvious one party is being favored over the other by the intended expropriation;

2) it must be demonstrated some irregularity has taken place with regards to the issue of the order;

3) the possibility of an irreparable damage must exist; or

4) a threat to the public well-being must exist.

"Now I have heard all the presentations both for and against the project which is being contemplated. While there are many convincing arguments on both sides, there is only one point, which disturbs me. It's this question of the ridge of gravel where the dam is to abut the river banks. If this is so, there may be a possibility of a threat to the public well-being. Now it may only be a minor problem, which could easily be overcome. As the gentleman who raised the point stated, he is not a civil engineer. It would require an engineering study presented by an expert witness in a regular Court of Law, according to established rules of proof, before any positive declaration could be made.

"Because of this possible threat to the public well-being, I am issuing a Temporary Injunction against the start of any construction on the Bickle Dam. When positive, independent evidence of the existence of this gravel ridge can be presented in Court, the party who raised this objection can apply to the Court in Nashua to have the Injunction continued or made permanent. Let me add that the simple existence of the ridge would not be sufficient to justify a Permanent Injunction. That would require an expert witness to testify about the danger."

"This Temporary Injunction will expire at 11.59 p.m. on Wednesday, July 24th. If a Motion has not been presented in court, in Nashua, by that date, the stop order expires and the construction may be carried forward."

The people who had come for the hearing waited until the Judge had left the room, before leaving themselves. On the way out, the Austin's were greeted with a mixture of sneers and smiles.

The former mill manager didn't waste any time. He knew exactly what to do. Out of his own pocket, he contracted the services of a geological testing company in Manchester. They came within a week in two sturdy pick-up trucks loaded with motors, portable generators, cables and pods.

The geological company started at the back of his property and moved south one hundred feet on either side of the proposed line for the dam. They crossed the river and continued on the other side of the bluff. Every ten feet, the pods, were relocated. The motor was revved up until the generator had built a sufficient charge. It was then shot into the ground.

The sensors on the edges of the pods awaited the electronic echo, which bounced back from the subsoil. The signals were coded and printed out on a graph. One could see more or less what could be expected to be found in the earth below, for up to 100 feet. The end result was similar to an ultrasound examination of the human body.

The two crews worked steady for three days. They took the raw data back to their office in Manchester, analyzed it and compiled it. Austin received a report from them on the fifth day of July. It confirmed without a doubt that there was a solid ridge of gravel running the full length of the bluff on either side of the river.

While the crews were working doing echo sounding, Austin had gone into Concord. It took him a full day, but he did manage to obtain a geological map of the riverbed near his property. Plans for the dam had also been made available to those who were interested in the project.

Hants

When the report came in, he took it, the map and the plans and drove to Boston to see a firm of consulting engineers whom he had spoken to over the telephone. They agreed to do a physical feasibility study of the proposed dam based on the data, which he was to supply them with. It was the middle of their busy season. However, the manager of small projects promised he would have something for him before Wednesday, July 24th. They called on Friday the 19th about 9:30 a.m. to say that their report was completed and that it could be picked up as soon as it was paid for. Brad drove straight to Boston when he hung up the phone.

At supper, that evening he and Angeline looked through the report from the civil engineers.

"I think you have them, dear. Look at these recommendations. We recommend an alternate site be found for the retaining dam. In addition to certain seepage and slippage caused by erosion, there is an eighty-nine percent probability with a two percent error factor the dam will give way at the base. It will either collapse or break in two under pressure of spring flooding."

"They even said they will provide one of their staff in Court next Wednesday morning to present the report. I was talking to Bert Hamstead right after I received the results of the geological tests. He said that given the results, he would represent me in Court and ask for a continuance of the Temporary Injunction. Wait until he sees this. Now I'm sure he will go for a Permanent Stop Order."

The Austin's spent a very quiet weekend together. It was very relaxed. The stress of the previous months was gone. On Sunday, Angeline made a picnic lunch, and they went up through the back pasture, hand-in-hand to the big oak tree, which was a little off to the west from the spring. While she unpacked the basket, he took the earthen pitcher she handed him and went to fill it with ice cold spring water. When they had finished eating, he stretched himself out and lay his head in her lap. Together they traded memories for the better part of the afternoon.

On Monday morning, Brad woke early. He felt youthful. He got up, shaved and dressed, then went to start breakfast. She appeared in a long cotton housecoat and saw him setting the table.

"I'll finish setting," she said, then added, "have you had a look outside?"

"Not yet."

"I don't know where it came from, but there's a heavy land fog. I could hardly see the garden from the bedroom window."

"I've got a few chores to do in the barn anyway, so I won't be out in it. Some rats gnawed their way in through the corner of the oat bin. I'm going to cut a piece of tin and nail it over the hole."

Brad was down in the barn when he heard a sound. At first he didn't pay much attention to it. When he finished nailing over the hole, he stepped outside. The land fog muffled the sound so it was difficult to tell from which direction it was coming. He stood very still and listened. It would fade and then come clear. He continued to listen. At length, he was sure it sounded like a pneumatic drill. After several minutes, he was able to pin point the direction from which the rattling sound originated.

It's coming from the orchard; he thought. This can't be. The Injunction isn't to be lifted until midnight Wednesday the 24th. Those bastards, they have no right to be up there drilling. I'll put a stop to this. He walked to the house. Angeline heard the kitchen door slam behind him.

"Is that you Brad?"

"Yes."

"Do you hear that sound?"

"They've started drilling up on the bluff."

"They aren't supposed to."

"I know, I'm going up there to tell them to get to hell off my property."

Hants

"Wait Brad, I'll come with you," she heard the door slam again. He hadn't heard her.

Angeline looked out the bedroom window and saw her husband walking towards the orchard. He carried their old shotgun in his right hand. Now there is no need for guns she thought, pulling on a coat sweater and hurrying downstairs.

Like Beowulf of mythical times, he disappeared into the mist-shrouded orchard carrying Hrunting, which he would use to drive out the evil. The noise had stopped, but he went forward anyway. They had no right. When Angeline came out of the house, she couldn't see him. She simply set off in the direction she had seen him walking, when she looked out the upstairs window.

Angeline Austin was just coming out of the orchard when an ear-shattering explosion rent the air. She felt the ground shake beneath her feet. The concussion sent the ground fog slithering in all directions. Not more than fifty feet ahead of her she saw her spouse reeling, then stagger and crumble to his knees. When she arrived alongside him, he was lying on his back. His body was still. His eyes were closed. She fell to her knees beside him.

"Brad! Brad! Talk to me," she cried and clutched at his coat.
There was a deep gash in the center of his forehead. Thick red blood oozed from it.

She put her lips down near his ear and called out, "Brad, can you hear me?"

His right hand moved and then grasped at her arm. "Is that you Angie?"

"Yes it is me. What is it?"

"I can't see you," he murmured, "it's too black."

"I'm here. Stay with me," she begged. "Fight it."

"I'm cold," he wheezed.

"I'll take you home."

"I can't hear you," he whispered. "The wind is too loud."

"There is no wind," she cried. "Please fight." Tears were streaming down her cheeks.

"I can't hear you," he rasped. "The wind, it's howling, it's taking me in."

"Fight it, please," she begged. "Stay with me."

"Angie I love you."

"I love you too, Brad."

"Angie, I can't make it. You'll have to live for us both."

"Nooooooo!" she cried.

"For us both." he gasped. "The wind, it is taking me."

She felt his grip on her arm go limp, and a loud sigh came from between his lips. A stream of red blood began to trickle from his right ear. The old man was dead. His wife buried her face in his chest and cried.

At the top of the bluff, the two workmen returned to inspect their blast site. It was much to their surprise that they found rocks as big as a man's fist strewn all over the crater.

"What are these rocks doing here?"

"I know, they told us that this was clay and dirt."

"We should have put the blasting mat down."

"We will for the next blast."

"Lucky thing it's early in the day. We could have hurt somebody. These rocks would be like flying hard balls."

The fog cleared for a moment.

What's that over there?" one blaster asked.

"I don't know. It looks like ...." The fog came back in. "It looks like someone slumped over."

"Oh, my God, I hope not. Let's go see."

The two men had to pry apart Angeline's fingers to get her loose from Brad's body. They set her on the grass several feet away and then turned their attention back to the man.

"Is he alive?"

"There's no pulse. He's old. Look at his forehead. He must have caught one of these rocks square on."

"Christ, why did this have to happen to us?"

"We should call an ambulance."

Hants

"We'll get the old woman to let us use her phone."

Angeline was in a state of shock, but while they were talking she had suddenly become crystal clear. She had first seen the civil engineers report in the grass. Brad must have been going to show it to them. She rolled it up and put it in her sweater pocket. Next she saw the shotgun and got hold of it. When the two blasters turned around to ask about a phone, they found themselves looking into the barrel of a shotgun.

"I think you better give that to us, missus," one of the men said taking a step towards her.

"Don't come near me or I will pull the trigger."

"Now missus, just take it easy."

"Who are you?" she demanded, regaining her feet.

"We work for Ivy Construction. They have a contract for the new dam."

"What are you doing here?" she demanded.

"The owner told us to come over and poke a few holes in the hill, to see what we were up against."

"Don't you know there's a Court Order stopping all construction?"

"We heard there was something, but the owner of Ivy Construction said nobody had contested it, so it was just a bluff. He told us to get to work first thing this morning, or he would give the contract to another blasting outfit."

"Pick him up," she ordered.

"Who?"

"My husband."

"We better do as she says."

One man took Brad under the arms and the other by the ankles.

"Now take him down to the house."

"Which way?"

She pointed with the barrel of the gun. The two men started to walk slowly in front of her. When they arrived at the house, she had them open the double hatch doors, covering the outside stairway leading down into the cellar.

There was a long table in the center of the cellar. She brushed the things off it onto the floor.

"Set him down on it," she ordered.

When they finished, she directed them to go back outside.

"We should phone an ambulance or the Police."

"No, I'll take care of him."

Both men were expecting to feel hot lead biting into their flesh at any moment.

"It was an accident missus. Why don't you put the gun away?"

She looked at them for a long moment then screamed.

"I want you two off my land."

"Anything you say missus." They started to back away from her. When they had gone about fifteen feet, they turned half sideways and started to canter, keeping one eye on where they were going and one eye on her. When the mist started to swallow them, Angeline shrieked and discharged the gun straight up into the air.

***

Contempt of Court

9

What had made its debut, Sunday afternoon, as a faint mist drifting down the California coast, soon showed its precise intention and drowned San Francisco in a stodgy, gray-smog. Twelve hours later, millions of condensed water droplets orchestrated from the city's dark alleys. Spasmodically, a muted foghorn warned of danger somewhere in the dark. Unaware of the voices outside in the night, a young woman, slept in an apartment, in a concrete silo, high above the city.

Abruptly, the telephone's vindictive ring sliced through the tranquility of the early morning. A groping hand reached to silence the intruder.

"Hello."

"Good morning!" an officious female voice announced. "This is Western Union calling on Monday July 22nd at 6 a.m. We have a telegram for Virginia Austin. This is our third call."

"I'm Virginia."

"Sorry to wake you Ms. Austin. The telegram reads:

'Tried to reach you by phone. STOP There was no answer. STOP Your father has passed away. STOP Please come home. STOP Mum.'

"A copy of this telegram is already on its way for delivery to you. Good Bye Miss Austin."

The words were like bullets, searing into her half-awake brain. Modern technology is extremely efficient. Death can spring from a coiled wire in the middle of the night, yet leave no mark. She switched on the bedside lamp.

Slowly her mind started the journey up over the mountains and east across the Midwest until it focused in on a little house, out in the country, near a small river in New England. An old man and woman named Mum and Dad lived there. Now there was only Mum.

The young woman felt her eyes filling with tears. She turned into the pillow and started to cry. It lasted half an hour. Then she dried up.

She rose and lit all the lights. Mum is all alone at Hants, she thought. I must leave right away.

It was 6:30 a.m. She put on the kettle then went back to the phone. First she tried to call her mother, but received a tone something like when the circuits are busy. Then she tried her work.

"Good morning, Hogan and Troy's answering service. May I help you, please?"

"Yes, my name is Virginia Austin. I work with Hogan and Troy. I'd like to leave a message for the Office Manager, Mrs. Wilson."

"Go ahead please."

"Mrs. Wilson, I've just been notified that my father has passed away. I am an only child. My mother is not young. I'm going to fly home first thing this morning. You'll find my parents' home address and telephone number in the file. Would you please have my upcoming Court duties assigned to someone else? I'll be back as soon as possible. Thank you"

I'll see she gets the message, Miss Austin," the receptionist assured her.

"Thank you."

When she came out of the shower, there was a Western Union envelope laying on the carpet in front of the apartment door.

Three hours later a young woman wearing a black cotton blouse, and light gray pant suit, boarded the morning flight from San Francisco to Boston at SFO. When it touched down at Logan International Airport, Virginia adjusted her watch to Boston time and made straight for the car rental concessionaire. It was getting late. There had been a stop in Chicago.

Her mind had been a blank in the airplane. She even dozed off several times. As the rented car sped up I 93, her thoughts zeroed in on home.

What could have happened? She felt guilty about missing Easter and then they hadn't been able to come when she took her oath, because of the Expropriation Hearing. How does a man just die who has never been sick?

The setting sun was reflecting off the white median line as the sub-compact automobile sped across the New Hampshire State Line. She was on the last stretch to the farm. Arriving at the lane, she pulled the car up abruptly. A Police cruiser blocked the entrance. A young patrolman got out and walked briskly towards her vehicle.

"Evening Ma'am."

"Good evening officer, I'd like to go in please."

Can't go in there; some crazy old lady has a gun. Captain said no one can go in."

"I beg your pardon, officer, that woman is my mother."

"Sorry Ma'am, I'll have to see some ID"

He checked over her driver's license. Then he went and drew the cruiser out of the way.

As they coasted up the long laneway, the car and its driver were submerged in a mysterious aurora of speckled twilight, which seeped through the leaves, of the trees, planted along the west side of the drive. At the end of the lane, the fieldstone house was as she had left it, except that someone had painted the steep black roof. The dwelling had an air of being uninhabited. A curtain ruffled in the arched window under the central gable. Before the automobile's door had clicked shut behind her, an ominous female voice rang out,

"What do you want?"

"It's me Mom, me Virginia," her daughter called out.

The exhausted woman stepped out in front of the heavy wooden door. Her lavender paisley dress was covered with a black apron, which had a crimson trim.

Virginia pulled her two cases from the back seat of the car and walked towards the veranda. When she reached her mother, she set down the cases and threw her arms about her.

"Oh, my baby, I'm glad you are here. It's been terrible. They started blasting this morning. The workmen wanted to take your father away. I told them to leave the property. Now they have a policeman out there."

"Poor mommy," Virginia said with tears in her eyes. "Why did they want to take daddy?"

"Come on in, I'll tell you the whole thing."

As the old woman explained, her daughter looked on and nodded. Angeline appeared to be near a state of hysteria. Perhaps it was only exhaustion Virginia thought.

"But there are laws Mum, you have to get a death certificate."

"I know all about the laws. They didn't protect your father this morning."

There was no sense in being antagonistic. The young woman tacked around and came back patronizing.

"There's nothing to raise our voices about mother." Then she probed a little deeper, "By the way, where is Daddy?"

"He's down in the cellar. It's cooler there. He doesn't even look dead. I washed him and dressed him.

There's a bandage on his forehead. That's where he was hit by a flying rock."

"I'd like to see him, Mum."

"Sure Virginia, you hop downstairs and say hello to your father. I'll put the kettle on. You must be hungry too?

"No, nothing to eat Mum, I'll only have something to drink."

Virginia felt relieved to close the kitchen door behind her. This is all so unreal, she thought as goose flesh began to form on her arm.

Even before she reached the bottom of the stairs, she could see the body of her father lying on a long solid wooden table. They had used the table during canning season, when she was at home. Her mother had covered the timber slab with a white sheet. A floor lamp cast a pale yellow light over the body. His head was resting on a white pillow. She approached the table.

It was her father. He was dressed in a black dinner jacket and was wearing black pants with a black silk ribbon running down the outside seam. His shoes were shined. His white accordion shirt was immaculate. A black bow tie closed the collar. He looked life like. He was still handsome. Virginia looked at him a long time. She expected him to open his eyes, swing his feet down off the table and say   "Hi!"

"I wish I had come at Easter, Daddy," she said with regret. Her hands closed around his. They were holding a Crucifix. She began to recite, "Our Father, who art in heaven........."

Upstairs the whistle of the kettle sounded. She bent over and kissed him on the cheek, then turned and started back upstairs. When she came through the kitchen door, her mother was spooning coffee powder, into mugs, at the counter. The telephone began to ring.

"I'll get it Mom," Virginia said.   "Hello."

"Who's speaking please?" a male voice asked.

"This is Virginia Austin. Who's asking?"

"This is Captain Anderson speaking. I had a call from Patrolman Robertson, who's on duty at the entrance to the lane. He said he allowed you go through. What's going on in there, Miss Austin?"

"My mother and I are about to have a cup of coffee."

"I had two men report an accident out there this morning. They said that an old man was killed near a blast crater. Then some crazy old woman ran them off the property with a gun."

"She isn't crazy Captain, just upset."

"They said that she fired a shot."

"The gun probably went off accidentally."

"Why didn't she tell me herself? I've called half a dozen times during the day, and all she would say was, don't come in, my daughter is coming."

"Well, I'm here now Captain."

"Miss Austin, there has been a death. The Coroner must see the deceased."

"Captain Anderson, I'm a lawyer. I understand all that. Give me a number where I can reach you. My mother and I are going to have a talk."

As she hung up the phone, Angeline was placing the mugs on the table.

"Who was that?"

"Somebody named Captain Anderson."

"I told him not to bother me. He's been a pest all day. You know Virginia, while I was making the coffee; I was thinking about the day I met your dad. He was on his first day in the office where I was working. He was really handsome. I remember I blushed when my boss introduced him to me."

"He still looks handsome downstairs Mum," her daughter reassured her.

"I know, didn't I dress him up fine?"

"I was half expecting him to open his eyes and get up." The daughter replied.

"We could pretend Virginia."

"Pretending won't change anything Mum."

"I've been pretending all day."

"The pretending has to stop mother. That was the Police on the phone."

Hants

When the coffee was finished, they decided to have a bourbon. Then it was something to eat. Around ten o'clock, Angeline's eyes began to flutter.

"You should go to bed now, Mum."

"What about you?"

"I'm three hours ahead of you, I'm going to stay up for a while. Do you have something that will help you sleep? I think you need a good rest."

"There are some envelopes of powder in the medicine cabinet."

"I'll go get one. You can have it here, before you go upstairs."

Virginia drew the sheet up over her mother's shoulders. Then she leaned over and kissed her on the cheek. Before leaving, she pulled the chain on the bedside lamp.

She went back downstairs and washed up the dishes they had used, before dialing the number the policeman had given her. The duty Sergeant took her name. Within five minutes, the phone rang.

"Captain Anderson speaking, Miss Austin."

"Good evening Captain."

"What's happening in there Miss Austin?"

"Nothing is happening Captain. I've just put my mother to bed. She has taken a sedative. It's been a very trying day. The Coroner can come in the morning."

"I'd prefer tonight."

"It's 11:08."

"It would still be better to get it over with now. It would look better for the report. The death happened today. I'm willing to forget a shotgun blast into the air. The Coroner is on call 24 hours a day; we pay him for that."

"As you wish officer, I'll wait up. Tell him to turn off his headlights coming up the lane. I don't want my mother to be disturbed."

"As you wish Miss Austin, he shouldn't be any more that 45 minutes."

The next morning Virginia was awakened by her mother standing over her holding a glass of orange juice.
"Did you sleep well?"

"What time is it?"

"Nine thirty."

"I guess the jet lag caught up with me."

"We have a busy day ahead of us."

"I know. I'll have to try to get a copy of that civil engineering report over to Mr. Hamstead. Tomorrow is the 24th. He'll need that if he is to apply for a Permanent Injunction."

"I forgot all about the Injunction. I was thinking we would need to make funeral arrangements."

"And there's the funeral too."

They were about to leave the house, to go to see the funeral director in Milford, when the telephone rang. Virginia went to get it.

"Good morning, Miss Austin, Captain Anderson speaking. I've just had a call from Dr. Johnston, who was out to your place last night.

"He has finished an analysis of the blood samples, which he took from the wound on your father's head. By analyzing the decomposition rate of the blood cells, he pinpointed the time of death. It was almost the same hour the blasters reported they exploded their charge. He said an autopsy wouldn't be necessary. However, he is calling for an Inquest. There's supposed to be an Injunction in place halting all construction until midnight tomorrow night."

"I understand. I have to see the lawyer who's handling it sometime today. He's presenting a Motion for Continuance tomorrow morning in Nashua Court."

"The Coroner has set his Inquest for 3 p.m. this afternoon. Do I have to send a Subpoena or will your mother be there?

"We'll be attending Captain."

Hants

"It will be held in one of the hearing rooms at the Nashua County Court. Look on the location roster, when you come in the front doors of the Court House."

"We'll be there."

"One more thing, Miss Austin."

"Yes."

"You should see about getting your father to a funeral home. I know it's cool in your cellar, but this is July. Dr. Johnson said the blood is decomposing. It is a natural process."

"We're just on our way out the door to make arrangements with the local undertaker."

The body of Brad Austin was picked up in a hearse which followed the mother and daughter back to Hants from the undertakers, an hour later. Virginia was able to get hold of Bert Hamstead, when the funeral director left. Bert said he didn't need her to bring him over the report. He simply had her read the recommendations and give him the telephone number of the firm, which had written the report. He would call to see if one of their men could be in Court, to present the recommendations as an expert witness.

That afternoon, the Austin women, made their way up the white granite steps of the Court House about fifteen minutes, before the Inquest was scheduled to begin. At 3 p.m., a woman carrying a file came through the door on the right hand side of the room.

"All rise, Coroner Dr. David Johnston presiding this afternoon in and for the State of New Hampshire."

A Court House clerk was called first to testify as to the content of the Injunction, which was on file in the Registry. A copy was labeled Exhibit A. Mrs. Austin was called to give her version of what happened on the morning of July 22nd. After her, the Coroner heard first one blaster and then the other.

"Place your right hand on the Bible."

"Do you swear the testimony, which you are about to give is the truth to the best of your knowledge."

"I do."

"State your name, occupation and place of residence."

"Larry Olds, registered blaster in the State of New Hampshire, 1098 Forest Dr., Manchester."

At first Dr. Johnston questioned Olds to see if his version of Monday morning's mishap was the same as that of his partner? Then he pushed his inquiring further.

"You say you told your employer you heard there was some kind of Court Order halting work on the Bickle Dam?"

"That is right Doctor."

"Who did you hear that from?"

"From him," the blaster replied

"From your employer?"

"He is not exactly our employer, Sir. We work on a contract basis. When Ivy Construction approached us about a month ago to get a quote, the President mentioned the Injunction."

"Are you referring to the President of Ivy Construction?"

"That is correct."

"What is the President's name?"

"Ward Shaw, Sir."

"How did you happen to be there Monday morning, if there was a Court Order?"

"Mr. Shaw came around the office in Manchester Friday afternoon and signed the work order. The Injunction was supposed to have expired. Nobody had contested it. It had been some kind of a bluff, a delaying tactic. He said if we didn't start the work Monday morning, he would give the contract to someone else."

A copy of the work order was filed as Exhibit B.

"Tell me Mr. Olds, how long have you been a blaster?"

"Ten years."

"Are you in the habit of letting off a charge without having mats placed?"

"No, Doctor."

"Then why did you this particular time?"

"We were in a bit of a hurry. We had another job scheduled for Monday and had to start it too. The ground was supposed to be nothing but dirt and clay. We were away out in the farm country. It was early in the morning."

When the hearse returned to the Milford funeral parlor, the undertaker had immediately moved Brad body to his workshop. Several years prior the funeral director had a woman wake up in his establishment, before any work had been commenced on her remains. From that day forward he always attached two electrodes to the skull of clients, as soon as they arrived, to verify that there was no brain activity keeping the body alive and recorded any activity on a print- out. When the electrodes were taped to Brad's skin and the machine switched on, the mortician went for lunch.

Upon his return, shortly after 1 pm he was amazed to find a consistent and regular ink trace on the roll of paper that fed through the EEG machine. Immediately he switched it off and wheeled the body out to his funeral vehicle. Once the still living man was loaded in the back, he drove straight to the hospital located in Nashua. There ER attendants placed the unfortunate old gentleman, who was still dressed in a black diner jacket, onto a hospital gurney and wheeled him inside where the duty doctor began to examine him, after having spoken with the Milford funeral home owner and having looked at the EEG print out he had brought.

Angie and Virginia were leaving the Courthouse after the adjournment of the Inquest into the accident on the Austin farm when they met lawyer, Bert Hamstead, who had just finished the hearing on the permanent Injunction.

"So was it granted?" Virginia questioned him eagerly.

"The judge took it under deliberation. He said he would render judgment in a few days and the Temporary Injunction is extended until then."

"I should have known. I always want them to decide from the bench, but it never happens." Virginia commented.

"It's a pity you hadn't come to see me, before going to the West Coast. I could have found you a place to article in Concord."

"Your thought is extremely considerate, but I doubt I would have found the same type of law to practice. I'm just at the entry level of corporate work involving fifty million and up."

"Stick with it. The closest place to here you'll find anything similar is in Boston. It's getting late in the afternoon. How would you ladies like to come out for supper with me? "

"I can't think of anything else I'd rather do. It's been such an exhausting day with the funeral arrangements and the Inquest," Angeline confessed.

"I'm always game for restaurant food," her daughter admitted with a broad smile.

"Then it's unanimous," Bert laughed, wedging himself in between the two women and taking hold of their arms.

When the funeral director arrived back in Milford, he called the Austin residence and left a message concerning the events that had transpired and the news about Brad.

It was 8:30 pm when mother and daughter returned home. They were both worn out. The supper invitation had been a stroke of good fortune. Neither would have had the inclination or the energy to cook.

"Let's go upstairs and straight to bed," Virginia suggested.

"You won't get any argument from me on that," her mother replied with sadness.

It was not until the next morning they saw the red light blinking on the phone when they came into the kitchen and found the message from the funeral director. Angeline felt weak upon hearing the news and had to sit down. Her daughter switched into office mode and began dialing the Operator. Within two minutes she had the telephone number for Admitting and was telephoning it.

"Yes, my name is Virginia Austin. I'm calling you from a bit west of Milford. My father was involved in a blasting accident out this way two days ago. We've had a message that he has been transferred to your Hospital. Can you confirm that?"

"One moment please, I'll check." There was a pause and then she was back. "Yes Ms. Austin, your father is here! He's in Room 204. Visiting hours are 2 pm to 4 pm and 7pm until 9 pm."

"Oh, thank you so much," Virginia gushed, "Thank you, thank you!"

As soon as she hung up she turned to her mother and whispered in a hoarse voice, "It's Dad, he's alive."

"But how," the old woman whimpered. "I washed him. The funeral man came and took him away. We attended his Inquest." Then she began to cry.

Virginia moved quickly towards her mother and pulled a chair up beside the stricken woman before wrapping her arms around her.

"Don't cry mummy, it's daddy, he's alive!"

They stayed hugging each other, rocking back and forth a long time and finally Angeline stopped sobbing. After her mother became quiet, Virginia said what they had both been wanting to hear,

"Let's get fixed up and go visit daddy. Visiting hours are 2 to 4 pm."

It was all Angeline needed. "Oh, I look a real fright. I haven't been to have my hair done in six months. I'll call Georgette in Milford to see if she can fit me in before noon."

"Okay Mom, you go call Georgette and I'll start to prepare us some breakfast."

At two o'clock that afternoon they walked up to the Nursing Station on the second floor of the Nashua Hospital holding hands.

"Good afternoon ladies," the Charge Nurse greeted them. "May I help you with something?"

Virginia spoke for them both. "My name is Virginia Austin and this is my mother Angeline. We're here to visit my father Brad Austin. I believe he's in Room 204."

The nurse looked at her chart and then asked, "Have you spoken with Mr. Austin's doctor?"

"No, we haven't seen him yet."

"Have you been told anything about your father's condition?"

"No nothing!"

"Your father is in a coma, but he has improved since being admitted. Also, he has a mild concussion. I'll show you in and then I'll let his doctor know you are here."

When they entered the room, Virginia had the strangest feeling that she had lived this before. It was like when she went down to the basement at Hants and had seen him spread out on the wooden table. The nurse told them they could move the two chairs from against the wall, up near his bed.

"Try talking to him in a low, regular voice. Sometimes they can hear, even when they are in a coma. Don't talk about the accident. Talk about what you had for breakfast or the garden or the past."

"Thank you nurse," Angeline said, beginning to feel stronger as she realized finally he really wasn't dead.

About fifteen minutes later Dr. Armstrong came in. "His vital signs have all improved since we admitted him. At his age, the body is still in shock from the blow to the head, but his mind is coming back. We're feeding him intravenously and on that screen we can see brain activity directing the nutrients that are absorbed to different parts of the body."

The two women stayed the full two hours, each sitting on opposite sides of his bed holding a hand and talking softly. He didn't move or twitch during the visit. At 4 pm they left and went off to a restaurant. They came back at seven and stayed until nine. The both of them did the afternoon and evening visit for the next five days.

Hants

On Monday Bert Hamstead called. The judge had issued his decision. He was granting a permanent Injunction. It would be in the afternoon papers. That afternoon Virginia bought a paper and read it during supper. At seven, both went back to Brad's bedside.

Virginia began to talk to her dad about Bert Hamstead. She told him they had got the geological report to the lawyer and about him going to the hearing on the Permanent Injunction. When she said the word Injunction, each woman felt the man's hand jerk.

Virginia kept talking. She told her father the judge had issued his decision and it was in today's papers. She had a copy of the paper and had read the reporting. The judge had issued a Permanent Injunction. She had the newspaper here on his bed.

All of a sudden both women were startled by the old man who began to cough. Virginia went for the nurse who called the duty doctor. When she returned to her father's bedside his eyes were open and he and Angeline were smiling at each other. The doctor asked the women to step out of the room, because he wanted to examine the patient.

Five minutes later he came into the hospital corridor where they were waiting. He's come out of it. It's amazing. It must have been something you said to him and that connected the inner brain back to reality.

Angeline looked at her daughter and turned towards the doctor, "Our little Ginny always knew what to say to him."

Virginia had planned to stay until the weekend. It was like a summer vacation although not planned. However, her plans were cut short. The following morning, the Office Manager Mrs. Wilson called from her law firm in Los Angeles.

"We can't seem to find the other half of the 'Saturnalia Corporation' file. The time card indicates you were the last person who signed out the first part of the file."

"I'm terribly sorry, Mrs. Wilson. I took it late Friday afternoon. I only planned to use it during the week -

end. I must have forgot to log it out. I would have had it back by now, but you know what came up."

"How are things going?"

"Better than I expected, but I'll explain when I get back. The file is in my apartment. Maybe if I phone security, they could use their pass key."

"No, I don't think we'll go that route. It was only one of the other lawyers who wanted to consult it. He can wait another few days. Actually, I've been in a panic. When I couldn't find it, and it wasn't logged out, I thought we might have accidentally thrown it out. It has happened before."

Angeline had been listening to the conversation and got the gist of what was going on.

"Virginia, tell her you will be leaving tomorrow. I'm going to be all right."

"Mrs. Wilson, I'm going to phone about the flights when we hang up. I should be back in San Francisco tomorrow evening."

"That's fine Virginia. Bring it in with you on Thursday. Give my regards to your mother."

"I will. Thank you."

Once she had hung up, she turned to her mother. "Get out your pen and paper. We've a lot to discuss and I don't want you to forget anything."

"Discuss, like what," her mother asked?

"Mom, that's a real herd out there in the enclosure. For starters, we need to get a man in here, at least on a part-time basis, to take care of the animals."

"Oh, those poor animals, I forgot about them. They're getting enough water through the automatic fill up trough outside at the back of the barn but they're probably getting tired of eating field grass though. We've been spoiling them.

"What do you feed them now?"

"Mostly barley this time of the year."

"We'll feed and water them before going into the hospital this afternoon."

"Okay, why don't you go phone about planes while I look for my pad and a pencil."

"Alright, I'll go phone, while you get yourself organized."

On the way into Boston Wednesday morning, Virginia stopped in Nashua to gas up the rented car. While she was paying the attendant, she picked up the early edition of the local paper at the same time. When she got back into the car, the newspaper went into the bag, which she would take to her seat on the plane.

The flight from Logan left at 1 p.m. She had enough time to return the car, get a ticket and find the loading Gate. When the aircraft had cleared Boston Harbor, it leveled off, and the flight captain gave the passengers permission to unfasten their seat belts. Virginia accepted a drink from the cabin steward, who was going up the aisle with a trolley and then settled back to read the Nashua paper.

There was an article about the 'Bickle Reservoir' on the bottom half of the front page.

'In light of the Nashua County Court's decision to issue a Permanent Injunction against the Bickle Reservoir, the State Department of Water Resources in Concord has announced it will go ahead with flood control on the Upper Souhegan. Instead of building a reservoir, it has been decided to build two smaller sluice gate dams at points along the upper river, the location of which are as yet to be determined.

Regarding the unfortunate accident, which seriously injured Mr. Bradley Austin, at the proposed site for the Bickle Dam, last Monday; a Coroner's Inquest has ruled criminal responsibility.

Nashua County Public Prosecutor has filed charges against the two blasters for negligence causing bodily harm. If found guilty, the two men could serve up to six months or face a fine as high as five thousand dollars. The Public Prosecutor has also filed charges against Mr. Ward Shaw, who is President of Ivy Construction. Mr. Shaw is in contempt of Court as there was an

Injunction issued by the State forbidding any work on the Bickle Dam before midnight July 24th.

Mr. Shaw is also facing charges of criminal negligence causing bodily harm. He insisted work begin at the dam site while knowing a Court Order was in place. Shaw could face up to five years in penitentiary if found guilty on both counts.'

The End

Made in the USA
Charleston, SC
13 September 2014